Body on the Bayou

Also by Ellen Byron:

Plantation Shudders

Body on the Bayou

A Cajun Country Mystery

Ellen Byron

CROOKED
LANE

NEW YORK

Copyright © 2016 by Ellen Byron

Published in the United States by Crooked Lane Books, an imprint of The Quick Brown Fox & Company LLC.

Crooked Lane Books and its logo are trademarks of The Quick Brown Fox & Company LLC.

Library of Congress Catalog-in-Publication data available upon request.

ISBN (hardcover): 978-1-62953-768-9
ISBN (ePub): 978-1-62953-789-4
ISBN (Kindle): 978-1-62953-790-0
ISBN (ePDF): 978-1-62953-791-7

Cover design by Stephen Graham and Louis Malcangi
Book design by Jennifer Canzone

Printed in the United States.

www.crookedlanebooks.com

Crooked Lane Books
34 West 27th St., 10th Floor
New York, NY 10001

First Edition: September 2016

10 9 8 7 6 5 4 3 2 1

Body on the Bayou *is dedicated to Harriette Sackler, chair of the William F. Deeck-Malice Domestic Grant Committee, as well as to committee members Arleen Trundy and Joan Gottesman, the Malice Domestic Board of Directors, and all of the volunteers who work so hard to make the Malice Domestic Convention a home for both mystery writers and readers. You have changed the lives of many, including this author.*

Chapter One

It was midafternoon and Maggie Crozat had already led five large tour groups through Louisiana's Doucet Plantation, a historic state landmark once owned by her ancestors. A storm had passed through at dawn, and remnants of rain dripped from the magnolia tree that shaded the employees' break area. Maggie sat on a bench under the tree. A fat raindrop fell on her nose and tumbled down the décolleté of the blue polyester ersatz 1850s ball gown that served as her tour guide uniform. She'd been starving when she went on lunch break, but her appetite disappeared and her homemade crawfish salad sandwich went untouched as she scanned the maid of honor to-do list that her coworker, Vanessa Fleer, had dropped in front of her.

"Here's page two," the bride-to-be said as she handed it to Maggie.

"There's a page two? Are you serious?"

"As a heart attack, which I could be in danger of having if all this stuff don't get done." Vanessa made a sad face and patted her rapidly expanding stomach. Maggie was skeptical of women who claimed that they had no idea they were pregnant. But while undergoing a medical evaluation before starting an all-liquid diet, Maggie's fellow tour guide at Doucet discovered that in addition to a food baby, she was carrying an actual baby. This scuttled her plan to milk a yearlong engagement to Rufus Durand, the lazy police chief of tiny Pelican, Louisiana. Instead, she was fast-tracking her nuptials, and Maggie reluctantly gave her credit for making sure that the ink was dry on the wedding license before popping out little Rufus or Rufette. Just because the woman was marrying "the man of muh dreams" didn't mean she trusted him not to duck out on child support if he wasn't legally bound.

"Since time's so tight, we're gonna have to do a lot of checking in with each other," Vanessa told Maggie, who noted that the woman's blandly pretty features were disappearing into a face that grew incrementally fleshier by the day. Maggie's artist eyes tended to pick up visual details that others missed. "Never, ever turn off your phone or put it on vibrate cuz I am gonna need twenty-four-seven access."

"What if I need to go to the bathroom?" Maggie asked in a dry tone.

"Twenty-four seven, Magnolia Marie, twenty-four seven. This is gonna be soooo fun! Oh dang, you said bathroom, now I gotta pee again."

The pregnant woman skip-waddled off, leaving a glum Maggie to pick at her lunch. She regretted letting Van strong-arm her into the position of head wedding cheerleader, but she was still trying to make friends and find her place again in her hometown. She'd barely been back a year after spending more than a decade in Manhattan and knew that many locals saw her as "that artsy-fartsy girl." At thirty-two, Maggie felt far removed from being a "girl," but in Pelican, that appellation applied to any female still single, be she seven or seventy. Signing on as point person for Vanessa's wedding party was also a strategic move. Van's fiancé was the archenemy of Maggie's family, so keeping her happy might lay the groundwork for a rapprochement between the Crozats and Durands. Reminding herself of this kept Maggie from exploding like an M-80 firecracker when Vanessa peppered her with inane demands.

A couple of other coworkers, Ione Savreau and Gaynell Bourgeois, strolled over to join her. Ione, who supervised the guides, was a slim, African American retired schoolteacher who reveled in surprising people with the news that not only were three out of every ten plantation owners women, there were also owners of color. Gaynell Bourgeois was a nineteen-year-old with angelic looks. Her ingenuous demeanor masked an intellect so sharp it had helped Maggie solve a murder that would have doomed her family's home and livelihood: Crozat Plantation Bed and Breakfast.

The women sat sidesaddle at the break area picnic table, their ball gowns poofing out around them like Miss Muffet's tuffets. "What's with you?" Ione asked, sensing Maggie's unhappiness. Maggie handed Vanessa's list to her. Ione took one look at it and burst out laughing, a deep basso guffaw. Gaynell peered over Ione's shoulder to view the list

3

and joined in with tinkling giggles. "Now we know why all of Van's relatives ran like a levee broke when she hit them up for the maid of honor job," Ione said. She pulled a tissue out of her cleavage to wipe the tears of laughter streaming down her cheeks.

"And she's got a big family," Gaynell added. "*Real* big."

Maggie glared at them. "Yeah, well, I'm going to think of myself as the foreman of this bridal party and assign as much as I can to the bridesmaids. So take that as a warning."

Ione and Gaynell, both of whom had buckled to Vanessa's entreaties that they serve as bridesmaids, stopped laughing. "Um, it's a bad week for me," Ione tap-danced. "My grandkids are coming to visit and things like that and—oh, never mind." She gave up trying to come up with excuses. "Fine. We'll help. Right, Gaynell?"

"Of course." Gaynell smiled at Maggie, who returned the smile. She knew that tease as they might, Ione and Gaynell would be there when she needed them. Which, given Vanessa's status as an archetypal Bridezilla, would be a lot.

"Luckily, or unluckily because we could use the money, there's a lull at Crozat between Thanksgiving and Christmas," Maggie said. "Some guests checked out this morning, and as far as I know we don't have any other bookings this week."

"What about people coming in for the wedding?" Gaynell asked.

Maggie snorted. "Please, like Rufus would ever let Vanessa give us the business."

The other women nodded. The whole town knew that Rufus Durand held a grudge against the Crozats dating back one hundred and fifty years. Maggie's great-great-great-grandmother was rumored to have put a curse on all Durand family relationships after catching her fiancé, Ru's great-great-great-grandfather, cheating on her with a New Orleans belle. "The only reason he okayed me as maid of honor is because he knew it would make my life hell," Maggie said, holding up Vanessa's list as evidence.

Ione frowned. "You'd think that since he's getting married again"—the "again" referring to this being the third marriage for Ru—"he'd assume the curse was broke and forget about it."

"At this point, hating my family is so ingrained in his DNA that I don't think anything could knock it out of his system."

"Shhh," Gaynell cautioned. "Vanessa's coming back."

Vanessa made her way to them, holding up the hem of the green-and-red, ill-fitting dress that had been cobbled together to hide her eight-month bundle. The goal had been to recreate an outfit that an antebellum belle might have worn during her confinement. But, as Vanessa griped, "I just saw myself in the mirror. I look like a Christmas tree." The other women were silent. "You're not saying anything."

"We would if we disagreed," Ione, ever blunt, replied.

"But it's okay," Gaynell said. "It just looks like you're celebrating the season."

Vanessa glared at them and then turned to Maggie. "I've thought of more stuff I need you to do. I'll text it all to you later."

"Oh come on, Vanessa." Maggie held up the list. "'Confirm contract with venue and caterers, order flowers, renegotiate rental prices . . .' A maid of honor doesn't take care of these things—a wedding planner does. You need to give this list to yours."

"I would if I still had one. Rufus fired ours. Said we should be spending that money on the house."

"The house," as Vanessa euphemistically called it, was La Plus Belle—the megamansion her fiancé was building with his share of the payout that the entire Durand family received for the sale of their family homestead, Grove Hall. At this point, La Plus Belle was just lumber and lawsuits brought on by the constant changes Ru and Van demanded and then refused to pay for. Maggie wasn't surprised that Ru had axed their wedding planner, a pricey hire from New Orleans. Nor was she surprised that Vanessa would try to foist those chores on her. "I'm sorry," she said, "but I can't take on all these duties. I don't have the time."

Vanessa grimaced and put her hand on her baby bump. She reached behind her, groping for a seat, then lowered herself onto the picnic table bench between Ione and Gaynell, shoving each of them to the side. "Dang, another pain. I can feel my blood pressure going up. I may need to call my doctor. She's real worried about me going into preterm labor."

"We know," Ione said. "You tell us every time we don't do what you want."

"Well, it's true."

Vanessa cast a pitiful glance at Maggie, who sighed. Vanessa might be bluffing, but Maggie didn't want to take the chance that she wasn't. Woe be it to anyone who caused the future Mrs. Rufus Durand to deliver early. "Okay, fine, I'll help you out. Just spare me another 'preterm labor' performance."

"Thank you." Vanessa popped up and then pulled out her cell phone. "Oooh, I got a text from my mama." As she read the message, Vanessa pulled off her old-fashioned, banana-curled wig and rubbed her scalp. She'd stopped coloring her hair after reading that it wasn't good for a gestating infant, so muddy brown roots dead-ended about two inches from her old yellow-blonde dye job.

Vanessa finished reading, put her phone away, and slowly sat down again, her face so pale that Maggie worried she might actually follow through with the threat to deliver early. "Van, are you all right? You don't look good."

"It's my cousin, Ginger," Vanessa said. The women waited for her to continue, but she stared straight ahead, her face stricken.

"Is it . . . bad news?" Ione asked gently.

"Yes." Vanessa nodded. "She's coming to my wedding."

And Vanessa burst into hysterical sobs.

Chapter Two

It took a while to ratchet down Vanessa's hysteria, but once she stopped crying, she refused to say anything else about her cousin. Ione sent the pregnant guide home to rest, and Maggie and Gaynell divvied up her tour groups.

"I wonder why she went off like that," Maggie said as the three women walked to their cars at the end of the day.

"Hormones?" Gaynell guessed.

Ione shook her head. "I popped out five kids, and believe me, I had some serious mood swings, but never a meltdown like that. There's something else going on. Something with that Ginger cousin."

Maggie nodded. "Still, whatever's going on with Vanessa isn't helped by the stress she's under right now. If I ever get pregnant, it better not be under such crazy circumstances."

"It won't be, because you're not her," Gaynell said. "And you won't be marrying Rufus Durand."

"Oh God, no." Maggie made a face and laughed.

The women got into their cars, and Gaynell and Ione drove off. Maggie sat for a moment behind the wheel of the '64 Falcon convertible she'd inherited from her late grandfather, Papa Doucet. Vanessa's anguish, so raw and real—and so unexpected from the woman nicknamed the "Loch Nessa Monster" by her coworkers—had unsettled her. Maggie felt worn out by the day. She shook herself to get her blood moving and then, despite the chill of a late-autumn day, put down the top of the car and peeled out of the parking lot, headed for home.

She drove fast, welcoming the cold slap of air the velocity created. She slowed down at the infamous town speed trap, just in case the Pelican Police Department was out trolling for tourists or Crozats to ticket. Once out of the danger zone, Maggie picked up speed again and quickly reached the family homestead. The sight of Crozat Plantation always rejuvenated her. Square columns encircled the elegant main house, which gleamed a crisp white. The first floor featured a wide, welcoming veranda; the second, a balcony that encircled the home. Maggie parked in the family's gravel lot at the far end of the property and then strolled past the garçonnière and carriage house, outbuildings that had been transformed into guest lodging. She pulled open the back door of the main house and walked down a wide hallway that led straight to the large front entrance. When both doors were open, it allowed for a lovely cross-breeze to sweep through, even on a hot Louisiana summer day. Her ancestors were no dummies when it came to ventilation.

She peeked into the dining room and back parlor but didn't see any sign of her parents. She found Grand-mère Crozat in the front parlor, seated on a dark-blue, velvet, nineteenth-century wingback chair. Gopher, the family basset hound, snored at her feet. Gran', dressed in gray wool slacks and a silk blouse a discreet shade lighter, looked elegant and immaculate as always, and not even close to her eighty-two years. She stared at a gold watch that she held in her right hand. Like almost everything at the plantation, it had been handed down through generations of Crozats. A Sazerac cocktail sat in a highball glass on the side table next to her. "And . . . it's five o'clock," Gran' said. She snapped the watch shut and put it down, then picked up the Sazerac and took a sip.

"Since when do you wait?" Maggie teased.

"Oooh snap, as the kids say. Now I won't make you your own cocktail."

"I'm good with a club soda."

Maggie went behind the bar tucked in a corner of the room and pulled a can out of a small refrigerator. She popped the top and chugged its contents. Gran' shook her head. "There are days I do wish you'd gone to Newcomb College instead of art school. You might have picked up a bit of etiquette."

"Sure, if I'd gone there in the nineteen-fifties, like you did." Maggie kissed her grandmother on the top of her head and sat down on the wingback chair next to her. "Where are Mom and Dad?"

"Out on a power walk," Gran' said, taking another sip of her drink. Ninette Doucet Crozat, Maggie's mother, had survived a bout with non-Hodgkin's lymphoma in her twenties. A recent health scare had inspired her to launch a fundraiser for lymphoma research, the Yes We PeliCAN! 10K Walk for the Cure. She trained for it by walking every day with family or friends. Maggie joined her whenever she could.

"Chère, are you home?" Maggie heard her father call.

"In the office," she called back.

Ninette and Thibault "Tug" Crozat, both in workout attire, strode in, bringing a whiff of perspiration with them. The couple held hands; petite Ninette subtly elevated her arm so that her husband, taller by more than a foot, wouldn't have to compensate for the height difference by bending toward her.

"We worked up an appetite," Ninette said. "I'm going to get dinner going."

"We got another booking for the week before Christmas," Gran' told Tug. "I think we'll be sold out for the holidays."

"Excellent," he said. "We will have some guests this week, but they're all freebies."

Maggie and Gran' exchanged a puzzled look. This was a surprise to both of them.

"Vanessa Fleer called and asked if we might have room for a few of her wedding guests," Ninette explained. "Her cousin Ginger's group."

"What?" Maggie exclaimed. "Are you serious?"

"Of course. Why, what's the problem?"

"I don't know, she wouldn't tell us. But there is one."
Maggie detailed Vanessa's unhappy reaction to the news that
her cousin would be attending the wedding. "I can't believe
that on top of a million duties she dumped on me, now she's
dumping a relative she obviously can't stand on my family.
And for *free*?"

"Charging her guests felt in bad taste. I told her it was a
wedding present."

"I'm already making them a wedding present, Mama.
I'm painting their portrait. If Vanessa lives that long. I swear,
I may kill her before I finish it."

"Watch your words, dear," Gran' said. "I'm guessing a
cocktail is now in order."

"Not right now. I have to drive over to Bon Bon. But
trust me, I'll be hitting the bottle as soon as I get back."

Maggie marched out of the main house to the small shotgun house that she shared with her grandmother. Gopher
tagged along with her. "I love them, I truly do," she com-
plained to the hound as she opened the creaky wooden door
and followed the dog inside. "But honestly, sometimes I
think my parents are so nice, it's dangerous." Gopher, distracted by some muffin crumbs he discovered on the floor,
didn't respond.

Maggie went into her bedroom, pulled off her clothes,
and threw them into the bathroom hamper. She took a quick
shower and slipped into faded brown ankle boots, jeans, and
a caramel sweater that brought out the orange in her hazel
eyes. She grabbed a leather jacket and headed out of the
house to her car.

As the sun began its twilight descent over the Mississippi River, Maggie drove down a two-lane road into the historic center of Pelican. The town featured a village green surrounded by centuries-old brick buildings sporting lacy iron balconies. One of them housed two quaint shops, Bon Bon Sweets and Fais Dough Dough Patisserie. Both were owned by her cousin, Lia Tienne. Maggie was thrilled when Lia, widowed young, found love again with a Crozat guest— Kyle Bruner, who'd lost his wife in a tragic accident. Some Pelicaners believed in magic; some didn't. But pretty much all agreed that Fate had a hand in uniting those two grieving souls.

Maggie parked behind the shops and hopped out of the Falcon. She opened the car's trunk, pulled out a small box, and walked into Bon Bon. The shop smelled of chocolate and salted caramel, a scent so delicious that Maggie felt she could bite into it. The walls boasted a display of paintings, vibrant contemporary renderings that celebrated Cajun Country's lush landscape and rich architecture. Small, discreet signs next to each painting indicated its name, price, and the artist. All were by Magnolia Marie Crozat—Maggie.

Lia and Kyle were behind the counter, huddled over what Maggie saw were interior design renderings for their new home. Kyle, a wealthy software engineer, had bought the Durand family homestead—Grove Hall. The couple planned to restore the run-down plantation, which suffered from years of neglect by Rufus Durand, who had enjoyed taunting concerned citizens like the Crozats with the plantation's dilapidated condition.

"Hi, sweetie," Lia greeted her cousin. "Tell me you brought souvenir thimbles and spoons."

"Yes, I surrendered to kitsch." Maggie, who'd channeled her artistry into a line of souvenirs, reached into the box and pulled out a thimble decorated with a colorful illustration of Doucet. "I've made them for ten of the local plantations. Same with the spoons. They may be cheesy, but they could also be big sellers."

"Exactly," Lia enthused. "Visitors can collect them." Lia opened the cash register and took out a check that she handed to Maggie. "Here's the money for your mugs and mouse pads. I'm also putting together a box of candy for the family."

"Yum! Sample, please." Lia tossed a chocolate rum truffle to her cousin. Maggie caught the truffle, popped it her mouth, and savored the marriage of tangy liquor and rich, bittersweet ganache. As she chewed on the sweet treat, she unpacked her box of souvenirs and began setting them out, moving them here or there to create a more interesting display.

"Maggie, what do you think of these drawings?" Kyle brought over printouts of the future Grove Hall dining and living room. Each room was so stuffed with antique furniture and knickknacks that they seemed more museum than home to Maggie.

"Truthfully? They're a little . . . overdone."

"We think so too." Kyle frowned.

"I can design a store, but I can't seem to design a house," Lia said, shaking her head as she filled a box with an assortment of homemade chocolates, pralines, and pastel bonbons.

"Don't worry about it," Maggie reassured them. "Anything you do will be a *huge* improvement over how that idiot Rufus left the place."

"Speaking of idiots . . ." Kyle muttered as he motioned to the door. The bell above it tinkled as rotund Rufus Durand walked into the shop. Maggie's pulse quickened when she saw that he was followed by his cousin and polar opposite, the tall, rangy Detective Bo Durand. Bo shot Maggie and the others a smile as Rufus went straight to the case of homemade candy.

"Gimme four chewy pecan pralines and a quarter pound of dark chocolate turtles," Rufus barked at Lia.

"Stress eating again, Rufus?" Maggie said as innocently as she could. She heard Bo turn a laugh into a cough.

"Anybody would if they had to deal with what I gotta," Ru grumbled. He chomped down on a coconut patty that Lia handed him as a lagniappe, a little something extra. "Van's all up in me with this dang wedding, and his royal-pain-in-my-keister, Mayor Beaufils, won't tell me when I get to go back to work." Ru was on leave from his job after getting into a scuffle with said mayor over a parking space. A Durand would never be given the boot from a town job, given their history in the area, but Maggie was happy to see Beaufils taking advantage of an opportunity to at least make the pugnacious police chief sweat.

"Rufus, I need to tell you something." Maggie relayed Vanessa's reaction to Ginger's RSVP. "And I know this won't make you happy, but Vanessa called my mother to see if Ginger and her group could stay with us."

"She did, huh?" Maggie was surprised to pick up a hint of glee in Rufus's voice. "And what did your mother say?"

"That they could stay. For free."

Rufus let out a roar of laughter so loud that it startled the others. "Oh, that is beautiful. Bee-you-tee-ful. Magnolia Crozat, you have made my day. That's exactly who I woulda wished on you." Lia handed Rufus a small bag. "I'll assume this is a small, free token of your appreciation for law enforcement."

"You're on leave, Rufus."

"Trust me, clock's ticking on that. I would not get too attached to my substitute." Rufus's phone made the sound of screeching brakes, and he checked it. "Text from Van. I gotta go with her to the lady doctor." He motioned to Bo. "Come on, I'll drop you at headquarters."

"You go ahead. I'll walk back," Bo said. "I want to get some treats for Xander. I have him tonight."

"Alrighty. *A bientôt,* Maggie. Get a good night's sleep. You'll need all your wits about you when Ginger shows up." Rufus guffawed again, then left the store with his hand in the bag of candy.

"Sorry about that," Bo said.

"It's okay," Maggie replied. "Ru was Ru long before you moved here."

Bo gave a slight nod and turned his attention to the candy display. "I'll take half a pound of the milk honeycomb, and if you don't mind—"

"I'll make sure the pieces don't touch." Lia and the others were sensitive to the fact that Bo's young son was on the autism spectrum. She wrapped up the candy and handed it to Bo. "On the house." He started to protest, but Lia cut him off. "It's either free or leave it be."

"Well . . . thanks." Bo gave Lia a grateful smile and headed out of the store. Maggie stared after him a moment, then shook it off and finished arranging her souvenirs. She exchanged good-byes with Lia and Kyle, took the box of candy Lia had assembled for the Crozats, and walked out of the sweet shop to her car. As she dug through her purse for her keys, she went over every detail of what she knew about Vanessa's cousin, which was only Vanessa and Ru's attitude toward her. That alone made her fear what might be in store for the Crozats if the woman stayed with them.

"Dang," Maggie muttered. She had yet to excavate her keys from the deep recesses of her purse, and the task was made harder by the darkness that enveloped the parking lot. The safety light had burned out. Maggie figured she better tell Lia.

She turned toward Bon Bon. But before she could take a step toward the store, a hand reached out of the pitch black and grabbed her.

Chapter Three

Maggie froze. She opened her mouth to scream, but no sound came out.

"I scared you," a male voice said. "Sorry."

Maggie recognized the hint of Texas in the man's Louisiana accent. Her assailant was Shreveport native Bo Durand. "I think my heart stopped," she said, placing a hand on her still-pounding chest. "I now know that in moments of extreme panic, I can't scream. Or move."

"Again, sorry. I thought you saw me. Let me make it up to you."

Bo pulled Maggie to him and kissed her. Her chest continued to pound—but this time for the right reasons.

The two broke apart. "Better?" Bo asked.

"Way better."

"I waited until Rufus was gone. But I had to see you."

Maggie leaned against Bo, resting her head on the smooth leather of his jacket. "I'm glad."

"I can't stand sneaking around like this."

"Come on." Maggie grinned. "Don't you find it a little sexy?"

"Okay, maybe a little," he admitted. "But I'm ready for it to be over. I'm hoping marriage mellows Doofus and he'll let go of his dumb-ass grudge against your family."

"We'll have to see how this marriage goes," Maggie said. "If it ends in divorce like his other two, we'll be in worse shape."

"Don't worry—I'm going to use my status as best man to access his good side."

"He has one?" Maggie wasn't being sarcastic. She truly wondered.

"He did when we were kids. It's buried pretty deep, but I'm going to apply a little emotional archaeology to dig it out."

"'Emotional archaeology.' Nice. I'm impressed."

"After Whitney and I divorced, I got pretty depressed. My captain talked me into getting help. That's the phrase my therapist used when he was trying to get me in touch with my feelings."

"And how are those feelings doing?" Maggie teased.

"Pretty great right now." Bo kissed Maggie again. "And I've got some good news. Whitney's husband Zach got a three-month transfer to Saudi Arabia, so she's relocating here while he's gone. That means I can cut out the drive back and forth to Lake Charles to get Xander, which'll give you and me way more time together."

"That's great. When is it happening?"

"Soon, but unfortunately, not tonight." Bo reluctantly pulled away. "I gotta go get him now. The I-10's calling."

"Okay. Text me a good time to come by and give him his lesson." Maggie had discovered that seven-year-old Xander, despite his challenges or because of them, was a preternaturally brilliant artist. Helping to nurture and protect the young boy's talent was one of the great joys of her return to Pelican.

After a final kiss, Maggie watched as Bo disappeared back into the night. The two first met when Rufus hired his cousin to replace a retiring detective, and they'd grown close during the investigation of three guests' deaths at Crozat B and B. By the end of the case, friendship had turned to romance, but the couple kept their three-month relationship clandestine so as not to poke the bear that was Rufus Durand. Both knew that relative or not, Rufus wouldn't hesitate to fire Bo for "cavorting with the enemy," an accusation he'd once flung at them. He also threatened to jail Maggie when she pointed out that the correct term was "*consorting with the enemy.*"

Maggie forced herself to focus. She resumed fishing through her purse for her keys, then gave up and walked back into Bon Bon to see if she'd left them in the shop. Lia saw her and held out a small, wax paper bag. "I knew you'd be back for a few pralines."

"I'll take them, but what I really need are my car keys," Maggie said, perusing the store shelves. "Ah," she cried triumphantly as she pulled the keys out of one of her souvenir mugs. "Problem solved."

Maggie's phone pinged, signaling a text. "Ugh. Another list of chores from Vanessa."

"I've been meaning to call her. I'm worried that being a bridesmaid will take me away from the shop too much, and I don't think I can—"

"No!" Maggie held up a hand to her cousin. "If I'm stuck in this crazy wedding party, so are you. No way are you coming up with some lame excuse to get out of it."

"It's not *so* lame," Lia said sheepishly. "But you're right. It wouldn't be fair to Vanessa."

"Forget her; it wouldn't be fair to *me*. I can't go through this nightmare without the support and help of my loved ones." Maggie's phone pinged again and she groaned. "God help me." She looked down at her phone and read the message out loud. "'BTW, watch Ginger on stairs.' What does that even mean? I'm very nervous about this woman staying with us. The fact that Rufus is happy about it can't be good."

"Who's Ginger?"

Maggie turned and found herself face to face with Little Earlie Waddell, whose family owned the *Pelican Penny Clipper*, a free community periodical. Little Earlie was a china doll of a man, with a slight build and delicate features. He'd recently graduated college on the five-year plan with a degree in journalism and carried around a laminated copy of his diploma that he'd had reduced to the size of a credit card. His late father, Big Earlie, had been happy keeping the *Penny Clipper* a collection of ads and paid-for puff pieces. But Little Earlie's goal was to turn it into an actual newspaper, albeit a trashy one, much to the annoyance of the town. Maggie had once witnessed the Pelican City Council break into a run when they saw Little Earlie coming toward them with his reporter's notebook.

"Oh hey, Earlie," Maggie said. "I didn't hear you come in." This was no surprise. Little Earlie had developed an ability to slink around on cat feet, the better to make himself invisible and eavesdrop on conversations that he could turn into gossipy banner headlines.

"Who's Ginger?" Earlie repeated.

"A friend," Maggie said, trying to be as vague as possible. But the avaricious look on Earlie's face told her she'd have to provide more information if she wanted to keep the newshound from tracking the scent of a story. "A friend of Vanessa's. A cousin actually. She's a wedding guest who'll be staying with us. It's no big deal."

"Then why do you have a bad feeling about it?" Little Earlie persisted.

"Because . . . I'm a Pelicaner," Maggie said, making her tone light. "That's what we do, have feelings and see signs in everything, right?"

While Maggie would never claim to have the second sight that some town residents were thought to possess, one thing she did see was that Little Earlie wasn't buying her explanation. But before he could press her with another question, Lia came to her rescue. "Little Earlie, we made a fresh batch of Coconut Haystacks this morning," she said, holding one out to him. "Your favorite. First one's on the house."

Little Earlie turned his attention toward the treat, and Maggie grabbed the chance to leave, blowing a grateful kiss to her cousin on her way out the door.

*

When Maggie returned to Crozat, she noticed two cars parked in front of the manor house. One was a dusty, nondescript, older-model hybrid sedan; the other, a late-model, white Mercedes SUV. She had no idea who owned the former but a pretty good one about whom the latter belonged to. She guessed that the infamous cousin Ginger had arrived. Maggie parked in the family lot and hurried inside.

She found Gran' in the front parlor holding court with three visitors. Each sipped from a goblet filled with a generous pour of red wine. The small group included a man in his late twenties with the vapid, blond good looks of a dating reality show contestant and a thin woman around thirty-five who had caved to the recent unflattering trend of dyed violet-grey hair. But the standout of the trio was the woman paying rapt attention to whatever tale Gran' was telling. Her platinum bob glimmered in the fire's light, and she had the kind of fine bone structure that made it difficult to define her age. She wore a winter-white cashmere turtleneck and matching nubby silk pants and, with her slim frame, resembled a delicate cloud.

"Maggie, dear, there you are," Gran' said. "Come meet our guests. This is Vanessa's cousin, Ginger Fleer-Starke," she said, indicating the cloudlike woman. "And her coworkers Trent and Bibi." Maggie exchanged curt greetings with the three. "Ginger is a Louisiana Fleer. She grew up in Ville de Blanc, just up the road."

Where there are plenty of B and Bs, but none that could be suckered into offering a free stay, Maggie thought grimly.

"I know we weren't expected until later in the week," Ginger said in a voice that was low and melodious. "I'm moving my interior design business from Houston to Baton Rouge, so this gave us the perfect opportunity to do some work on the new location."

Maggie did the math in her head, considering what the freeloading threesome's week-long stay would cost her family. "It is a bit longer than we'd anticipated," she said as diplomatically as possible while she steamed inside.

"I know," Ginger said. "It was very generous of you to offer us a complimentary stay, but I insist on paying for myself and my employees."

Maggie was speechless for a moment. This was not what she expected. "Oh. Maybe you could pay until the wedding—"

Ginger shook her head, and the scent of orange blossoms wafted toward Maggie. "I'll pay for the entire stay. No argument, please."

"You won't get one," Maggie said, surprised and relieved that Ginger was being so reasonable. The designer was hardly a she-devil, despite the intimations of Vanessa and Rufus. Maggie was starting to wonder if pregnancy hormones had made the bride-and-mother-to-be paranoid.

Ninette stuck her head into the room. "Dinner's ready."

Maggie's positive impression of Ginger grew during the dinner that Ninette laid out. Their recent guests from

Japan had requested an all-American turkey dinner for the last night of their visit, and Ninette had veered from her famed Cajun cooking to devise a delicious recipe for the leftovers that wrapped them all in crescent roll dough. "Turkey-dinner-in-a-braid," as Ninette called it, wasn't the sort of authentic Louisiana cuisine that the family usually served to guests, and Maggie prepared herself for complaints. But Ginger raved about the dish. She also entertained the Crozats with anecdotes about the wacky clients she'd dealt with in her interior design business while Bibi sat thin-lipped and silent and Trent spent most of his time checking his phone. When the group said their good-nights after dinner, Ginger hugged Maggie, telling her, "I feel like I've known you forever."

"I feel the same way," Maggie responded, surprised at how true the statement felt.

Ginger had requested that she and her assistant Trent room in proximity to each other and have a living area from which to conduct business. Tug led Ginger and Trent off to their rooms in the carriage house. Bibi, who described herself sourly as "the world's oldest intern," was assigned a room in the garçonnière.

Maggie offered to lead Bibi to her lodgings. As the two walked, Maggie noted that everything about Bibi seemed tight, from the skin that stretched over her almost-anorexic arms to her thin, pursed lips. "It sounds like your business is challenging, but fun," Maggie said in an attempt to break the ice.

"I wouldn't know about the fun part," Bibi said with a grimace.

Not sure how to respond, Maggie went with "Oh."

"I was an accountant for ten years," Bibi said, "but I'd always wanted to be an interior designer. I took classes at night and got my certificate, but it was hard finding a job. When Ginger offered me the internship, I grabbed it. I figured I'd live off my savings while I trained, and she promised me a job within three months. I've been with her a year. And I'm still an intern."

"Ah," was Maggie's choice of generic comment this time.

"Ginger started off staging houses to sell, which wasn't even a career until TV invented it. Then she started doing decorating and then she got her real estate license. So now she can decorate, stage, and sell houses."

"That's very entrepreneurial," Maggie said, impressed by Ginger's business savvy.

"'From Starke to Finish.' That's her advertising slogan."

"It's a good one."

"Thank you. I came up with it. For free, of course." Bibi gave a mirthless laugh as Maggie opened the door to her room. The intern took her suitcase from Maggie, nodded good-night, went inside, and closed the door behind her.

Maggie stood there, mulling over Bibi's bitter words. Ginger seemed smart, generous, friendly—nothing at all like what Maggie expected. Either Bibi had a serious attitude problem or Maggie was missing something. She shuddered, despite the unseasonably warm evening.

*

Maggie slept fitfully. She dreamt that she had fallen off a boat into the Atchafalaya Swamp, and when she screamed for help, no one came. She began to drown, and as she gasped for air, she woke up with a start.

"Hmm," Gran' said when Maggie shared her dream that morning as the two ate a breakfast of soft-boiled eggs and beignets. "A drowning dream symbolizes a loss of property—or life. You might want to have Helene Brevelle make you a gris-gris bag for success and health when she returns to town." Many Pelican residents put as much stock in local spiritualists as they did in priests and preachers. Helene Brevelle, the town voodoo priestess, was currently on a cruise to Mexico—paid for by gris-gris bag orders from college girls looking for some mojo that might help them land dates to their sorority formals.

"If I have the dream again, I'll call Helene." Maggie paused. "I had the shudders last night."

"Oh dear," Gran' said. Pretty much everyone in Pelican viewed the shudders, a sudden physical reaction that seemed to come from nowhere, as a psychic premonition.

"I know," Maggie said. "It's a sign. I just wish I could figure out what's bothering me. It's not about the whole maid of honor thing. That's just aggravating. It's something else, but I don't know what."

Gran' nodded. "Listen to your instincts, chère. You'll pinpoint what's troubling you eventually."

As soon as Maggie and Gran' finished breakfast, Maggie changed out of her sleep tee into her painting clothes and left the shotgun for the old plantation schoolhouse that she'd turned into an artist's studio. Vanessa had promised to drag Rufus over so that Maggie could work on her portrait of the couple, and they were due shortly. As she walked down the dirt path that ran through the plantation grounds, she almost bumped into Ginger, who was out for a morning jog.

"Sorry," Ginger said. She pulled her headphones off her ears. "I was in the zone."

"No problem," Maggie replied. Ginger's workout top and leggings were the same shade of winter white that she'd worn the night before. The woman was certainly committed to her fashion theme.

"My favorite time to run is sunset," Ginger said. "I have to really ramp up to get into a morning run groove like this." She gestured to her headphones almost apologetically. "It just fits better with my schedule on this trip."

"I get it. My friends and I have been power walking lately, and sunset is definitely our favorite time, too," Maggie said. "We're training for a cancer fundraising 10K that my mom's sponsoring. We'd love to have you join us while you're here."

"That would be great. But I have to keep a certain pace, and it can be tricky for other people to get in the rhythm of it." Ginger shrugged her shoulders. "You know what I mean?"

"Sure. Got it." In the light of day, Ginger's age was more apparent; she looked like a woman in her early forties who'd had some work done. The taut skin around her eyes and a lack of mobility in her upper lip area indicated a few Botox shots. Maggie berated herself for being so shallow.

The designer worked in a highly competitive business. She wouldn't be the first woman who felt the need to smooth a few years off her face.

Ginger checked her fitness watch. "I better go. I'm only up to four thousand steps."

Ginger took off down the service road that ran alongside the plantation and then made a left onto an old, abandoned road that disappeared into the dense woods. It was eight thirty in the morning. Maggie did a little math regarding her own activity thus far. She guessed that if she counted looking for her sunglasses, she might have hit four hundred steps. She wondered if Ginger was a woman who inadvertently set the bar very high for herself and others. *Or was it inadvertent?* Maggie chastised herself for being so suspicious. *That dream messed me up,* she thought. *Shake it off.*

*

Maggie's sessions with Vanessa and Rufus followed a pattern—an hour of the couple bickering with each other followed by a few minutes of criticizing whatever Maggie had created. She'd positioned them so that they were bathed in the sunlight flooding through the large windows of the old schoolhouse. Vanessa sat in a chair and Rufus sat on a stool slightly above her, with an arm draped around his bride-to-be's shoulder. "This stool always digs into my butt," he said as he pulled at his slacks.

"That's because all your pants are getting tighter," Vanessa snapped at him. "Ow! You just yanked my hair."

"It was an accident."

29

Vanessa squinted and looked at him with suspicion. "I'm not so sure about that."

"Hey, you lovebirds," Maggie intervened. "Time's up for today. I've decided to take some photos so that I can alternate between them and actual sittings. It'll make your lives easier." *And mine,* she thought. She snapped a dozen photos with her digital camera. "Alrighty, we're done for today."

"Good, cuz I gotta get to my anger management class," Rufus said, throwing air quotes around the "anger management" part of the sentence.

"Not sure what you need the air quotes for, Rufus," Maggie said as she screwed tops onto her tubes of oil paint. "Nothing ironic about you taking that workshop."

Rufus snorted. "I'm only there cuz the acting chief wants to bust my hump. He's making all these changes so that he looks like some kind of management genius and takes my job. I know the boys on the force, and all I can say is, it ain't gonna happen." Rufus gave Vanessa a desultory kiss on the top of her head and then glanced at Maggie's canvas. "You gave me jowls."

"You have jowls."

"Doesn't mean I want 'em in my portrait."

Rufus headed off, but Vanessa lingered. She made sure her fiancé was gone and then turned to Maggie. "Can I talk to you?" she asked.

"Sure," Maggie said. "What's up?"

"I've got a big problem with Ginger, and Rufus can't know about it," Vanessa confided, kneading her hands anxiously. "You know how she's an interior designer and all? Last month she gave me some advice for decorating La Plus Belle. She did a couple of computer drawings and said they were a wedding present. But then she just sent me this ginormous bill for a 'consulting fee.' I reminded her how she said it was a present, but now she's saying that she never said that, and if I don't give her the money, she'll sue us. I can't say anything to Rufus because he'd be so mad at me for getting involved with Ginger in the first place. He hates her. Says he's put people in jail who were less sneaky and underhanded than she is. I don't know what to do. It ain't like she needs my money. Her husband, Fox, is an oil exec and makes a bundle."

Beads of sweat on Vanessa's forehead combined with her makeup and dripped beige blobs onto the white caftan she wore. "Here," Maggie said, handing her a hand towel. Vanessa took it and dabbed her face. Maggie was discomfited by Van's story. "This has to be some kind of misunderstanding. Why don't you try talking to Ginger again? Worse comes to worse, you can play the premature labor card and see if she caves. It works with me."

Vanessa managed a weak smile. "It does, dudn't it? But I don't think Ginger would fall for it. She's not as nice as you." Maggie couldn't help but be touched by Vanessa's backhanded compliment. "Can I have a piece of paper?" the bride-to-be asked.

"Sure." Maggie ripped a sheet from a drawing pad and handed it to her. Vanessa pulled a pen out of her fake Louis Vuitton purse. She scribbled some words on the page and handed it back to Maggie, who read it aloud. "'Talk to Ginger for me.'"

"It's now one of your maid of honor duties," Vanessa said. "Maybe the most important one."

Maggie was about to protest but changed her mind when she saw the look of desperation on Vanessa's face. "Okay. I'll see what I can do."

"Thank you, thank you! I cannot tell you how much I appreciate it." Vanessa hoisted herself up from her chair and hugged Maggie. "I gotta get to my gyno appointment. He's on my case about gaining too much weight. That's the problem with a male doctor. They've never been pregnant, so they don't understand how it makes you crave donuts and fried food all the time." Vanessa picked up her purse, walked over to Maggie's canvas, and grimaced. "I look superpregnant."

"Van, you're due in three weeks."

"Yeah, but I don't have to look like that. You need to thin me out."

Vanessa left, and Maggie squelched the urge to paint horns and mustaches on the portrait's subjects. She reminded herself that despite Van's blunderings, she was a good person at heart and desperately wanted friends but had no idea how to make them. And the problems piling up on the bride-to-be certainly weren't helping her mood or behavior.

Maggie dunked her paintbrushes into a can of turpentine and wiped them off with a damp cloth. As she cleaned each brush, she thought about Vanessa's dilemma with Ginger. There was probably a simple explanation. Still, Maggie couldn't shake her sense of foreboding.

Her cell phone rang. She pressed "Accept" when she saw the call was from Tug. "Hey, Dad."

"Can you come over to the main house?" Tug's voice sounded grim.

"Sure. Is everything okay?"

There was a pause. Then Tug spoke, clearly choosing his words carefully. "We have a situation."

Chapter Four

Maggie found her father in the guest parking area with Ginger, Trent, and Bibi. All four were staring at Ginger's Mercedes. Maggie noticed a pool of dark liquid underneath the car.

"Hey, chère," Tug greeted his daughter. "Ginger's car seems to have sprung a leak."

"I ran over a rock in your driveway," Ginger said. She was dressed in a cotton top and pants, both in her signature soft white. "It's very upsetting. The car was in perfectly good shape until we got here, wasn't it, Trent? Bibi?"

"Yup," Trent seconded.

"I wouldn't know," Bibi said. "I drove here in my beater."

Tug rubbed his forehead. "I'll call Bertrand's garage for a tow. I'm waiting on a delivery of feed for our chickens. Maggie, could you drive Ginger over to Bertrand's so she can hear his diagnosis?"

"Of course."

Tug smiled reassuringly at Ginger and her employees. "Not to worry, we'll make sure everything's taken care of. And we'll take responsibility for any damage."

Tug turned away. As soon as his back was to the visitors, Maggie saw his smile fade. She headed back to the manor house with her father. As they walked, she noted the pristine, decomposed granite drive, packed hard as cement, under their feet. There wasn't a loose stone anywhere to be seen.

"Oh, one other thing," Ginger called to them. "I noticed that one of your back steps is loose. I thought I should tell you. You certainly wouldn't want guests to fall and hurt themselves."

"Thank you. I appreciate that," Tug called back, then muttered to Maggie, "I rebuilt those steps right before you came home. They're tight as a tick."

Maggie nodded but said nothing. All she could think about was Vanessa's ominous text warning: "Watch Ginger on stairs."

*

Bertrand's tow truck arrived within half an hour and carted the SUV off to the repair shop. Maggie chauffeured Ginger and Trent over to the shop; Bibi chose to stay behind. By the time they reached Bertrand's Gas and Auto Repair, the owner, Leontel "Lee" Bertrand, already had the car up on a lift. Lee was a tough ex-Marine in his mideighties whose energy defied his age. He and a sandy-haired man in his early twenties, whom Maggie didn't recognize, were examining the car's undercarriage. Maggie and Lee exchanged hellos.

"I don't think you've met my great-nephew, Chretien," Lee said. "Chret for short."

Chret moved forward to shake Maggie's hand. She noticed that he walked with a limp. "Hello, ma'am," he said shyly. As he took her hand, she felt a tremor in his.

"Chret's back from a couple of tours in Afghanistan," his uncle said with pride. "He's a Marine. Took some shrapnel in the leg, so he got an honorable discharge. Since none of my kids or grandkids is interested, I'm teaching him the business."

"Nice to meet you, Chret," Maggie said with a warm smile. "Welcome to town."

Chret gave a small nod, then returned to work. Maggie saw Ginger and Trent staring at the young war vet and whispering to each other. She glared at them, and they looked away. "So what's going on with the car, Lee?"

"There's a crack in the oil pan." Lee pointed to it. "That's where the leak is."

"Oh. I guess Ginger was right. She must have driven over something in our driveway."

Lee shook his head. "No one drove over nuthin'," he said, keeping his voice low so Ginger and Trent wouldn't hear. "This car sits too high up. And see that? It's epoxy. This pan's been damaged before and someone tried a cheap fix."

Maggie examined the oil pan and saw that Lee was right. "We can't confront Ginger about this," she said, her voice equally low. "For one thing, she's our guest, and it would be bad form to accuse her of scamming us. But also, and I hate to say this, I don't really trust her. I feel like she might get back at us some way."

Lee nodded. "Revenge reviews. As a businessman, I can tell you that there's few things worse than a customer posting nasty comments on some dang online site."

Maggie nodded. While Crozat had managed to stay on the positive side of Internet travel sites, she'd heard horror stories from other hoteliers forced to mop up the online mess created by a terrible review. "We have to pick up the tab for Ginger's car repairs," she told Lee.

"I'll give you the best price I can, but parts for this make and model are expensive. At best, we're looking at a grand, easy."

"What?" Maggie yelped. "A *grand?*"

"I should be charging twice that. That's just for parts. I'm waiving the labor charge. Anyway, should be ready in a day or two."

"Thanks, Lee. I really appreciate your generosity." Maggie strode over to Ginger and Trent, who were standing behind a metal rack filled with oil cans, still whispering as they watched Chret, albeit more discreetly. Maggie suppressed the urge to grab Ginger by her off-white shirt and call her a scam artist. Instead, she mustered up a polite tone and said, "Excuse me." Trent turned to her, but Ginger's attention remained focused on Chret. "Excuse me," Maggie said, louder and much less politely. Ginger tore herself away from gazing at the handsome young repairman and focused her pale-grey eyes on Maggie. "Lee can fix the car," Maggie told her, "but it may take a couple of days."

Ginger shrugged helplessly. "I can't be without a car."

Maggie gritted her teeth. "Well then, we'll just have to rent you one."

Fortunately, Lee always had a few rudimentary cars on hand for clients. He insisted on loaning one to Ginger for free. Maggie was grateful but figured Lee's generosity was based on the whopping repair bill the Crozats faced.

"Thanks for the help, Maggie," Ginger said as she took a set of car keys from Lee. "I am *so* sorry about all this."

No you're not, you manipulative witch, Maggie thought but managed not to say. Instead, she decided to grab the moment of fake goodwill to plead Vanessa's case. "We're the ones who should be sorry for putting you through this," Maggie said, matching Ginger's fake sincerity beat for beat. "There is something else I wanted to talk to you about." She shared Vanessa's concern about Ginger's decorating bill.

"Oh dear," Ginger said, scrunching her face in a performance of discomfort. "Poor Vanessa really messed up. I told her our phone consult was free, but I'd have to charge her for any actual drawings. If I did everything for free for my family and friends, I'd go broke." Ginger gave one of her trademark helpless shrugs.

Yeah, but working Bibi like a dray horse for free doesn't seem to bother you, was Maggie's acidic thought.

"By the way," Ginger continued, "Trent and I won't be having lunch at Crozat."

"Yeah," Trent said. He grimaced. "That turkey thing your mother made did a number on my system, if you catch my drift."

Maggie burned with anger. "I have an IQ over fifty, so yes, I catch your drift," she shot back at Ginger's snarky second-in-command. "Whatever's going on with your 'system,' I would not lay it on my mother. She happens to be one of best cooks in Pelican. One of the best in the whole parish."

"Trent didn't mean to insult anyone," Ginger said. Her tone, meant to be soothing, came off as patronizing. "I'm sure your mother's a fabulous cook. But everyone has an off day, don't they? Anyway, if you don't mind, would you tell Vanessa that I'm so sorry about the mix-up, but I need payment ASAP? Thanks so much."

With that, Ginger and Trent folded themselves into the subcompact loaner and took off.

"She's not very nice, is she?" Chret said, rolling himself out from under a car. He'd obviously heard Maggie and Ginger's conversation.

"No," Maggie said grimly. "She is not. But she's smart. She's got a way of putting things that makes it hard to argue with her."

*

Since one of Maggie's many maid of honor obligations was throwing Vanessa's bridal shower, she put Ginger out of her mind and focused on organizing the party, which was scheduled for the next evening. Crozat Plantation, a popular location for weddings, featured a permanent tent and all the equipment necessary for event planning. Unfortunately, hosting this particular event also meant picking up the cost of the food. Rather than the simple girls-only shower that

Maggie originally envisioned, Vanessa had blown it out to the point where the party might rival her wedding as a Pelican social extravaganza. To save money, the Crozats planned a menu featuring ingredients from the family's organic garden. Pelican attendees would ingest more fiber in a night than they usually did in a month.

Sunday dawned clear and dry—perfect weather for the shower, much to Maggie's relief. As she left for church, she saw Ginger running her usual route down the plantation's side road, with a left turn down the ancient, abandoned dirt road. After Mass at St. Theresa's—Saint Tee's to locals—Maggie hurried home to set up for the event. She headed into the main house and heard an "Ow!" come from the front parlor, uttered by her father. It was followed by a few expletives. Maggie, Gran', and Ninette all hurried into the room. As they did, they bumped into furniture, letting loose with a few "ows" and expletives themselves.

"What the hey?" Tug said as he and the others examined the room, which looked the same yet completely different. Every piece of furniture had been rearranged.

Maggie noticed a note card on the table and tore open the envelope. "'The arrangement of this room had negative chi, so I took the liberty of applying fêng shui as a thank-you for fixing my car. Best always, Ginger Fleer-Starke.'"

"Fêng what?" a frustrated Tug said as he rubbed his bruised shins.

"Fêng shui," Maggie repeated. "It's a Chinese philosophy for finding harmony in your environment. Although right now, all I'm finding is bruises on my shins."

"Either Ginger is well-intentioned," Ninette said as she tended to her own bruises, "or this is some kind of passive-aggressive act. For what, I don't know."

"Oh, I think it's definitely the latter," Maggie said.

"That woman is the worst kind of Glossie," Gran' declared, using an acronym she'd invented that stood for "gracious ladies of the South." "She's a . . . a . . . Flossie—a fake lady of the South." Gran' crossed her arms and looked pleased with herself.

"I'm going to find that woman and tell her to put the room back exactly the way it was," Maggie declared. She marched upstairs and knocked on Ginger's door, ready to let loose with a few "fêng yous." There was no answer. She left the house and scoured the grounds, but there was no sign of the interior designer. Maggie found Bibi struggling under a load of carpet samples. "A delivery for the new place in Baton Rouge," she explained as she piled them into her car. When Maggie asked after Ginger, Bibi pointed toward the bayou behind the plantation. "Last I saw, she went that way."

Maggie made her way through the woods and was within reach of the bayou when she heard the murmur of voices. She froze. The murmurs turned into giggles. Maggie peeked through some branches and saw that a couple had rendez-voused in a small clearing. Maggie caught a glint of platinum hair, then a brief flash of blonde. The couple was Ginger and Trent. And the embrace they were locked in made it clear that this was no business meeting.

Chapter Five

Maggie crept away from the bayou as quietly as possible, although she doubted any noise she made would disturb the illicit lovers.

"Did you find Ginger?" Ninette asked when Maggie returned to the manor house.

"Uh . . . no," Maggie lied, not wishing to delve into what she'd witnessed. "Let's not worry about that now. We have guests coming in a few hours."

Maggie debated waiting until after the party to let Vanessa know that Ginger refused to budge on her due bill but decided that it was better to pull off the Band-Aid, so she texted the bad news. Then she, Ninette, and Gran' set the tables under the tent with the purple-and-gold colors of Louisiana State University that Vanessa had requested, although the only time she'd ever stepped foot on the campus was to crash a frat party. Belles Fleurs, the town florist shop, had cut the Crozats a great deal on fleur-de-lis, and Maggie arranged the beautiful, purple bearded irises in glass vases as centerpieces on each table. Lia, Gaynell, and Ione showed up early to help set a table with cheeses and hors d'oeuvres. Per Vanessa's request, the future bridesmaids were dressed in violet, as was Maggie, who wore a silk slip dress and matching shrug sweater. "You look gorgeous," Lia told her.

"But not too gorgeous, right?" Maggie asked. "Bride's orders—no one outshines her."

"God knows I don't," Ione muttered as she tugged at her ill-fitting pencil skirt. She motioned to Gaynell. "But you look like an angel. Violet is definitely your color, honey."

"Stop," Gaynell said as she blushed. "Let me help you, Ione." She straightened the older woman's skirt, which had wrinkled and bunched up on the car ride over. "There. Much better."

Maggie's cell rang. She looked down. "I need to take this," she told her friends, then walked to a quiet spot in the tent. "Hey," she said into her cell, keeping her voice soft. "Can't wait till you get here."

"Bad news," said Bo. "Acting Chief Perske put me on desk duty."

"What?! Why? Doesn't he know you're Ru's best man?"

"He sure does," Bo said, his tone terse. "It's part of the mayor's payback campaign against Rufus. Not helped by the fact that Perske and I do *not* get along."

"It's going to be a long night without you," Maggie said. She was bitterly disappointed. Although she and Bo had to keep their relationship a secret, they found ways to connect at most social events—a gentle touch here, a moment alone there.

"I'm sorry. Have fun tonight," Bo said.

"Given what's gone on the last few days, I'm not sure that's possible."

But much to Maggie's relief, the party got off to a festive start. Guests streamed in, gifts in hand, as Cajun and zydeco favorites thumped cheerfully from speakers. Rufus arrived with an entourage of fellow officers, all of whom immediately hit the bar. Little Earlie Waddell showed up, his reporter's notebook sticking out of his jacket pocket.

"If you see Ginger Fleer-Starke, lemme know," he told Maggie. "She asked me to put together an advertorial for her company's relocation, so I been working like a dog on it."

Little Earlie pulled out a mock-up of a two-page ad designed to look like a newspaper. It trumpeted Starke Homes' move to Baton Rouge and featured a stunning portrait of Ginger.

"What do you think?" Earlie asked, clearly proud of his work.

"It looks great, Earlie," Maggie said. "She'll love it."

Lee Bertrand came into the tent with his great-nephew, Chret, who was quite handsome when cleaned up and out from under a car. His hair shone from the pomade that held it in place, and there was more life in his grey-green eyes than she'd seen before. "Chret's my date tonight," Lee said. "I'm a lucky man." Lee winked at Maggie and slapped Chret on the back. But the ex-soldier didn't notice. He was staring at Gaynell, who gave him a shy smile in return. Maggie couldn't resist a bit of matchmaking and motioned for Gaynell to come over. "Gay, Chret is new in town. Why don't you tell him about some of Pelican's best bets, like Bon Bon and Fais Dough Dough and Junie's Oyster Bar and Dance Hall?"

"Sure," Gaynell said. "But I hope I don't bore him silly."

"I don't see how that could happen, Miss," Chret said, and followed Gaynell to a quiet table. Maggie noticed him trying to hide his limp.

Lia nudged Maggie in the ribs. "All hail the queen," she said, pointing to where Vanessa had entered with her mother, Tookie Fleer. The bride-to-be had timed her appearance so that she made a grand entrance. She was heavily made up and clothed in a bright purple, green, and gold caftan, accented with a raft of matching beaded jewelry.

"She looks like a Mardi Gras float," Maggie muttered.

"Shhh," Ione admonished. "Be nice."

"You're just jealous because you didn't say it first," Maggie retorted.

"A little," Ione admitted.

"Hello, everyone. Hey, y'all." Vanessa knocked a knife against a glass to get everyone's attention. It didn't work.

"Hey!" Tookie roared. That silenced the crowd. "My baby and I wanna thank y'all for coming."

"Thanks from me too," Rufus called out.

Tookie and Vanessa ignored him. "I can't help but think," Vanessa said, taking over from her mother, "that as I journey toward this big moment in my life, I—"

"Vanessa!" a woman's voice called out. All eyes turned toward the tent entrance. Ginger floated in, flanked by a smirking Trent and an unhappy-looking Bibi. The party-goers stared at Ginger, captivated. She wore a flowing lace dress—off-white, of course—and a tiara of baby's breath. Diamond studs sparkled in her ears. She looked like an angel—or a bride.

Ginger glided toward Vanessa and gave her cousin an air kiss. "I'm so happy for you."

Tookie, a momma bear if there ever was one, literally pushed Ginger aside. "We're in the middle of something here."

But it was too late. Vanessa couldn't recover from Ginger's showstopper of an entrance.

"I think maybe we should all eat," she said in a monotone as she looked down at the ground, too mortified to make eye contact with anyone. Maggie felt terrible for her.

"You heard the lady," Rufus echoed. "Chow call!"

He took Vanessa's hand and led her to the buffet tables. The rest of the guests lined up behind them. Maggie felt someone grab her arm. It was Tookie, who was hopping mad. A tiny, peppery woman, Tookie was in her early fifties but looked much older thanks to years of smoking and a failure to use sun block on her job as a swamp airboat pilot.

"Can you believe that woman?" Tookie barked. "She's nothing but a—" Tookie released a stream of cuss words that burned Maggie's ears. "She don't deserve to live," Tookie said, finishing her rant.

"I don't blame you one bit for being so upset, Mrs. Fleer," Maggie said in her most soothing voice. "Let's get you a drink. Lia's boyfriend, Kyle, volunteered to work the bar, and he's using my dad's Ramos Gin Fizz recipe." She guided Tookie to the bar and deposited her with Kyle. "Make her a stiff one," she whispered to him. He nodded and poured a double shot of gin into a glass. Maggie saw Vanessa sitting by herself, picking at her food, which was unusual for the robust woman. Rufus was preoccupied with entertaining a group of his police department buddies as he wolfed down a plate of shrimp étouffée. Maggie looked for her fellow bridesmaids. Gaynell and Chret were busy blushing and smiling at each other, and not wanting to disturb the blossoming romance, she left them alone. She spotted Ione and Lia in line for food and marched over. "I need you," she said as she pulled them out of line. Before they could protest, she pointed to Vanessa. "One duty I'm proud to fulfill as maid of honor is making sure the bride-to-be isn't miserable at her own party." Maggie herded Ione and Lia over to Vanessa's table. "Okay if we join you?" she asked. Vanessa's relieved grin told her it was, and the three women sat down.

"Great party," Vanessa said as she dug into her plate of food, appetite restored. "Thanks, Maggie."

Maggie faked shock. "Did you just actually thank me for something I did?"

"Yes, ma'am."

"Lace up your ice skates, ladies, because hell just froze over."

All four women burst out laughing. They didn't hear Ginger approach. "Vanessa," she said, in her soft, smooth voice. Vanessa started, then tensed. "I wanted to tell you how lovely you look."

"Oh." Vanessa relaxed slightly. "Thanks, Ginger."

Ginger shook her head sadly. "You would have made a beautiful bride, except for . . . you know." Ginger made a wan gesture toward Vanessa's bulging belly and then shrugged in a way meant to convey sympathy. "But what can you do? You're a Pelican Fleer."

Having thrown that verbal harpoon, Ginger glided off, leaving the others in stunned silence. Ione finally spoke. "Did she just insult our entire town?"

Lia pursed her lips. "I believe she did."

Vanessa pushed away her food, appetite gone once again. "Does she think I *wanted* to walk down the aisle like this? Of course I didn't. No dang bride does. But stuff happens even when you don't want it to, if you know what I mean."

"We do," Maggie replied before Vanessa could deliver a more graphic explanation. "Ignore Ginger. She's a horrible human being."

"A horrible human being that I owe lots of money to." Vanessa got up and stomped away, ignoring the chair that she knocked over. The others, not knowing what to say, watched her go.

The drama continued after Ginger's nasty barb. Little Earlie was furious when she proclaimed his advertorial "garbage" and refused to pay him. Then Rufus blew up when Trent dropped a bill in his lap for Starke Homes' "detailed designs regarding Maison La Plus Belle."

"I swear, I've put out so many fires tonight, I feel like I should have a hose and a ladder," Maggie told Gran' after managing to calm down both Little Earlie and Rufus.

Gran' smiled and sipped her gin fizz. "I know this has been a nightmare for you, chère. But take comfort from the fact that it's been very entertaining for the rest of us."

A man Maggie had never seen before approached her. He was in his early forties and wearing an expensive-looking suit and silk tie, but with his thinning hair and sagging skin, his good looks had turned a corner. "Hello," he said, his tone polite but tentative. "I was told you're the party's hostess. I'm looking for Ginger Fleer-Starke."

Just then Bibi rushed by, eyes blazing with fury. "Uh-oh," Gran' said to Maggie. "Better get your hose and ladder."

"Excuse me for a minute," Maggie told the stranger, and took off after Bibi. The intern was screaming at Ginger, who seemed unfazed by the display of anger. "Trent just told me the news. You swore to me that I would get a promotion. How can you lie like that, Ginger? And how can you make *him* a partner?"

"I reward talent," Ginger said calmly.

"No, you don't," Bibi shot back. "He's a useless buffoon. You rewarded him for sleeping with you!"

"I thought so but didn't want it to be true," the stranger said. He stepped between the two women and faced Ginger. "Is it?" he asked. Maggie saw that his face was red mutating into purple. "I want to hear it from you, Ginger. Is what Bibi's saying true?"

Ginger didn't answer. Instead, she turned and strode off, out of the tent. The man followed. "Glad you could make it to the party, Fox," Tookie Fleer called after him. She was smiling for the first time all evening.

"Is that . . ." Maggie asked Bibi, who seemed glued to her spot on the floor.

"Yes," Bibi said almost inaudibly. "That's Ginger's husband, Fox Starke."

Chapter Six

There was a brief pause in the action after the scene between the Starkes, but then the festivities resumed. "You'd think something like that would shut down this shindig," Kyle commented as he worked himself into a sweat, mixing and pouring drinks for a long line of thirsty celebrants.

"Not in Pelican," Maggie said. "It takes more than a marriage breaking up in front of everybody to put the brakes on a party in this town. But I better go see if the Starkes are okay."

Before leaving the tent, she scanned the crowd for Trent, the stick of human dynamite that had exploded the Starkes' relationship. She didn't see him and assumed that, motivated by self-preservation, he'd made himself scarce.

As soon as Maggie stepped outside, she heard the couple. "You want a divorce? Huh? Is that what you want?" Fox yelled. Ginger's response was low and unintelligible. "Of course not, because that would mean the gravy train pulled outta the station," Fox continued. "That's all I am to you anymore, a credit card with no limit. A checkbook filled with blank checks." There were more murmurs from Ginger. "I don't care. I'm done," Fox responded. "I'm going back to Houston. But you better tell your boyfriend to keep on hiding, because if I see him, I swear to you—I will kill him."

Fox stormed off to his car and tore out of the parking lot. Ginger watched him drive away, her face a mask. Then she sauntered off toward the bayou, where Maggie was sure the designer would find Trent waiting at their trysting spot. *That is one ice-cold woman,* she thought as her eyes followed Ginger, appalled yet fascinated.

Vanessa peered out of the tent entrance. "Did they leave?" she asked hopefully.

"Fox did. Ginger went for a walk by the bayou."

"Maybe we'll get lucky and someone'll push her in."

Vanessa's barb made Maggie nervous. "I should check on her," she said.

The party guests erupted into a drunken chant of "Cake, cake, cake!" It grew louder. "Forget about my stupid cousin," Vanessa ordered. "This is my party. And Ru's. Now, let's go. This baby," Vanessa said, pointing to her face, "and *this* baby," she continued, pointing at her stomach, "need us some Caramel Dobash Cake."

"I could use a big slab of Dobash, too," Maggie said, then followed Vanessa back into the tent, attributing her nerves to prior events at Crozat that made her sensitive to even a callous semijoke about murder.

*

The festivities continued deep into the night. Even Gran' made it onto the dance floor, unable to resist Lee Bertrand when he bowed and presented his arm as an escort. The couple wound up surrounded by cheering guests as they performed some old-fashioned, intricate dance steps to traditional Cajun tunes.

Maggie booted out the last revelers around four in the morning. She caught a few hours' sleep and then staggered down to the kitchen to fortify herself with chicory coffee and a hearty breakfast of biscuits and scrambled eggs before tackling cleanup. She found Gran' sitting at the kitchen table, chuckling as she read a copy of the *Pelican Penny Clipper*. "Is that a new issue?" Maggie asked.

Gran' held up the paper. A banner headline screamed, "SPECIAL EDITION! MARRIAGE MAYHEM AT BRIDAL SHOWER BASH."

"Let me see that." Maggie grabbed the paper from her grandmother. She skimmed the article to see if Little Earlie had said anything disparaging about her family or the B and B. But he'd spared them, choosing to heap his vitriol on Ginger. If anything, the Crozats came off as suffering at her expense, as did Vanessa and Rufus. Little Earlie had even managed to snap a cell phone shot of the moment Ginger began to rain on Van's parade. There she was, with a smile so devious that Maggie wondered if Earlie had done a bit of photoshopping. "I had no idea Earlie could be so brutal," she said. "I'm kind of impressed. Yet also terrified."

"Yes, you do want to stay on his good side," Gran' said. "I'll need the paper back. There's a coupon for my favorite shampoo on page ten." A bell tinkled. "Our guests have made their way to the dining room. I'm surprised they still have appetites after last night's kerfuffle. Oh, I almost forgot. This was under the paper."

Gran' handed Maggie a manila envelope addressed to Ginger. Maggie put it under her arm, picked up a coffee carafe, and left the kitchen for the dining room. She found Ginger and Trent sitting at the antique black oak table, chatting with each other. They seemed so relaxed that it was as if the night before had never happened.

"'Morning. We'll just take coffee," Ginger said.

"We're still a little iffy about the food here," Trent added as he did his variation on Ginger's helpless shrug.

"No problem—less work for me," Maggie said. After she filled their cups, she dropped the manila envelope in front of Ginger, who opened it and pulled out a copy of the *Pelican Penny Clipper*. Her eyes widened.

"Agh!" she shrieked.

Trent pulled the paper away from her. His mouth dropped open as he scanned the front page. "What the . . ."

Ginger waved the *Clipper* in front of Maggie. "What's the circulation of this rag? Do they get it in Baton Rouge?" Maggie nodded. She couldn't help but get some pleasure from watching the unflappable Ginger lose it. "He can't do this. He mentioned Starke Homes and the relocation. It'll kill our business." Ginger whirled around to Trent. "Get this Earlie idiot on the phone," she demanded.

"I'm on it." Trent was already punching in a telephone number he'd found on the Clipper. Ginger stood up and paced while the phone rang. "It went to voicemail," Trent said.

Ginger let loose with language so foul it would have made swamp boat pilot Tookie Fleer blush. "Then we'll flush the rat out of his nest and make him destroy every copy of this piece of garbage. And get Les Robbins on the line. I want him to sue this SOB for character defamation." She grabbed the expensive designer purse that she'd slung over the back of her chair and marched down the hall and out the back door. Trent sprinted behind her, punching numbers into his phone as he ran.

"Good luck," Maggie called after them. She picked up the paper that Trent had thrown down and made a note to buy Little Earlie a box of his favorite Coconut Haystacks from Bon Bon.

*

The *Pelican Penny Clipper* cover story was the hot topic of conversation among the tour guides at Doucet. Vanessa lapped up the attention and pity she received from her coworkers. Maggie grew tired of rehashing every moment of the Ginger-Fox debacle and was glad when the workday ended.

She drove home, enjoying the bright pink, purple, and orange sunset that painted the sky over the Mississippi. When she got out of her car, she noticed a pile of carpet samples next to the plantation dumpster. She recognized them as the ones Bibi had been loading into her car. Then she saw Bibi walking toward her with another armful of samples. She was struck by how relaxed and almost happy the intern looked.

"Do you mind if I dump these here?" Bibi asked as she threw the load she was carrying on top of the pile.

"No, it's fine. But don't you need them?"

"Ginger might, but I don't. I quit."

"Really?" Despite recent events, Maggie was surprised that the put-upon intern had shown such initiative.

"Yep, and get this. I called the Labor Board, and nothing I've been doing classifies as an internship. I've done the work of an employee and should be compensated for it. So for a change, someone will be suing Ginger instead of the other way around. FYI, you might want to make sure all your stairs are in good shape. Nothing like a 'fall' to bring up a lawsuit."

"Yes, I've been warned about that."

"It was seeing Fox so hurt that made me do it," Bibi said, her voice emotional. "He's such a good person. He deserves way, way better than that horrible woman."

It became clear to Maggie why Bibi had suffered through a year as Ginger's lackey. Also clear was why she hadn't quit even sooner. She was in love with Fox.

"I'm packing up my stuff," Bibi continued. "I'm leaving in the morning. Oh, that Vanessa person is here. She's been looking for Ginger, who's probably going at it with Trent in the woods somewhere."

Maggie was distracted by a strange sound. "Do you hear that?" she asked Bibi.

"Yes. It almost sounds like a baby crying."

Gopher began barking furiously. "Excuse me, I need to make sure our dog's okay," Maggie told Bibi. "It sounds like he's down by the bayou."

Maggie trudged through the woods calling the hound's name. Finally, he came bounding up to her. "There you are, buddy," she said, bending down to rub his ears. But the dog, which usually collapsed at her feet and begged for more ear love, wouldn't stay still. He ran a few circles around her and then took off, looking back now and then to make sure she followed. They reached a clearing near Ginger and Trent's rendezvous locale, and Maggie heard the thin cry again. Gopher nudged her leg with his nose, and Maggie looked down. She was stunned by what she saw. "Oh my gosh." Nestled on a bed of leaves was a beautiful but thin calico cat. Three kittens were nestled between her legs.

As were three Chihuahua-mix puppies.

"Sweet, sweet babies," Maggie murmured as she dropped to her knees and petted the mama cat and tiny creatures. "We've got to get you to the house. But where's Momma Doggy?"

Maggie looked around but saw no sign of another dog. "Come on, Gopher, she must be here somewhere." Gopher barked and wagged his tail, then headed toward the swampy stream. "You found her?"

Gopher stopped at the edge of the bayou and barked furiously. "I hope you didn't find that poor little doggy lying in the water," Maggie said as she made her way to the basset hound. She looked to where the basset hound was standing and screamed. Gopher hadn't found the puppies' mother. But he had located another body . . .

The lifeless body of Ginger Fleer-Starke.

Chapter Seven

Ginger lay on her side, her head resting on a rock. Her platinum hair floated in the shallow water at the bayou's edge; she might as well have been napping. But three Crozat guests had died only months earlier, leaving Maggie all too familiar with what death looked like. A small stream of blood leaked from the back of Ginger's head into the bayou.

Maggie pulled out her cell phone. Before she could place a call, she heard footsteps and heavy breathing. Vanessa shoved her way through some bushes and made her way toward Maggie. "I really should follow my doctor's orders and get some exercise," Vanessa said between huffs and puffs of breath.

"What are you doing here?" Maggie asked, stunned to see the woman.

"I tried texting you, but you didn't answer."

"Yes. There's a reason for that."

"Whatevs. Anyway, I'm glad I tracked you down. We have an emergency. The rental company called and they've discontinued carrying the chairs I want for the reception."

"Vanessa," Maggie responded, choosing her words with care as she dialed 9-1-1. "Something has happened."

Vanessa's eyes followed Maggie's gaze and landed on Ginger's body. She let out a shriek and then fainted.

The 9-1-1 operator came on the line. "Hello, help!" Maggie cried out. "There's a dead woman and an unconscious one, and she's pregnant, and there are puppies and kittens and a cat, but no mama dog!"

"All right, honey," the operator said cautiously. "Now are you able to tell me exactly what drugs you've taken?"

"I know this sounds crazy, but it's all happening. Send the police and an ambulance to Crozat Plantation. Tell them to go up the side road to the back where the bayou is."

"Maggie Crozat, is that you? It's Delphine Arnaud. I'll get someone out there right away."

Maggie ended the call and then speed-dialed her father. "Dad, emergency! GPS me and bring Mom and the wagon and blankets. Get Ru here, too." She hung up without waiting for a reply and rushed to Vanessa. She lifted her to a sitting position, which was no easy feat since the pregnant woman had added sixty-five pounds of baby weight to her already-zaftig figure. She slapped the unconscious woman's face a few times. "Van, wake up. Wake up!"

Vanessa started, then heaved in a big gulp of air and opened her eyes. "Wha . . ." she said in a weak voice. She saw Ginger's body and started to sway.

Maggie shook her to prevent another faint. "Stay with me."

"Okay," Vanessa murmured, still in a daze.

"Maggie! Maggie, honey, where are you?" Tug called.

"Here, Dad! Down by the bayou."

Maggie heard her parents push through the heavy brush. They appeared seconds later, pulling the red wagon from Maggie's childhood that now conveyed items around the plantation. Ninette let out a small scream when she saw Ginger. "Oh my God!" she cried out, clutching at her heart.

Tug took a step toward the body, but Maggie pulled him back. "No, Dad, don't touch anything. The police are on their way, and we have to leave everything exactly as it is for them. I need your help with this." Maggie jumped up and ran over to the puppies and kittens, which made tiny, mewling sounds. "Mama, bring the wagon over."

Ninette didn't respond or move. She seemed frozen in place. Tug ran his hands through his hair and looked from Ginger to Vanessa to the puppies and kittens, then back to Ginger. "You know how much I love animals," Tug said, "but that doesn't seem to be the biggest crisis here."

"I know, but it's the one I need you and Mom to handle right now," Maggie said, her tone urgent. Maggie ran back to Vanessa and dropped to her knees next to the disoriented woman. "I want to stay with Vanessa, and the authorities will have to investigate what happened to Ginger." She motioned to the animals. "Someone needs to take care of these babies or they'll die."

This snapped Ninette out of her stupor. "Yes, right. Of course. Tug, lay a blanket on the bottom of the wagon. I'll bring them up to the house and call the vet. Vanessa, chère, are you all right?"

"I . . . I . . . I . . ." Vanessa stuttered.

"I've got her, Mama." Maggie took a blanket from the wagon and draped it around Vanessa. She kept an arm wrapped protectively around Van's shoulder. "It's okay. An ambulance should be here any minute."

Tug and Ninette carefully moved the mother cat, kittens, and pups into the wagon. The cat didn't give them any trouble; Maggie figured the poor thing was too dehydrated to make a fuss. Ninette headed back to the main house, pulling the wagon as carefully as possible to protect its delicate cargo.

"I'm going out front to meet the police," Tug told his daughter and sprinted off.

Maggie's cell rang again. She looked down to see that Bo was the caller and answered. "Hey," Bo said. "Just wanted to see if you were up for Xander's lesson in an—"

"Ginger's dead, out back by the bayou. Get here. I'll explain."

Bo hung up without a word, and Maggie knew he was on his way. She turned back to the crisis at hand. Vanessa had transitioned to weeping. "No, no, no, no," she moaned. "How could this happen?"

"I am so sorry," Maggie said as she gave her a sympathetic hug. "I know it's a huge shock."

Vanessa's nose started to run, and she wiped it with the Crozats' blanket. She risked a quick glance at Ginger's lifeless body and then turned away. "How could Ginger drown like this? It's awful. Poor her."

Maggie nodded sympathetically but said nothing. It was not the time to point out the wound on the back of Ginger's skull that indicated a much more sinister demise.

*

The Pelican first responders arrived simultaneously. EMTs examined Vanessa and pronounced her vital signs strong but insisted on taking her to the hospital to be thoroughly checked out. Maggie bundled the pregnant woman into the ambulance and texted Rufus where to find his wife-to-be. Officers Cal Vichet and Artie Belloise taped off the area while Acting Police Chief Hank Perske barked orders at them. Maggie tried to hide the instant dislike she felt for Perske, a tightly muscled giant in his early fifties. Where Rufus had opted for casual business attire while on the job, Perske was never out of uniform. He struck her as a rigid, humorless autocrat. She introduced herself and said, "I'm the one who found poor Ginger."

"A detective will be here shortly." Perske's terse, cold tone reaffirmed Maggie's first impression.

"Yes," she said. "Bo's on his way."

This got the taciturn man's attention, much to Maggie's regret. "How would you know that?" he demanded.

"We're friends. I give his son art lessons sometimes. And Bo's helped out before, so I called him." Maggie made herself maintain eye contact with the chief. Looking away would indicate weakness; the last thing she wanted the man to see was how vulnerable she felt.

"Exactly what kind of help did you need?"

"Just support. It's horrible finding someone who's . . . passed away . . . on your property."

"This would be the fourth time in only a few months."

Perske glared at her, eyes narrowed to suspicious slits. Maggie flushed. She felt her underarms start to perspire and wished she'd gone with something stronger than an all-natural deodorant. "I have an alibi. I was at work," she blurted.

"Interesting you think you need an alibi considering we haven't even determined Mrs. Starke's cause of death."

Maggie's heart raced so fast that she felt faint. *Too bad I can't flag down Vanessa's ambulance and hop in there with her,* she thought. "I saw the back of Ginger's head," she explained to the chief. "I don't see how she could get a wound like that and wind up face down in the water."

"There are few things I hate more than an amateur sleuth,'" Perske said. "Very few things."

"Honestly, I don't mean to be. But I'm an artist. I'm very visual, so I tend to pick up things other people might miss. Not the police, of course. They don't miss a thing."

Perske was unimpressed by her ham-fisted attempt at flattery. In fact, Maggie's visual instincts picked up downright disgust in his expression. She was searching for a way of climbing out of the verbal hole she'd dug when a welcome voice called out her name.

"Back here, Bo," she called to him.

Bo pushed aside thick foliage and made his way to her. He was clad in his off-duty attire of jeans and a T-shirt, his hair slightly mussed up from colliding with branches. Maggie tamped down the surge of attraction she always felt at the sight of him and was always forced to hide— now more than ever given Chief Perske's mistrustful glare.

She greeted Bo with a stiff "Hello. Thank you for coming."

Bo nodded a greeting to his chief and then responded to Maggie with equal stiffness. "Just doing my job. If you'll show us somewhere to sit, I'd like to get the details of how you discovered Mrs. Starke."

"Yes. We can talk on the veranda. Just follow me."

Chief Perske held up his hand and shook his head. "Yeah, that won't be happening," Perske said. "I don't know what the deal is with you two, but I'm picking up a little too much personal history. You can supervise the boys here, Durand. I'll be taking Ms. Crozat's statement."

Perske motioned to Maggie, who snuck an anguished look at Bo and then glumly led the chief to the veranda of the main house. She had the terrifying feeling that if Ginger's cause of death really was murder, the chief considered her a prime suspect.

Chapter Eight

Maggie's grilling by Perske did nothing to allay her fears. His tone was so suspicious and skeptical that Maggie felt compelled to remind him of what he himself had pointed out. "We don't know yet that Ginger was murdered," she said.

"No, we don't," the man had to acknowledge. "But we will know very soon." He studied her. Maggie held his glance and studied him right back. While an unexpected heat wave had soaked through many a Pelican shirt, the chief was almost unnaturally dry. Even his skin had a matte finish instead of a dewy sheen. Was the man human or a cyborg? "Being a chief in a small town means listening to gossip," Perske continued, "and from what I've heard, this Ginger had become a problem for your family. A very expensive problem."

Maggie was stunned. It was one thing to consider her a suspect, but quite another to drag in the rest of the Crozats. "She wasn't dishing out anything that my family couldn't take," she responded evenly. "And when it comes to Ginger, gossip can point a finger at a lot of people around here."

"Anyone in particular?"

"I think finding that out is your job. You certainly wouldn't want to hear the ramblings of an 'amateur sleuth.'" Maggie stood up tall, claiming every inch of her five-foot-four-inch height. Even with the inch-plus heels on her black espadrilles, she was still only about a head taller than the sitting Perske. "I've told you everything I know about the circumstances of finding Mrs. Fleer-Starke. I need to help my mother with the puppies and kittens that we found. You have all my contact information if you need to talk to me again."

Maggie marched off, feeling pretty proud of how she'd schooled the bully of a chief. She made her way to the B and B office, where her family was tending to the new arrivals. Ninette had commandeered one of Gopher's beds for the animals and placed it inside Maggie's old playpen; her parents' sentimental attachment to it had proved fortuitous. The mama cat, looking full and sated, rested on the bed while her kittens nursed. Ninette, Tug, and Gran' were feeding the hungry puppies with syringes. Gopher guarded the group so tightly that he even barked at his beloved Maggie's approach. She reached down to pet him and massage one of his floor-length basset ears. "Good boy. You watch out for the little ones. Were y'all able to reach the vet?"

"The service tracked down Dr. Waguespack, and she's sending over special formulas for puppies and kittens in the morning," Ninette said as the pup in her lap sucked on the syringe. "We may not need the kitty formula, since Mama Cat seems to be responding to the food and drink we gave her. Since the pups are motherless, it appears they were feeding from her as well, which is another reason she was dehydrated. The doctor gave us instructions for making something called 'glop,' which will nourish them just fine until the puppy formula comes."

"It smells kind of yummy. What's in it?"

"Evaporated milk, Karo syrup, raw eggs, and gelatin, warmed up enough to go from custard to liquid."

"I'd hold onto that recipe, Ninette," Gran' said. "Throw in some pecans and you've got a delicious pie."

"Did you talk to Chief Perske?" Tug asked his daughter. "What did he tell you?"

"He didn't say much. You know the police. They're pretty tight-lipped until some facts start rolling in." Maggie, who constantly feared that stress might bring on another bout of her mother's cancer, opted not to mention that Perske had the Crozats in his crosshairs.

"I think Vanessa was in shock," Ninette said. "I hope she's all right."

"That poor girl can't seem to catch a break," Gran' commented.

Tug gave his mother an admonishing look. "A woman died, Mama. The term 'catching a break' doesn't exactly seem appropriate."

"My age allows me the occasional blunt observation," Gran' responded. "It's very sad that Ginger died, but she was a horror of a human being. And I dare anyone to deny that the timing of it couldn't be worse for Vanessa."

Maggie paced the room. She felt an overwhelming urge to resume an old habit of biting her nails, but since she'd recently trimmed them to facilitate her ability to draw, there was nothing to chew on. "I just hope the coroner's report comes back fast."

"So you think it might be . . ." Tug didn't finish his sentence. He didn't have to.

The family fell silent for a moment. Then Ninette spoke. "Whatever happened to Ginger probably scared off the mama of these little ones. I feel terrible thinking that she might be out there looking for her babies. Maggie, why don't you and your grandmother check with a few neighbors to see if they've noticed a stray lately?"

"Good idea," Maggie said, grateful to her mother for offering a distraction from Ginger's death.

"I'll wash up and change into my walking shoes." Gran' stood up and placed the pup she'd been feeding back in the playpen, then picked up a lint roller and deftly swiped it over her navy silk slacks.

Maggie hastily typed and printed some "Lost Dog and Found Cat" fliers to put up around town. As soon as Gran' was ready, the two took off. They went from one neighborhood to the next, ringing doorbells to ask if anyone was missing pets or had seen a stray dog in the area. No one had. As they trudged down another dusty street toward the final house on the block, Maggie noticed Gran' pull a tissue out of her purse and pat her forehead with it. The eighty-two-year-old was also breathing heavier than usual.

"Maybe you should go home," Maggie said, concerned. "I can keep looking."

"No. This is merely proof that I don't get enough exercise. Chère, I need to talk to you about Ginger. Do you really think someone killed her?"

Maggie nodded, her face grim. "She was facedown in the water with a deep wound in the back of her head."

Gran' shuddered. "How ghastly. Well, PPD won't lack for suspects. There's her husband, of course."

"And Bibi, who obviously hated her and was in love with him," Maggie said. "Then there's Trent, who was having a thing with Ginger. Who knows what the real story was there?"

"True. And one can't rule out Vanessa or her gorgon of a mother, Tookie."

"There's also the remote possibility—*extremely* remote—that Rufus might have been driven to get off his duff and defend his fiancée from Ginger's machinations," Maggie said.

"And these are just the people we know about. I'm guessing that woman left a trail of bad blood between here and Houston."

Maggie hesitated before saying, "And there's us." Gran' looked at her, confused. "I got the impression that Perske thinks Ginger's death was very convenient for the family, as was my discovering her body."

Gran' gave a derisive snort. "That man suffers from a serious lack of imagination."

"I just hope he doesn't fixate on us. And that once the coroner establishes a time of death, we all have alibis."

Maggie stopped at the end of the country cul-de-sac. She and Gran' stood in front of a small but charming house. It was painted a pale green with bright, white gingerbread trim and a deep, forest-green door. "This is lovely," Gran' said.

"Adorable," Maggie agreed. "Do you know who lives here?"

"An older couple, but I've never met them. I heard from Alicia Benoist up the street that it's a vacation home and they bought it not that long ago."

Maggie surveyed the cheery scene. She noticed that the street numbers on the house were painted in dark green but shaded in the paler green, an artistic touch she appreciated. The home had been renovated so recently that the smell of sawdust and fresh paint still clung to the air.

"They've put a lot of work into the place. They're either planning to spend more time here or fixing to sell." She and Gran' walked up three wooden steps that led to the front porch, which featured an oak-stained Adirondack chair surrounded by potted pink azaleas. Maggie rang the doorbell, which responded with a few church-like bongs.

"A bit pretentious for a spit of a house," Gran' said.

"Don't be judgy," Maggie admonished.

"Be right there," a man called from inside the house. Maggie and Gran' heard a few sturdy footsteps, then the front door opened a crack, and a man who appeared to be in his midseventies stuck his head out. He had a thick thatch of pure white hair and alert, light-brown eyes that peered through gold, wire-rimmed glasses. "Sorry, I'd open the door more, but I'm taking care of a dog and I don't know if she'll bolt."

"Is she a stray?" Maggie asked. "We found some pups without a mama. We've been out looking for her."

"You know what, I may have your girl," the man said. "Come on in. I'm Stevens. Stevens Troy."

"I'm Charlotte Crozat and this is my granddaughter, Magnolia," Gran' said.

"Maggie for short," Maggie added.

Maggie and Gran' followed Stevens into his home. The living room was stuffed with moving boxes and a collection of furniture that was traditional in style. Maggie noticed a heavy glass award jutting out of a box, anointing Stevens as Houston Lawyer of the Year. "Forgive the mess," Stevens said. "I just sold a home in Houston and moved everything here permanently. My wife passed away about four months ago. I felt like I could use a fresh start."

"We're so sorry for your loss," Gran' said. "I'm a widow myself. I admire your courage. Except for college in New Orleans, I've never lived anywhere but Pelican."

"Well, then, you're the perfect person to fill me in on what I need to know about my new home," Stevens said, smiling.

Oh my gosh, he's flirting with her! Maggie thought. As she wondered if her grandmother noticed, Gran's behavior answered the question. "Of course I will, of course," Gran' fluttered. When nervous, she cranked up her inner Southern belle and repeated phrases in what was almost a parody of her soft Louisiana accent. "You simply must let me give you a personal tour of the area. You *must*."

"I'd love that," Stevens said. "Let's set a date."

"Why don't you both do that after we see the dog, so you're not distracted?" Maggie said, interrupting the senior singles' mingle.

"Yes, sorry," Stevens said. "Follow me."

"I see you face west," Gran' said as they walked. "You must catch some lovely sunsets."

"That's why Wynette and I bought this house," Stevens said as he led them through a small galley kitchen. "She had a passion for a pretty setting sun."

They exited the kitchen onto an enclosed patio at the back of the house. A small tan-and-white Chihuahua mix paced the room, whimpering. "She came in through the doggy door the previous owner installed for his Doberman," Stevens said. "The cover to it is missing, and I ordered a new one, but lucky for her, it hasn't shown up yet. She goes outside and wanders around, then comes back in. Poor thing seems agitated."

Maggie knelt down next to the animal, which shivered and pulled away. But as Maggie murmured soothing reassurances, the dog crept closer and allowed Maggie to pet her. Maggie took advantage of the proximity to peek at the pup's belly. "This sweetie has given birth recently," she told the others. "We found our girl."

"No wonder she was so distressed," Stevens said. "She missed her babies."

Stevens offered to drive Gran', Maggie, and the pooch back to Crozat. The dog, still weak from her ordeal, didn't protest when Maggie wrapped her in a blanket and carried her to Stevens's Prius. Maggie had texted her parents that they were on their way, so Ninette and Tug met them at the back door. Gran' introduced Stevens to Ninette and Tug as Maggie brought the dog into the B and B's office and placed her in the playpen. The mama cat gave a happy meow, and the puppies squeaked with joy. They leapt on their mother, who was equally happy to see them.

"She needs a name," Maggie said. "I think Stevens, as her rescuer, gets that honor."

"Ooh, lotta pressure," Stevens said. He thought for a moment. "We're in Cajun Country, so it should be French. What about Jolie Fille? Pretty Girl?"

"I think it's lovely," Gran' said. "We'll call her Jolie for short."

"Could call a lot around here '*jolie*,'" Stevens said, eliciting a blush from Gran'.

Tug pulled Ninette and Maggie aside. "What's going on?" he whispered.

"I know it's been a while, chère," Ninette whispered back, "but it's called flirting."

The Crozats' landline rang. "I'll get it," Ninette said. She picked up a cordless phone and stepped into the hallway. Gran' and Stevens didn't even register her departure.

"You could be on the road to getting a stepdaddy, Daddy," Maggie teased her father.

"Huh," Tug said, wrinkling his forehead. "Not sure how I feel about that."

Ninette reappeared in the doorway. "That was Pelican PD," she said, her voice tense. "They're on the way over."

The others exchanged worried glances. "Everything okay?" Stevens asked.

"We have a problem with a guest," Maggie said. Unsure of how much to reveal, she opted for being vague.

"A Houston woman," Gran' said. "I'm not going to ask if you know her because I despise when people do that. 'Oh, you're from Louisiana, do you know my friend Mary Smith?' Let me run through the names of the five million Louisiana citizens in my head and see if that one rings a bell."

"Now I'm curious. Try me. What's her name?"

"Ginger Fleer-Starke," Maggie said.

To the surprise of the others, Stevens burst out laughing. "Oh, I've heard all about Mrs. Ginger Fleer-Starke, as has pretty much every litigator in Houston—which is what I was in my former life. I don't think a month went by when that woman wasn't suing someone. What's your problem with her? Maybe I can help."

"That's very generous, but I don't think you can." Maggie held up her cell phone. "Bo just texted me. PPD received the coroner's report. It's official. Ginger was murdered."

Chapter Nine

Stevens looked stricken. "My God, that's awful. What happened?"

"We don't know," Maggie said and then described how she'd found Ginger by the bayou. "I assume the police will have more questions. Unfortunately for us, we're on their list of suspects."

Stevens grimaced. "If you don't mind, I think I'll stick around. Just in case you need a lawyer at some point. You know, to at least run interference."

"That's both reassuring and terrifying," Maggie said. "Thank you, but here's hoping the only reason we need you is to help nurse animal babies."

"I just heard a car pull into the back parking area," Tug said. "I'll see what's going on."

"I'll put on another pot of coffee," Ninette said. "Thank goodness I made a Bananas Foster coffee cake this morning. Food earns a lot of goodwill with at least some of the PPD officers."

Maggie followed her father outside, where Cal Vichet and Artie Belloise had parked their patrol car. "Sorry, Crozats," Cal said. "I've got some bad news. According to the coroner's report, the cause of death for Mrs. Fleer-Starke was blunt force trauma. Translation—she was murdered."

Before Tug could respond, Maggie jumped in. She didn't want to give away that Bo had already shared the news. "Oh, no!" she cried out, hoping the officers wouldn't question her overly dramatic tone. "What a tragedy! We had no idea." Tug gave her a confused look but didn't say anything.

"We're sorry to put you through this again," Artie said, "but we got stuff to do. I'm gonna examine what's now officially a crime scene. And Cal's gonna take statements. He'll need to talk to everyone here—guests, you guys. You know the drill."

"Sadly, we do." Maggie's heart pumped. She had a question—an important one. "Was the coroner able to determine a time of death?"

"Yeah, we got lucky," Cal said, hastening to add, "Begging your pardon regarding the circumstances. The victim was wearing one of those fitness watches. It must have cracked on a rock when she fell. Anyway, it stopped working, and the time on the watch corresponded with the coroner's estimation."

"Which is . . . ?" Maggie prompted.

"3:07 PM. On the watch. Coroner estimated between two and four PM."

Maggie let out the breath that she'd been holding. "I have an alibi. I was still at work."

"And your mother, grandmother, and I were at the grocery store picking up ingredients for dinner," Tug said. He hesitated a moment before saying, "Wait, that's not completely true."

"It's not?" Maggie asked, nervous again.

"No. Your grandmother was at Junie's having a late afternoon cocktail."

Maggie controlled the urge to burst into highly inappropriate giggles. "That counts as an alibi. Three o'clock at a bar in Pelican? I'm sure there are loads of witnesses."

"I'm one of 'em," Artie declared. The others looked at him. "It's all good. I was off duty. And I remember saying hi to your Gran'."

"Y'all can relax," Cal assured Maggie and Tug. "We never would have suspected you."

Maggie noticed that he emphasized the "we," indicating that others did—the others being Hank Perske, she assumed. "So," Cal continued. "If you don't mind, we best get started. If you could round up whatever guests are staying here, that'd be great."

"Of course," Maggie said. "With Ginger gone, it's just her employees Bibi and Trent. You can talk to them in the front parlor. Mama has coffee and dessert waiting for you, Cal."

His face lit up as Artie's dropped. "Artie, why don't you come too? You should probably fuel up before you start the search."

Artie brightened. "Amen to that. Wouldn't want to do a murder investigation on an empty stomach." He patted his rotund belly. In Artie's case, empty stomach was purely a figure of speech.

As the four walked toward the main house, Maggie realized something was bothering her about the scenario. "Where's Bo?" she asked. "I thought it was his job to get statements."

Cal shrugged. "You know small-town departments. We all do whatever's asked for."

Maggie nodded, but she wasn't satisfied with Cal's evasive response. Bo had clearly landed on the wrong side of Chief Perske, and she feared that could have serious ramifications. It might even endanger his job.

Maggie texted Bo to ask what was going on. His response was "I'm on filing duty," confirming her fears. She then went looking for Bibi and Trent and found them in the living area of Ginger's carriage suite, side by side in front of a laptop computer. They snapped the computer closed as soon as Maggie entered. "I assume you know about Ginger's death," she said. "I'm sorry."

Bibi uttered a couple of perfunctory comments about Ginger being taken too young, blah blah blah—an expected response considering she wasn't on the payroll and was in love with her boss's husband. But Trent's reaction to the loss of his lover-slash-paycheck bothered Maggie. There was no grief or even panic. "Circle of life," he said with a shrug and a headshake. Perhaps realizing how cold he came across, he quickly added, "I believe in the Buddhist tenet that death isn't the end of life but the end of the body inhabited in that life." Maggie, who had a feeling Trent would have trouble spelling "Buddhist," no less following the religion, found his callousness suspicious.

"The police are here," she told the two. "They've confirmed that Ginger's death wasn't an accident."

"Are you saying she was murdered?" Bibi asked. She seemed genuinely shocked.

"Yes. I'm sorry."

"Oh no. I don't believe it." Bibi put her hand on her heart and looked at Trent, who closed his eyes and took a few deep breaths.

"Namaste," he said.

"That's more a sign-off at the end of a yoga class than a send-off to the next world," Maggie couldn't stop herself from pointing out. "Anyway, the police need to interview all of us."

"Why?" Bibi looked panicked. "Are we suspects?"

"Not if we have alibis," Trent jumped in. "Did the police happen to say when this horrible event took place?"

Oh no you don't, Maggie thought. *I'm not buying you time to come up with some manufactured alibi.* "Officer Vichet will tell you everything you need to know," she said. "I'll walk you over to him."

The three left the carriage house and made their way in silence to the main house's front parlor. Maggie pulled Cal aside before depositing Bibi and Trent with him. "I have some information for you," she said. She revealed how she'd discovered Ginger and Trent's romantic rendezvous and the subsequent blow-up with Ginger's husband, Fox. She also shared Trent's low-key response to the news of his inamorata's demise. "And even though Bibi and Trent seem to hate each other, I just found them together doing something on the computer that they couldn't hide from me fast enough."

"Good stuff," Cal said. "Thanks." He motioned for Bibi and Trent to precede him into the room. Bibi nervously clenched and unclenched her fists; Trent was preternaturally calm.

"Good luck," Maggie told Bibi. "Namaste," she couldn't resist calling over her shoulder to Trent as she walked away.

*

The officers didn't leave the B and B until midnight. Maggie fell into bed after they left but woke up wide-awake at three AM. After trying and failing to fall back asleep, she gave up and decided to distract herself from the murder by working on Vanessa and Ru's portrait. Dawn broke and the sky streaked pink as Maggie trudged to her studio, crunching on fallen spruce pine needles and releasing their pungent scent. She printed out the photos she'd taken of the couple and pinned them to a bulletin board, the goal being to incorporate the best elements of each picture into the painting. But concentration was hard to come by. Maggie's thoughts ricocheted between feeling badly about Ginger's death and realistic concerns about how news of a homicide might affect Crozat B and B. The venerable old place had survived everything from the Civil War to the Great Depression, but another murder might do in the family business.

After working on the portrait for a couple of hours, Maggie closed up her studio and returned to the shotgun to get ready for work. After sending Bo a quick text to check in, she changed into the jean shorts and T-shirt that she wore under her hoopskirt. Then she pulled her chestnut hair into a tight bun, put on a tinted moisturizer that allowed the smattering of freckles on the bridge of her nose to shine through, and circled her hazel eyes with brown eyeliner. Maggie locked the door of the shotgun behind her and headed for the Falcon convertible. She was startled to see Cal standing next to the car.

"Hey there. Us again," he said apologetically. "Artie's at the crime scene, but I need to get your statement. I know you gave one to Perske, but he wants me to go over it again."

Maggie fumed. The chief was clearly looking to catch her in inconsistencies. But she politely responded, "Of course," and motioned to a picnic bench under an oak tree. The two sat down, and she shared every detail she could think of about Ginger, from her scams to her death. She also gave him Ione's number so her boss could corroborate Maggie's alibi.

"Alright, I think I got what I need from you," Cal said, putting away his notepad.

"I'm curious—how did the interviews with Trent and Bibi go last night?" she asked.

"Interesting. They alibied each other."

"Really? I got the impression they can't stand each other."

"That may be," Cal said. "Or . . . maybe it's the opposite. Maybe Trent was catting around with Bibi too, and they were putting out that negative vibe to throw everyone off."

"But that would mean Trent was having an affair with both his boss and his competition. It doesn't make sense."

"You can't make sense of a horndog."

"True," Maggie acknowledged. "But I get the impression that Trent is more of an opportunist than a horndog."

Cal was about to reply when he and Maggie heard Artie Belloise shouting, "I got someone!" They ran toward the bayou and met the officer just as he emerged from the brush. He was dragging a handcuffed Little Earlie by the arm.

"I swear, I didn't do anything," Little Earlie protested. He looked terrified. "I was just trying to get a story."

"You been on your police scanner again, Earlie?"

"Finding stuff to write about's my job. And this is a big story."

Maggie knew it was true but hated hearing it. The last thing Crozat B and B needed was for Little Earlie to use the tragedy as a way of bumping up the *Pelican Penny Clipper*'s visibility. "I think it would be disrespectful to turn this into some salacious tabloid feature," Maggie said. She searched for another angle that might put the brakes on Earlie's editorial enthusiasm. "Plus, you need to be very careful about what you publish. Releasing any information about the . . . incident . . . could hamper PPD's efforts to ID the suspect."

"Well put, Maggie," Cal complimented. "I see you've picked up some lingo from being around so many murders."

Little Earlie jumped on this. "Considering how your bookings took a downturn after the last 'incident,' are you worried about the negative effect this one will have on your business?"

"Of course she is, you idiot," Artie barked. "Who wouldn't be? Now you get to take a ride with me to the station where you can explain to the captain what you were doing contaminating possible evidence." Artie stuffed Little Earlie into the back of the PPD patrol car and got in the front passenger seat. The patrol car took off with Cal at the wheel.

Maggie returned to the Crozat office, where Tug was paying bills. Gran' was tending to the animal babies with Stevens at her side. "Morning, chère," Gran' greeted her. "Look who volunteered his services." She addressed her helpmate. "You are quite the gentleman, sir."

Stevens smiled bashfully as he replaced the soiled paper at the bottom of the playpen. "It's my pleasure. This is all new to me. Wynette and I never had kids, and she had respiratory problems, so we couldn't even have pets. I'm telling you, I had no idea how exhausting it is to be a parent."

"Yes, but so worth it. Especially if they tend to your every need when you're in your dotage. Right, dearest son?" Gran' winked at Tug, who shook his head affectionately. "Maggie, what was going on out there? I could swear I heard Little Earlie."

"You did." Maggie filled the others in on the aggressive young journalist's antics.

"That's all we need," Tug said. "Little Earlie Waddell turning this into 'the story of the century'!" Tug finished the sentence with a dead-on impression of an old-time newsreel reporter's stentorian tones.

"Did Cal interview y'all?" Maggie asked.

"Yes," her father said. "But once he realized we weren't around the house during the time of the murder and our alibis would check out, he kept the interviews brief."

"Since I was here, I also told the officer that I knew Ginger from Houston and shared a bit about her reputation there," Stevens said.

"Good. It sounds like H-Town is teeming with potential suspects."

"Just ask any lawyer whose client got hit with one of her nuisance suits," Stevens agreed.

"I should let Bo know about that angle." Maggie pulled out her phone and tapped out a text. "I texted him already this morning, but he hasn't gotten back to me. I hope he's okay."

"I'm sure he is, chère," Gran' said. "He'll get back to you when he can. Stevens, you have a bit of puppy spit-up on your shoulder. Let me get that."

Gran' pulled a tissue out of a box and wet it in a nearby glass of water. She patted the small stain while Stevens smiled appreciatively. Maggie and her father exchanged glances, hers amused, his bemused.

Maggie left the others and got in her convertible to make the drive to work. The day was once again unseasonably warm, and she put the top down, reveling in a moist breeze as she drove. She sailed along the river road until about a mile from Doucet, where she hit stop-and-start traffic. Maggie put on her Bluetooth and called Ione to warn her that she was running late.

"No worries," Ione said. "I heard something was going on out there."

Ione signed off the call. As Maggie inched toward the stoplight, she began losing patience with the traffic tie-up. She motioned to a driver coming toward her from the opposite direction, and he slowed down.

"Hey," she asked. "Do you know what's causing this mess?"

"Stoplight's out at Bonneville, and they got some idiot traffic cop directing everyone," the man responded before he drove on.

After another excruciating ten minutes, Maggie reached the light. She felt for the traffic officer, who had to contend with the honks and curses of irate drivers. "Thank you," she called to him. Maggie was stunned when he turned around to acknowledge her.

The "idiot traffic cop" was Bo.

Chapter Ten

Maggie pulled over and parked on the side of the road. She made her way through the cars to Bo. She'd never seen him in a uniform. He looked uncomfortable . . . but still sexy.

"Bo?" she said. "What the heck is going on?"

"Perske, that's what," he replied as he directed three cars to make a left and then held up his hand to stop the annoyed driver of the fourth car. "He said my 'friendship' causes me to show favoritism to your family. I disagreed using a few choice words, so here I am."

"I'm so sorry."

"It's not your fault. The guy's a—hey!" A car snuck by Bo and zoomed off. "Dammit."

"I'm behind in giving Xander his lessons," Maggie said. "Do you want to come by tonight? I can get him started on a new painting, and you and I can talk through this whole Perske thing."

"Sure." Another car tried to ignore Bo. He banged on the hood and glared at the driver. "Yeah, I don't think so, buddy." Intimidated, the driver waited for Bo's signal to move forward. "I'm sorry, Maggie, I need to focus here," Bo said as he directed the man on his way.

"Right. Sorry. I'll go."

Maggie wended her way through traffic back to the Falcon. She felt responsible for Bo's demotion. And she wondered if, despite his words, Bo didn't feel the same way. He had been curt with her, which made sense given the circumstances. But Maggie feared an underlying resentment in his attitude.

She continued the drive to Doucet in a funk that she knew she'd have to shake off before taking on the day's tourists. Since part of her draw as a Doucet guide was the fact that she was a descendant of the original owners, she needed patience and a positive attitude—especially when asked for the millionth time if it bothered her to work as a guide at a home that the Doucets had owned until the mid-1950s, when the family agreed it would be better served as a historic landmark. The answer: it didn't. Maggie was thrilled with its beautifully preserved manor house and outbuildings and deeply affected by the silent power of its restored slave cabins. She loved that Doucet offered visitors the full range of plantation experience, from brutal to beautiful. Still, the question grew tiresome, and there were days when she just didn't feel like seeing the skepticism on visitors' faces when she answered it. Today was one of them.

As soon as Maggie parked in the field that served as the employee lot, Gaynell and Ione ran over and interrupted her brooding. "Vanessa's here and she's in a state," Ione said.

"I thought she was going to take a few days off."

"The police let her know that Ginger didn't die a natural death," Gaynell said. "Somehow that set her and Rufus at each other even more than usual, and she said she had to get out of their trailer."

"You have to talk her off the ledge. It's your maid of honor duty," Ione declared. She steered Maggie through the plantation's kitchen garden into the overseer's cottage, which housed the employee break room. Vanessa sat sobbing on a faded club chair.

"Why, Maggie?" she cried. "Why, why, why, why, why?"

"Okay, you need to calm down." Maggie pulled a glass out of the drainer by the sink and filled it with water. She handed it to Vanessa. "Here. Drink this. Slowly."

Vanessa obeyed the order, and as she drank, her hysteria morphed into fury. "That evil see-you-next-Tuesday. It figures that she'd find a way to make this wedding all about her."

"I assume you're talking about Ginger, and I don't think that's what she had in mind when she got herself murdered."

Vanessa grabbed Maggie by her faded purple T-shirt. "You need to help me. You're good at finding out who killed people. With Rufus on leave and that stupid chief acting like besties with the mayor, no one's gonna do anything to find out what happened."

"I think that's a little unfair, Vanessa. Despite personal differences, Chief Perske is a professional. Besides, it'll look bad for him if he can't solve the crime."

Vanessa released Maggie and slumped in her chair. "Yeah, but will he do it in time for my wedding? It's not gonna be much fun if everyone's looking at their neighbor in the church pew wondering if they're the one what killed Ginger."

Maggie had to acknowledge that Vanessa had a point. "If you really want quick action, you and Rufus should hire a private eye or something."

"With what money? Every dime is sunk in that stupid mansion. And did I mention Rufus is on *unpaid* leave? That was one expensive parking space he fought over. Please, Maggie. I know Bo will help, but I need more than that. I need you."

"Of course," Maggie said. "I'll do whatever I can."

Vanessa brightened and downed the rest of the water. She made a face. "Dang, more peeing." She got up and disappeared into the bathroom. The others looked after her.

"Great," Maggie said when Vanessa was out of earshot. "I can now add solving a murder to my list of maid of honor duties."

*

Maggie raced home after work, put on her workout clothes, and met up with Ninette, Ione, Lia, and Gaynell for a twilight power walk. The five women had signed up as a group for Ninette's Yes We PeliCAN! Walkathon. The weather was perfect, with a sixty-five degree temperature that prevented the fifty percent humidity from feeling clammy.

Maggie led a few warm-up stretches, and then the women took off down the plantation's side road at a brisk pace. "Are we done yet?" Ione asked a few minutes after they started. She took a tissue out of her fanny pack and dabbed at a spot of perspiration on her forehead.

"Ione, you're terrible," Maggie chided. "Aside from the fact this is for a good cause, you need the exercise. We want you to stick around for a good long while."

"Maybe I'd rather sit on my duff eating pecan pie and stick around for a *really* good short while," Ione grumbled. But she kept up with the others, even upping the workout by grabbing a couple of rocks to use as hand weights.

The fivesome used the time to catch up with each other. Ninette and Maggie filled the others in on their newfound infant animal brood, eliciting a chorus of "awws." Gaynell blushed scarlet when teased about her admirer, Chret. But the casual chatter faded into silence as they passed PPD's evidence van, once again parked at Crozat.

"Poor Ginger," Lia said. "I pray that she didn't feel any pain."

"Amen," Ninette said.

"Amen," the others chorused.

"She ran this route twice a day while she was here. She always went down that old road." Maggie gestured to the overgrown drive that melted into a thicket of shrubs and trees.

"Do you have any idea who might have done it?" Gaynell asked.

Maggie shook her head. "Not yet."

"Do the police?"

"Lots of ideas, but I don't think they have any strong leads. If they do, they're not clueing us in on them."

"At least we have Bo in our corner," Ninette said. "He was so helpful with the last . . . incidents." Ninette could never bring herself to call the previous tragedies at Crozat what they were: murders.

"Bo's been a great friend," Maggie said, keeping her words purposefully bland. She knew her friends suspected that she and the detective were involved in some way and appreciated that they never pressed her about the relationship. "But I'm not sure how much he'll be able to help us this time." Maggie told them about Bo's demotion.

The women gasped and muttered angry epithets. "That Perske's a total jerk," Gaynell declared.

"The worst," Maggie agreed. "If you ever tell anyone I said this, I'll deny it to my death. But . . . I kind of miss Rufus as chief."

"It's a classic case of 'the enemy of my enemy is my friend,'" Lia said. "You both despise Perske."

"'Despise' is such a strong word," Maggie said. "And yet, in this case, not strong enough."

*

The women finished their trek in enough time to allow Maggie a chance to shower before Bo brought Xander over. Considering their strained last exchange, she searched her closet for an outfit that would be appropriate to the occasion yet put a desiring gleam back in his dark-brown eyes. She settled on a snug, black pleather tank top that she paired with black jeans. She was just adding mascara to her curled eyelashes when a car scrunched to a stop on the gravel drive in front of the shotgun.

Maggie finished her beauty routine and hurried to the front door. She opened it to find an absolutely stunning woman standing there. She appeared to be in her early thirties, like Maggie. But that's where any resemblance ended. The woman was tall and had the natural figure of a Playboy Playmate. Her hair was golden, her eyes sapphire blue, and her bone structure the stuff of sculptures.

"Hello," Maggie said, wondering who the vision on her doorstep might be. "Welcome to Crozat Plantation and B and B. I can check you in at the main house."

"Oh, I'm not a guest," the woman said. She smiled, revealing dimples and perfect teeth. "I'm Xander's mom, Whitney. Bo's wife." She slapped her forehead with a beautifully long-fingered hand. "Wow, what was that? Sorry. I'm Bo's *ex*-wife."

Chapter Eleven

For a moment, Maggie just stared at Whitney. She wondered why Bo had never mentioned that his ex was gorgeous enough to appear on the cover of *Vogue* or the *Sports Illustrated Swimsuit* edition. Then again, why would he? *She's his ex,* Maggie reminded herself. *As in over. Done. It's history.* But that's what Bo and the enticing Whitney shared. A history. And a child.

The last thought jogged Maggie out of her stupor. "Well, hey, nice to meet you, Whitney," she said, hoping to pull off a casual friendliness that she didn't feel. She stepped outside and pulled the door shut behind her. She felt like a circus midget compared to Bo's statuesque ex and discreetly checked out the woman's footwear, hoping to find a pair of six-inch heels. Whitney was wearing ballet flats. "Where's Xander?" Maggie asked.

"With the chickens. He loves y'all's chickens." Whitney gave a throaty chuckle. Even her laugh was sexy.

"What's not to love about chickens?" Maggie said. "Especially fried." *Oh my God, did I just say that?! I sound like an IDIOT.* "I mean, not those chickens. We'd never fry those. They lay eggs." *Like me in this conversation.* "Anyway, I'm all ready for him. I thought we'd paint in my studio tonight."

"Sounds great," Whitney said as they walked toward the chicken pen. "I'm sorry Bo couldn't drop off Xander, but this Chief Perske has him on a short leash, poor guy. I was hoping that once my husband Zach and I moved to Pelican, Bo would get more time with Xander. But he's had even less time since Ru got put on leave. It's killing him. Bo is such an *amazing* daddy."

She spoke the last with so much warmth that it set off an alarm bell for Maggie. Whitney's phone buzzed and she checked it. "Oh. Zach landed in Riyadh." She put her phone back in her purse. There was silence for a moment.

"You can talk to him," Maggie said. "Don't worry about me."

"It's okay." More silence. "I'll call him later tonight. Or tomorrow. He's probably tired."

"Okay, then. Well . . ." Maggie forced an enthusiastic tone into her voice. "Welcome to town. Bo told me you were coming, but he wasn't sure when or for how long. You used the m-word—moved. It's sounding pretty permanent." Afraid the last sentence sounded snarky, she tacked on a weak "Neat."

"It's not permanent," Whitney said. "At least . . . not yet."

There it was. Maggie's intuition had picked up a vibe from Whitney that all was not well with her current marriage, and the "not yet" confirmed it. Weighted in those two words was the intimation that Whitney was grappling with important decisions in her life. The question that remained to be answered was the one that troubled Maggie the most: when "yet" came, would it be with or without Bo? It didn't take clairvoyance to sense some unresolved feelings about him on the part of his ex.

The women found Xander outside the chicken yard, staring thoughtfully as the animals scurried around, squawking at each other. Xander's serious expression rarely wavered, but Maggie was pleased to note the hint of a smile when he saw her.

"Hey, baby," Whitney said, bending down, taking her son by the shoulders, and looking him straight in the eye. Bo had taught Maggie to do the same thing with Xander as a way of encouraging him to hold eye contact and connect with people. "I'll be back in a couple of hours. You behave yourself, okay?"

Xander nodded. His mother kissed him on the top of his head, thanked Maggie, and headed to her car. Maggie and Xander watched in silence as she pulled out of the driveway. Then Maggie took Xander's small hand in hers.

"Come on, buddy," she said as she led him toward her studio. "Let's make some awesome art."

Teaching Xander meant helping him create a specific shape or detail but otherwise staying out of his way so his imagination could let loose with colors and images that seemed channeled from another world. The young boy had a condition known as selective mutism. He knew how to speak and, according to Bo, did so until he was four. Then he simply stopped. Since Xander never spoke, there was silence as he worked, and Maggie's thoughts began to drift. She was torn between brooding over Whitney's bewitching ways and debating who murdered Ginger. Since the former was rough on her ego, she went with the latter.

Ever since the murders at Crozat a few months earlier, Maggie had been haunted by the question of why people kill. Was Ginger's murder a crime of passion? If so, her cuckolded husband Fox was the frontrunner. Or was it a crime of means? That required some insight into who might gain from her death. Ostensibly, that would rule out Bibi and Trent because they'd both be out of jobs. Or would they? Up until Ginger's passing, Maggie had sensed nothing but loathing between the two, yet they'd provided alibis for each other. Maggie was suspicious of their newfound chumminess.

Her phone pinged, and she looked down to see an e-mail from Vanessa with an attached spreadsheet of updated maid of honor duties. Maggie found it ironic that a woman who couldn't make change from a twenty in the Doucet souvenir shop was a computer whiz when it came to her wedding festivities. Maggie's cell rang, and Vanessa's name flashed on the screen. "Yes?" she said through gritted teeth as she answered the call.

"Did you get my e-mail?"

"Yes."

"Do you know who killed Ginger yet?"

"No."

"Dang. Well, then, let's focus on my bachelorette party."

"You're going through with that?"

"Of course. You haven't read the spreadsheet yet, have you?" Vanessa scolded.

"I looked at it."

"That doesn't count. If you'd *read* it, you would've seen that Mama and I had a great idea for the theme. It'll be a memorial to Ginger. The kind of blowout she would have wanted us to have if she was still among us. And we'll do it at Junie's."

Maggie lacked the energy to point out how insincere Vanessa's idea sounded. Instead, she said, "I'll check into it," and ended the call. She looked up and was startled to see Xander standing there. He handed her a painting-in-progress of two chickens in the Crozat chicken yard. Some of the details were rudimentary; others, like the feathers of the birds, were meticulously detailed and shadowed. The painting was fascinating.

"Buddy, I love this," she said and then hugged him. The boy stiffened only slightly, pointing to still more progress in their relationship. "You can finish it next time you come over. Now, let's get you a treat."

She took Xander to the kitchen of the main house, where they enjoyed slices of Ninette's coffee cake. "And now I have a really special treat for you," Maggie said. She motioned for Xander to follow her into the office, where Gopher had parked himself in front of the playpen. He barked a happy greeting to Xander and padded over to get a pet. Xander obliged, but his attention was focused on the puppies and kittens. The tiny creatures lay by their mothers, occasionally letting out a squeak. Maggie had initially feared for the health of all the animals, but they'd blossomed under her family's care.

"It's like one of those Internet videos where cats help raise puppies or a mama dog helps take care of kittens, isn't it?" Maggie said, and Xander gave a slight nod. Maggie pointed out each puppy to Xander by name. "These are both boys and they seem attached, so we call them Rice and Beans. We named the girl Jasmine, and the mom is Jolie." Maggie reached into the playpen and gave Jolie a pet, then stroked the mama cat's fur. "And I named her Brooke, which is short for Brooklyn, where I lived before I came back home."

Brooke purred and stretched, jostling her kittens. They mewed their displeasure and then went back to sleep. Maggie had an idea. "I'm supposed to name the kittens, but I haven't come up with anything yet. Why don't you name them, Xander? You can make a list and give it to me."

Xander gave a slight nod and leaned over the edge of the playpen to study the kittens. He smiled. A real smile, full of joy. Maggie's eyes welled with tears.

Bibi appeared in the office doorway, and Maggie pulled herself together. "Hi, can I help you with something?" she asked the guest.

"I just wanted to let you know that I'll be checking out in the morning. Should I pay you now or then?"

"Then will be fine." Maggie noticed that everything about Bibi seemed lighter since her boss died. Her hair seemed fuller; her face was no longer fixed in a tight grimace.

Maggie could swear she'd even put on a few pounds. And she'd made a fashion choice that she never would have dared to make when Ginger was alive—she was dressed in the late woman's signature soft white. "Are you going back to Houston?"

"No." Maggie picked up a slight hesitation before Bibi continued. "Ginger set up her company so that Trent would take over if anything happened to her."

Oh, really? Maggie thought. *That's an interesting development.*

"Trent and I had a long talk," Bibi continued, "and it turns out that he really likes my work. He wants me to stay on and finish setting up the new location in Baton Rouge. He's renaming the business Starke-Socher Design and hiring me as a full-time designer. I'll do the day-to-day work while he courts clients. I might even get my name in the title eventually. I'm so excited—" Bibi caught herself. "Although I'm very upset about the way all of this happened."

"Of course," Maggie said, feigning sympathy. She marveled at Trent's machinations. He had used his romantic sway over Ginger to guarantee himself a career and then somehow maneuvered Bibi into working twenty-four-seven while he gadded about with wealthy potential clients, among whom there might be a bankable replacement for Ginger. He made the leap in Maggie's mind from slacker opportunist to evil genius. And an evil genius might include murder in his master plan.

Bibi excused herself to finish packing. Maggie heard a car pull into the driveway and recognized the sound of Bo's sedan. "Your dad's here," she told Xander, then went to meet him, doing a quick makeup check on her way out the door. Her heart flip-flopped when she saw Bo's lean figure saunter toward her, and she suppressed the urge to fling herself into his arms. But before she could even utter a greeting, an SUV pulled into the gravel drive, and Whitney jumped out. She threw her hands up in mock frustration when she saw Bo.

"Oh my goodness, did we get our wires crossed? I thought I was picking up Xander."

"Didn't you get my text? I thought I'd take him tonight since I had to work late last night."

"No, my battery died and I couldn't find my car charger."

"How you find anything in that car mess of yours is beyond me."

As the exes chatted and joked, Maggie fought off the urge to throw up in the bushes by the side of the house. "Xander's in the office with the puppies and kittens we found," she said, motioning for the couple to follow her inside. Their casual exchange continued, leaving Maggie to feel like the definition of a third wheel.

When the three reached the office, they found Xander reaching inside the playpen as he took turns petting Brooke, Jolie, and their respective broods. "Oh, Bo," Whitney whispered. "How sweet is that?"

Bo nodded, too moved to speak. Maggie watched the tableau of mother, father, and son. Whitney and Bo may have divorced, but they still shared a bond that she could never compete with.

"Why don't you take him home tonight?" Bo said to Whitney. "I have to be up early anyway."

"Okay." Whitney addressed her son. "Sweetie, we need to go now."

Xander pulled himself away from the animals. "You can see them whenever you want," Maggie told him. "And don't forget that list of names for the kitties."

Bo hugged his son, then he and Whitney shared a quick hug, and she left with Xander. Maggie felt a resentment that she knew was unjustified. "Nice to see you," she said to Bo. It was an awkward, chilly dismissal.

"Huh?" Bo looked at her, confused. Then his expression cleared. "I get it. This is about how I blew you off when I was in the middle of being the world's worst traffic cop. I'm sorry. It's rough going from detective to the guy in white gloves trying to keep ticked-off drivers from banging into each other."

"I know. It's not that. It's just . . ." Maggie couldn't bring herself to admit that she was jealous of Whitney. "It's just . . . everything that's been going on here lately."

Bo nodded his head in sympathy and wrapped his arms around her. She felt heat course through her body.

"I want to kiss you so much right now," he murmured. Then he gently pushed her away. "But not here."

"I know where we can find some privacy," Maggie said, unwilling to let him go. "My studio."

"Oh, you're going to 'show me your etchings'?" Bo teased. "I like it."

Maggie and Bo were about to leave when they heard two men shouting outside. "What is *that*?" Maggie said as she ran out of the office and down the hall to the plantation home's front door. She met up with her parents, who'd made their way from their bedroom.

"What's going on?" Tug asked.

"No idea," Maggie replied as Bo ran past her and out the door. She, Tug, and Ninette followed. They found Fox Starke on the front lawn, raining down punches on a cowering Trent Socher.

"You killed her!" Fox yelled as he pummeled Trent. "You killed my wife!"

Chapter Twelve

Bo broke up the fight—if it could be called that, since it basically consisted of Fox wailing on a whimpering Trent. "You didn't love her, you used her," Fox accused his adversary. "You just wanted her money and career."

"I'm suing you!" Trent yelled back. "For character assassination and pain and suffering!"

"Just try it, you sonuva—"

"Hey, enough, you guys," Bo said as he held Fox back.

Trent pointed to Fox. "I want him arrested for assault."

"I'm off duty," Bo said.

Ninette stepped in and laid a hand on Trent's shoulder. "No need for anyone to get arrested, Trent. Why don't you come with Tug and me? I'll get some ice for your bruises and then Tug will put some ice where it really counts—in a nice, tall drink of your choice."

Ninette's soothing tone seemed to assuage Trent's anger, and he let her and Tug lead him back to the main house. Fox glanced down at the ground. He seemed too embarrassed by his actions to make eye contact. "Sorry about that," he mumbled.

"You don't have to apologize to us," Bo assured him. "We get it."

Fox looked up, relieved. "Thank you. I only came back to Pelican to get Ginger's things. I'm having her brought home to Houston tomorrow. When I saw that . . . that . . . poor excuse for a human being, I just lost it."

Despite the fact that there was every possibility Fox had murdered his cheating wife in a fit of rage, Maggie felt for him. "If there's anything we can do, please let us know."

"I appreciate that," he said, then walked back to his car, head down. Maggie and Bo watched him drive away.

"He's sure making himself the number one suspect," Bo said.

"I know. But Trent can give him serious competition for that spot." Maggie filled Bo in on Trent's machinations with Ginger's design company.

"Wow, he's some schemer," Bo said. "He's almost too obvious a choice. Of course, the jails are filled with guys dumb enough to think they could pull off a murder and a business coup." Bo kicked at the gravel and spat out an epithet. "I hate that I've been sidelined on this case. Nothing against Cal and Artie, they're good cops, but they're missing the detective gene. They do a fine job using their good ol' boy charm to get information, but they don't know how to put it together. And they're bored by the tedious part of the job, like going through phone records and credit card statements." Passion intensified Bo's voice. "I love all that. When

I pick up a thread through receipts or a cell phone log, it's like I won a contest. I wanna high-five the world."

Maggie was inspired by Bo's devotion to his job. "I can't believe Perske would rather play politics than utilize an amazing resource like you. He's an *idiot.*"

Her cell rang, and she pulled it out of the back pocket of her jeans. The caller was Vanessa's mother, the pugnacious Tookie Fleer, who barked at Maggie before she even got out a greeting. "You need to get crackin' on Van's bachelorette party. My girl needs something to look forward to."

"Her wedding isn't enough?"

"I am in no mood for sass, missy. Do you know what that Fox did? He's set Ginger's funeral for the day after tomorrow. So now the Texas Fleers are going to Houston, and who knows how many of them will wanna come back here for the wedding? You'd think he'd do the right thing and keep that woman on ice a few more days, until after the wedding. But no, he's not thoughtful like that. Anyway, let's see some progress on that party."

Tookie hung up without a good-bye. "I think the murderer got the wrong Fleer," Maggie muttered.

"She was so loud that I heard the whole conversation," Bo said. "I sympathize with you. But if you want to feel better about everything you have to do for this wedding, remember that I'm stuck planning Ru's bachelor party. I can't even tell you what he's asking for. Some of it's not even legal. Anyway, I gotta take off. The river road's going to be down to one lane tomorrow due to construction, and I get to manage the rush-hour traffic flow."

Bo took off without even the promise of a phone call, and a dejected Maggie dragged herself inside the main house, where she found Bibi waiting. "I heard the fight," Bibi said. "Is Fox okay?"

"Physically, yes. Emotionally, not so much." Maggie wasn't surprised that Bibi hadn't tried to intervene in the men's struggle. She was caught between her new boss and her unrequited love. "I'm sure he'd appreciate knowing that you're concerned about him. You should give him a call."

Bibi clenched and unclenched her hands. "I will." She looked toward the kitchen, where Ninette was nursing Trent's bruises. "Fox'll get over Ginger. He just needs someone to remind him that he's better off without her. Way, way better off."

"Whoa," Maggie said, "that's rough. I think you might want to show a little sensitivity, if not to Ginger, then to Fox. He *was* married to the woman, and it's perfectly legitimate that his feelings about their relationship and her ugly death would be complicated."

Maggie had to finish her sentence calling to Bibi's back as the woman moved quickly down the hall. Bibi shot out the back door of the house, almost bumping into Gran'. "Someone's moving like the devil's on her tail," Gran' said, glancing after the retreating figure.

"Long story, which I don't have time to go into because I need to go to Junie's and price out Van's bachelorette party. I'm torn between two themes. I can't decide whether to go with 'In Bad Taste' or 'Incredibly Clueless.'"

"Either seems to fit. You're going to Junie's? I'll come with. I wouldn't mind a brief respite from the melancholy atmosphere around here."

"I'll get my car keys." Maggie hesitated a moment.

"Having second thoughts?"

"No, no. It's nothing. It's just that when Bibi and I were talking about Fox and the fight and Ginger, she wasn't melancholy at all. It was more like she was gloating."

"Hmmm. Perhaps she's past the point of pretending to care about a boss she despised. Or perhaps she's a murderer. One thing I know for sure—it's a conversation that will go down better with a few cocktails."

*

Since it was a weeknight, Junie's was filled with locals. Hipsters from New Orleans and Baton Rouge didn't infiltrate the popular bar and restaurant until the weekend. Old Shari, the hangout's ancient bartender, shook her head when Maggie ordered a glass of chardonnay. "Nuh-uh," Old Shari declared. "I feel you for a Pimm's Cup tonight." Maggie knew better than to argue with Shari's psychic ability to read a person's cocktail needs. The nonagenarian had retired a few years back, but after almost literally dying of boredom—she had a heart attack while watching a women's golf tournament—she'd returned to Junie's and reclaimed her title as Pelican's Cocktail Queen.

Maggie sipped her Pimm's Cup, which did indeed hit the spot. Gran' was off socializing, thus tabling any further discussion about Bibi. Instead, Maggie vented about Vanessa's bachelorette party to Junie's proprietor, JJ, the son of the late Junie. JJ, who had a predilection for caftans, was dressed in a flowing zebra-print number and had his long hair in a classy updo.

"Van's wedding festivities are going to bankrupt me," Maggie said. "I won't have a dime left for my own, should that miraculous event ever take place."

"Don't worry, chère. A, of course it will, and B, I'll give you the fairest price I can on Van's shindig." JJ laid a hand with beautifully manicured nails on top of Maggie's unadorned mitts. "Wait, I just had a brainstorm. Why don't you impose a small cover charge for guests? Say, ten dollars each? That's not too high, but it'll save you a bundle."

"That's kind of tacky. But then, so are the Fleers, so yes! It's brilliant. They'll hate it, of course, but I'll give them a choice. Suck it up or kick in the money yourself."

"That'll shut down any argument, I gar-on-tee. But you might not want to put it on the invitation—nobody will come. We'll just tell them at the door. They'll grumble, but they won't go away."

Gaynell and her Cajun-zydeco band, the Gator Girls, were on Junie's small stage getting ready to do a set, and Maggie wandered over to her. She filled her friend in on the new twist to Vanessa's party. "Sounds good," Gaynell said. "And I can save you even more money. We'll perform for free as the entertainment."

"Oh, that's fantastic! People will really get their money's worth now. It's almost too good for Vanessa."

Maggie realized that Gaynell wasn't listening. She followed her friend's gaze and saw that Chret Bertrand had arrived, along with his great-uncle Lee. "Hey," she called, waving the two men over. The foursome exchanged hellos. "Let me buy you a drink, Lee," Maggie said, then pulled the older man away, leaving Chret and Gaynell with each other.

"That was pretty bald," Lee laughed.

"I don't think they even noticed."

"It's good to see some life back in him," Lee said, gazing at his great-nephew. "Kid's had it rough. My nephew Wayne and his wife adopted him as an infant. Wayne died a year later in a car accident, and his wife passed the summer after Chret graduated high school."

Maggie felt a catch in her throat. "I can't imagine that kind of pain."

"It was bad. Real bad. Poor kid didn't know what to do with himself after that, so he joined the armed forces, which turned out to be its own set of problems."

"That's so sad. But he's lucky to have you."

Lee shrugged, embarrassed. "I do what I can." He smiled as he saw Gran' sauntering over with her favorite cocktail, a Sazerac, in hand. "Looky-look who's gracing us peasants with her presence," he teased.

"Hello there, Mr. Bertrand," Gran' said, extending her hand.

"Madame." Lee took her hand and kissed it, then stood up and bowed to her.

"Stop that, you silly man." Gran' giggled.

"Isn't that how I'm supposed to greet Pelican's grande dame when I see her?"

"What you're supposed to do is promise her a dance when the band starts."

"Of course. I'll see if they'll play a minuet fit for royalty."

"I believe you were around when that dance was invented."

"Ouch! Good shot, Queenie." Lee turned to Maggie. "Now I truly do need that drink you offered me."

"I'll put it on my tab," Gran' said, then held out her arm, which Lee took. "You may escort me."

"Yes, your ladyship. And I promise not to get any motor oil on your frock."

The two headed for the bar as Maggie marveled at her octogenarian grandmother's casually flirty way with men. Somehow that Crozat gene had passed her by. Hopefully it would reappear in the next generation—if Maggie ever got the chance to procreate. Her spirits lifted when she saw Bo come into Junie's. They immediately dropped when she saw Whitney right behind him. She tamped down an urge to sneak out the back door and forced a smile when Bo started her way. Whitney followed. "Hi, Maggie," Whitney said, her tone bright. "Bo's being gallant and taking me out for dinner. I've been kind of lonely with Zach gone."

"That must be hard on you."

"It is, but it helps having this guy looking after me. He hired a sitter for Xander and whisked me off for a night on the town." Whitney squeezed Bo's arm affectionately, and Maggie choked back the bile in her throat.

"Why don't you join us?" Bo said.

"Yes, good idea," Whitney echoed.

It didn't take Maggie's keen visual sense to detect Whitney's lack of enthusiasm. "That's okay. You two have a nice dinner. I need to talk to Junie about some party plans."

Maggie escaped and planted herself at the bar. Old Shari studied her, poured Maker's Mark into a shot glass, and placed it in front of Maggie. "Here's what I feel you for now," she said.

"Dead-on as always, Shari."

JJ, who was paying bills behind the bar, looked up and raised a perfectly plucked eyebrow as Maggie drained the glass in one gulp. "You wanna talk about it?" he asked.

"Nope."

"Okay then." JJ was a good enough friend to know that Maggie would share when she was ready. She set her shot glass down, and Old Shari refilled it. This time, Maggie sipped the bourbon, mulling over who might have killed Ginger as she drank. Like the ancient bartender, she had a specific and finely honed instinct about people. Old Shari's was for their drink order; Maggie's was for their predilection for murder. But she had zero instinct about who might have caused Ginger's death, and that bothered her.

Junie's front door flew open, and a tied pile of *Pelican Penny Saver*s came flying in. "I got a stack of those yesterday," Junie said, surprised.

"So did we. Maybe Little Earlie's making it a daily," Maggie said. She got off her barstool, went to the stack, and pulled out a copy of the paper. "It's a little heavier than usual. Earlie must be pulling in more advertising."

"I gotta say, people are reading it these days. I blew through my supply in a couple of hours. Little Earlie sure found himself a way to hook people."

"Yes." Maggie held up the copy. She was furious. "By printing trash." She pointed to the paper's headline, and this time both of JJ's eyebrows went up. "'Special Edition,'" Maggie read. "'Killing at Crozat! Murders Bedevil B and B.'"

"Oh dear." JJ pursed his lips. "Judging by that look on your face, I think the next victim might be Little Earlie Waddell."

Chapter Thirteen

Maggie's anger grew as she read the story. "That little . . . ! Listen to this, JJ, just listen. 'Magnolia Marie Crozat labeled any mention of the murder as salacious and threatened a reporter with trouble if he pursued the story.' That's not what I said at all—I warned him to be careful because he could compromise the investigation with his stupid, cheesy tabloid story! He makes me sound like a mob goon. And here, listen to *this*—'A nearby police officer attributed Ms. Crozat's dismissive attitude to a desperate and perhaps futile desire to protect her family's business at all costs, even if it meant belittling a heinous crime.' Now he's putting words in Artie's mouth too! But does he name him? Of course not. He knows Artie would clean his clock, which is exactly what I'm going to do when I get my hands on that weasel."

Maggie leaped off her barstool and ran out the door. Seeing Little Earlie a block ahead, casually strolling to his car, she tore down the street after him. "Hey!" she yelled. "Hey, Earlie, wait up, do you hear me? I said, wait up!"

Little Earlie did the opposite of waiting up. He picked up speed and ran for his car. But Maggie's outrage fueled her with superhuman power, and she blazed toward him like a rocket, reaching his car before he could beep the lock open. "You lying piece of dog poo!" she yelled. "How could you do this to me? To my family? You print a retraction of that article tomorrow or I swear, I will pull a lightning bolt out of the sky and smite you with it. And by lightning bolt, I mean that I will get the best lawyer in Louisiana to take you down!"

"You'll have to take the First Amendment down with me," Little Earlie retorted as he fumbled with his car key.

Maggie planted herself in front of his PT Cruiser's driver's-side door. "You completely distorted my words."

"Aha! You admit they were your words."

"Oh, stop it, you know what I mean."

Little Earlie pulled himself up to his full height, which barely put him eye-to-eye with Maggie. "Like the song says, 'here's a quarter, call someone who cares.' Whether you like it or not, this story is big news, especially in a pissant town like Pelican. It's the break I've been praying for, so I'm gonna write the heck out of it and keep writing until it's all over the national papers and TV and Internet. You'd have to lock me in a chest and toss it off the side of a boat in the middle of the Gulf to stop me—and even then, I want this so bad that

I'd figure out a way to get out of that chest, swim back to shore, and cover the story. Now if you'll get out of my way, I got papers to deliver."

"Hello, you two." Both Maggie and Little Earlie jumped, startled. Neither had noticed Bo walk up to them.

"Hey," Little Earlie said, but his focus remained on Maggie. She caved to his glare and stepped away from his car.

"Earlie, buddy, there's something I wanted to tell you." Bo took a step toward Little Earlie and, without warning, punched him hard in the gut. Maggie gasped as the reporter let out an "oof" and doubled over.

"What was that for?" Little Earlie gasped as he clutched his stomach.

"That was for bothering my friends, the Crozats. If you liked it, there's plenty more where it came from."

Little Earlie pulled himself up to standing. "I'm reporting you for police brutality!" he screamed.

Little Earlie, still clutching his stomach with one hand, pulled open his car door with the other. He revved the PT Cruiser's engine, and as he peeled out of the parking space, he yelled to Bo, "I'm gonna write about what you did, too. It's all going in the paper. I'm gonna sue and report and write, so you better watch out, mister!"

He roared off. Maggie, who'd watched the whole exchange in mute shock, found her voice. "Bo, what . . . ? You didn't have to . . . Your job . . ."

It was hardly articulate, but she formed enough words to give the Bo the gist of what she was trying to say. "It's all good," he said as he leaned against a parking meter. "I wanted to take a few vacation days and go to Houston to meet up with a college friend from LSU who's a detective there. He's gonna help me do a little snooping into Ginger Fleer's past and see if we can dig up any suspects in Texas. That's not what I told Perske, of course. I told him I needed a little R and R. And he turned down my request. But as of Little Earlie's complaint, which I'm guessing he's filing right now, since he took off toward the station, I'm on administrative leave—paid leave—while it has to be investigated. So Houston, here I come—and on PPD's dime, since it's not coming out of my days."

Bo flashed a mischievous grin, and Maggie matched it. "And you won't get in trouble," she said, "because you have Little Earlie's 'victim' to testify that he was harassing her."

"If it even goes that far. I'm guessing there'll be a lot of lip service about an investigation, and then they'll give it a few days to blow over. Little Earlie doesn't want to get on the bad side of PPD. No one will feed him dirt for his rag."

"Wow," Maggie marveled. "I'm superimpressed by your plan."

"And hopefully a little turned on," Bo teased. He looked at her with his dark, bedroom eyes. *Why, oh why,* she lamented internally, *are we on a public street, where we can't give in to our obvious desire for each other?*

"I'm coming to Houston with you," Maggie blurted. "I promised Vanessa I'd help find whoever killed Ginger, and I've gotten nowhere so far. I know you're an amazing investigator, but I spent some time with her, and your friend might have information that reminds me of something Ginger said or did that might be a clue. The funeral's the day after tomorrow. I can tell people I'm going to represent the Louisiana Fleers there. Everyone will think that it's just another to-do on my maid of honor list."

"Great idea. Now I'm the one who's superimpressed."

Bo laid a hand on Maggie's shoulder; with that slight touch, Maggie felt a bolt of electricity course between them. Then Bo dropped his hand. "I better get back to Whitney before she calls the police to file a missing person's report," he said. "I'll call you tomorrow."

And the spark instantly flamed out.

*

The next morning, Maggie rearranged her schedule with Ione and cleared her upcoming trip with Tookie. As predicted, the Fleers were on board. "Those Texas Fleers will grab any excuse to stay put in their dang state," Tookie griped. "I wouldn't care except that they're not the kind of folk who'll send a present if they don't show up at the wedding. We need their butts in the seats. Tell 'em that the best way to get over grief is to celebrate life. Sell it, Magnolia Marie."

"Yes, ma'am," Maggie grumbled, then ended the call before Tookie could strafe her with any more orders.

She drove toward Houston alone, having reluctantly agreed with Bo that driving together would be the Pelican gossip equivalent of throwing chum to sharks. "It's KISS," Bo had said as they coordinated their plans.

"Huh?" Maggie responded, confused.

"K-I-S-S," Bo explained. "Translation: 'Keep it simple, stupid.' It's how we operated when I worked undercover in Vice. You tell the same story to everyone and you keep it lean. The more complicated you make it, the easier it is to mess up. So we're not dating. That's our story, plain and simple. Even with my friend, Johnny. KISS."

The irony that the operation was titled the one thing Maggie longed to do with Bo was painfully obvious to her. She also got the sense that even though the two men's relationship went back to college, Bo didn't completely trust Johnny.

It was an easy, flat ride on Interstate 10, which allowed Maggie's mind to wander. She examined every moment of contact that she'd had with Ginger. There was some clue in those interactions, but she hadn't landed on it. It remained mere intuition, which frustrated her. She hoped that Bo's friend might help her hone in on whatever she was missing.

Maggie crossed the Sabine River, a dividing line between Louisiana and Texas, and the 10 continued its bland way into Houston. Never the most scenic drive, the late-fall weather had turned a muted green palette into one of pale grays and dull browns. Maggie had done an online search for lodging in or near Ginger's upscale neighborhood, figuring that at least one resident might be meeting mortgage payments by operating a clandestine hostelry. Given the still-precarious economy, she wasn't surprised when the search yielded a flood of options. Maggie had gone with proximity, choosing a home only blocks from Ginger and Fox's abode.

She followed directions sent by the owner, a Mrs. Anna
Ward, and found herself on a leafy street in front of an elegant, slightly faded, red-brick Georgian house in an area
described on the site as "River Oaks adjacent"—River Oaks
being the toniest neighborhood in the city. She parked the
Falcon on the street, grabbed her overnight bag, and headed
for the front door. It opened before she could ring the bell.
A woman in her late seventies flashed a wide smile and held
her arms up in a welcoming gesture. She was dressed in yellow from head to toe, with a perfect, blonde, bouffant hairdo
that Maggie guessed was a wig.

"Hello there, I'm Anna," she said. "But my friends call
me Sunny. I've been waiting on you, honey. Welcome to
the 'My Husband Died and Left Me With a Lot of Bills
B and B.' Come on in. And if my neighbors ask, you're my
grand-niece who's visiting for the first time."

"I wouldn't worry about what your neighbors think,
given how many other secret B and Bs popped up around
here when I did my search," Maggie said as she followed
Sunny into a foyer with a black-and-white marble-tiled floor
and buttercup-yellow walls. A staircase carpeted in a paler
yellow led to a second floor.

"Oh, really now?" Sunny said. "I want names. It'll
give me something to hold over them next time anyone in
the neighborhood association complains that my hedges are
'scraggly.' Can I fix you a drink?"

"No thank you. It's a little early for me."

"Alrighty, but remember that it's always five o'clock
somewhere."

Maggie was amused to discover that she was staying with Grand-mère's Houston twin. "It also feels a bit wrong since I'm here for a funeral," she said, grabbing an opportunity to steer the conversation toward Ginger's death.

"Oh, you mean that woman who was murdered?" Sunny said. "I heard about that."

Maggie noted that Sunny hadn't described Ginger as "that *poor* woman." For an effusive, yellow rose of Texas like her, Maggie suspected the choice of words—or lack of them—was intentional. "I don't mean to be forward, but I'm sensing you didn't think much of her," Maggie commented as the women strolled through a kitchen splashed with yellow Formica counters and wallpaper populated with smiling lemons.

"I'd hate to speak ill of your friend," Sunny demurred.

"To be honest, I hardly knew her," Maggie replied. "I'm here as a favor to some of Ginger's relatives who were unable to make the trip." Maggie hoped this half-truth might help Sunny overcome her hesitation to trash-talk the late woman, which it did.

"I never met her myself, but she almost perpetrated a scam on a close friend," Sunny shared. "But that's for a conversation over sweet tea. Let's get you to your room."

Sunny led Maggie to a small bedroom with an en suite bathroom off the kitchen. It had obviously once been a maid's room but was now cheerfully appointed with yellow-and-white-striped wallpaper that matched the comforter on a white wrought-iron bed. The nightstands, also white, were of wicker. "It's charming," Maggie said. She glanced out the window. "And your hedges aren't the least bit scraggly."

Sunny chortled and slapped Maggie on the shoulder. "For that, you get an extra cookie with your tea. Get settled and come join me."

Sunny left the room. Maggie didn't want to put her hostess off by appearing too eager to hear the story, so she threw down her bag, washed her face and hands, and counted to thirty before sauntering onto the home's brick patio. Sunny was sitting at an old-fashioned café table and motioned for Maggie to join her. Maggie sat down and accepted the tea as well as several cookies; she'd skipped lunch and was starving.

"So . . . Ginger . . . Fleer . . . Starke," Sunny said. She shook her head and sighed. Maggie hoped the story lived up to the drama of its introduction. "It's quite a tale."

"Yes, Ginger inspired a lot of those," Maggie said. "I'm curious to hear yours."

"Well . . . a couple of years ago, my dear friend Nancy Brown Bradley inherited her parents' home, a lovely Victorian in the historic neighborhood of Houston Heights. Financial circumstances forced Nancy Brown to put the place on the market, but it was paramount to her that the house be sold to someone who loved its architecture and was committed to preserving it. Then Miss Ginger comes along with a whole story about how she's always dreamed of owning one of our city's grand painted ladies and how she eventually wants to deed it to the Heritage Society, and blahbidiblah, blahbidibloo. She completely wins over Nancy Brown and is chosen as the buyer. Then, in the middle of escrow, a neighbor who volunteers for the Heritage Society shows up at Nancy Brown's door, fit to be tied. She'd learned from someone in City Planning that Ginger had applied for a demolition permit! Nancy Brown immediately pulled out of escrow, but Ginger took her to court and forced my poor friend to pay court costs and all fees incurred up to that point."

"What an awful story," Maggie said, truly outraged. "I can't even imagine how upset your friend must have been."

"Nancy Brown had been in remission for breast cancer. Within weeks of the whole debacle, it came back. She died not long after. But she did live long enough to see some measure of justice enacted by yours truly." Sunny got a look of grim satisfaction on her face. "My family goes back many generations in this city, and I am not without some important connections. A few well-placed words from me spread amongst the right people, and Ginger was just about reduced to designing the interiors of takeout restaurants for a living."

"Good for you."

"Thank you." Sunny picked up a small carafe of a brown liquid that Maggie assumed from its scent was rum, then added a splash to her sweet tea. "Now, enough about that poor excuse for a human being. Let me tell you about my roses. I've collected every shade of yellow that I could find . . ."

As her hostess chattered on about her roses, Maggie pretended to pay attention, but her mind was focused on the latest addition to the catalog of Ginger's evil deeds. She wondered if there was a connection between Nancy Brown Bradley's sad saga and Ginger's death. Nancy Brown was gone, but there might be Bradley family members around who carried a grudge against Ginger—a grudge so strong that it led to murder.

Chapter Fourteen

As Maggie readied herself for dinner with Bo and his friend, she contemplated Sunny's story. It made anyone connected with Nancy Brown Bradley a suspect. But she doubted that it had been Ginger's only attempt at a shady development transaction, which widened the field of her victims—and potential killers.

She finished applying a swipe of teal eyeliner and switched her attention to critiquing her ensemble in the full-length mirror attached to the bathroom door. Presented with an opportunity to see Bo somewhere besides a bar, a parking lot, or a murder scene, she opted for a look that would be appropriate for the barbecue joint where they were meeting but also amped up the sexy. She subbed out her usual jeans for a snug denim miniskirt and equally snug teal top, an outfit that highlighted her curves. She slipped on a pair of wedgie sandals that added a few inches to her height and then headed for the front door, teetering slightly on the heels that she wasn't used to wearing.

She followed GPS instructions from Sunny's to the Barbecue Inn, an iconic Houston restaurant in its seventh decade of serving comfort food. The place was all wood-and-red-vinyl booths and suffused with the scent of barbecued meats. Maggie glanced around and spotted Bo and another man in the farthest reaches of the restaurant. He waved to her, and she headed over. Both men stood up as she reached the booth. "Hey," Bo greeted her. "This is the friend I told you about, Johnny Tucker. Johnny, this is Maggie."

Johnny shook Maggie's hand with a hard grip. With his cowboy hat, lanky build, and weathered skin, Johnny seemed cast in the role of Texas lawman. Maggie couldn't imagine what he'd look like without his ten-gallon straw Stetson. She blushed when his blue eyes, made bright in contrast to his tanned face, gave her an admiring head-to-toe once-over. "Nice to meet you, Maggie," he said. "Glad you'll be joining us. Real glad."

Johnny's interest seemed to spark Bo's territorial instinct, and he motioned for Maggie to sit next to him. She did, and he moved closer to her. The three made small talk while they perused the menu. Johnny asked after Xander and expressed regrets that Bo's marriage had broken up. "We just grew in different directions," Bo said. "But we're still friends. We're close." Maggie focused on the menu to prevent herself from blurting out, "How close?"

"Now you can get out there and catch up on what you missed by getting married straight from college," Johnny said. "After my divorce, there wasn't a website or app I didn't hit."

"Not my style," Bo responded, his tone terse.

"Hmm," Johnny said as he looked from Bo to Maggie. "Wouldn't be much of a detective if I didn't get that there's a story here. But I won't interrogate you."

A waitress came over and took their orders: beers for all three, ribs for the men, chicken for Maggie, which elicited teasing from Johnny about her "girly" order. As soon as the waitress left, his demeanor became serious. "So I've been looking into this Ginger Fleer-Starke, and let me tell you, she was a piece of work."

"Clue us in to her life here," Bo said.

"She was basically run out of town because no one would work with her. She was an equal-opportunity suer. Clients, tradesmen, contractors—you name it. She'd accuse people who made the mistake of working for her of doing a crappy job and then refuse to pay them. They'd have to settle for pennies on the dollar. She also sued a couple of clients for 'falls' she took on their property. Their liability insurance had to pay up."

"She was about to pull that scam on us," Maggie shared. "She was setting the stage for a 'fall' due to a 'bad step.'"

"Yeah, that was one of her favorites. She was equally good at getting sued. Clients who found overcharges, workmen who'd been stiffed. Her husband Fox is well liked, by the way. No one understood why he stayed with her. He was probably terrified of what she might do if he left. And she had charisma, no doubt about it. Most grifters do."

"Yes, I got a big dose of that the first time I met her," Maggie said. "She sucked me in, but only briefly, thank goodness. Now, thanks to my Houston hostess, I discovered another scam that you haven't mentioned." She filled the men in on the sad saga of Nancy Brown Bradley.

"Wow," Johnny said when she was done. "That is some nasty stuff. Nice job sussing that out." He motioned to Maggie. "She's a sharp one, Bo."

"Yes, she is," Bo said. She felt his hand on her knee under the table and placed hers on top of it, allowing for a brief moment of contact.

"There's one other thing I'm looking into," Johnny said. "There are rumors that Ginger had a little side business going." Maggie and Bo looked at him quizzically before he said, "Prostitution."

"What?" Maggie tried to process this new, dark information. "She slept with men for money?"

"That's the basic definition of prostitution," Johnny said. "But this little lady did it less for money than for blackmail—which is a way bigger payoff in the long run."

"Sort of a grifter's five-year plan," Bo said dryly.

"I don't get it," Maggie said. "I just don't understand how anyone could have as much as she did and be that horrible."

Johnny shrugged. "Some psychopaths are born, some are made. Bottom line—who cares? They're still psychopaths. Anyway, I'm gonna work the Houston angle. I'll go through everyone who had an issue with her, which is one damn long list."

"Sounds good," Bo said. "Get in touch with me on my personal cell. I'm working the case on my own. My a-hole boss doesn't know about it."

"Maybe I should go through Miss Maggie here," Johnny said with a grin. "You know, just to keep you totally clean."

"Go through me," Bo said, glaring at his friend. His cell rang and he checked out the caller. "It's Whitney. We arranged for me to say good-night to Xander."

Bo got up and left the table so he could take the call in private. As soon as he was out of earshot, Johnny leaned in toward Maggie. "I'm not gonna ask questions about what's going on with you two. But I will tell you this. Watch out for Whitney. Truth be told, none of us liked her too much. She's one of those women who keeps going and going until she gets what she wants. I know she's remarried and all, but I have a bad feeling about it."

"So do I," Maggie confessed.

Johnny grinned again and pointed a finger at her. "See? Sharp." He leaned in even closer; the brim of his cowboy hat touched Maggie's forehead. "I'll say this for my buddy, Bo. His taste in women sure has improved."

*

Dinner finished uneventfully. Johnny shelved his flirting, which Maggie wasn't sure she was happy about. She found it both annoying and flattering but definitely enjoyed seeing the rise it got out of Bo. Johnny, Maggie, and Bo concentrated on analyzing every detail they knew about Ginger's life. Maggie and Bo agreed to be on alert at the funeral. "Her murderer could show up just to make sure she's really dead," Johnny said. "It sounds like a joke, but it's happened."

"More than once," Bo concurred. "In fact, I can think of three times when I was on the force in Shreveport." He and Johnny shared war stories and then segued into memories of their college days at LSU. After an hour of this, Maggie excused herself for the night, leaving the men to their law enforcement male bonding.

In the morning, she dressed appropriately mournfully in a vintage, black wrap dress that she'd found in a Brooklyn thrift store. She shared coffee and croissants with Sunny, who gave her directions to the funeral home Fox Starke had chosen for his late wife's service. "I've been there many times," Sunny said. "People like it because there's a great Mexican restaurant right next door. It's real convenient. You can pay respects and then shoot right over to El Paseo. They make their own tortillas. I like when there's an early evening wake because El Paseo has a terrific happy hour."

"I'm not sure what Fox has planned after the service, but I'll keep El Paseo in mind," Maggie said politely, then paid her bill and bid Sunny good-bye. She planned to drive back to Pelican as soon as she was done nosing around Ginger's mourners.

Sunny's directions proved easy to follow, and it took only fifteen minutes for Maggie to find the Barnard Family Funeral Home. The home was a nondescript but dignified building that looked to have been built sometime in the

1980s. She parked and walked into its hushed lobby, respectfully decorated in whites and neutrals. The air was thick with the perfume of lilies, a scent that Maggie had come to associate with funerals. A sign directed her to Ginger's service, and she made her way into what had to be the smallest room in the facility. Like the rest of the place, its palette was subdued. A large urn rested on a pedestal at the front of the room, flanked on each side by some desultory flower arrangements featuring the ubiquitous lilies. Fox Starke sat in a chair in front of the urn, staring at it.

"Fox?" Maggie said. She spoke softly, not wanting to startle him. He turned around, but his gaze was so foggy that he seemed to look through her. "Maggie Crozat. From Crozat Plantation B and B. I'm here on behalf of the Fleers. And my family, too."

Fox's expression cleared. "I'm so sorry for not recognizing you right away. I'm still in kind of a daze. Thank you so much for coming."

"Of course."

They fell into the awkward silence of two people who barely knew each other brought together by extreme circumstances. "I should pay my respects to Ginger," Maggie said.

Fox nodded. She made her way to the urn, closed her eyes, and assumed the position of prayer. This turned out to be a handy stance for eavesdropping, so she hung out that way for a while. Most of the guests seemed to be there for Fox, but no one seemed so passionately supportive that they'd kill for him. A few made disparaging remarks about Ginger, then caught themselves and covered with a perfunctory "may she rest in peace." The only genuine grief Maggie heard was from Ginger's hairstylist and masseuse. Judging by their bemoaning the loss of a good client, she had tipped both well and never sued either.

Having learned nothing useful, Maggie grew bored and stepped away from the urn. She wondered where Bo was and was about to text him when he strode into the room. He wore a black button-down shirt with his requisite jeans and the unexpected addition of cowboy boots. Maggie didn't need to note the admiring glances of pretty much every woman in the room to know that he looked, as usual, totally hot. The women were disappointed when he zeroed in on Maggie and made his way to her. "Sorry I'm late," he said, "but Whitney texted me this."

Bo called up a photo on his phone and showed it to Maggie. On his own, Xander had used paints Maggie had given him to create a portrait of the Crozats' rescued animal brood. The puppies and kittens nestled against their mothers, rendered in the prodigy's unique stylistic balance of rudimentary and beautifully detailed. "It's . . . fantastic," Maggie said, overwhelmed by the young artist's natural talent.

"It is, isn't it? Lord knows where he gets it from. Whitney and I we were laughing about how neither of us has a lick of artistic talent." Bo flashed a boyish grin, and Maggie felt heartsick. There was a lightness to him that she'd never seen before. The photo, his demeanor, his teasing relationship with his ex—it all served to remind Maggie once again that he and Whitney shared the immutable bond of parenthood.

"Incoming," Bo muttered to her, nudging her to look at the front of the room. She saw Bibi and Trent walk in together. Bibi immediately peeled away and went to Fox. She hugged him and whispered in his ear. The widower shot daggers at Trent and then switched to pointedly ignoring him. Bibi released Fox and watched wistfully as he moved on to greet other guests. Her love for him was so palpable that Maggie noticed a couple of women subtly point at her and whisper to each other. Bibi's longing confirmed for Maggie that there was at least one person at the service who would kill for Fox.

A somber chaplain arrived, and the guests took their seats. The chaplain delivered a short service full of the kind of generalities men in his position delivered when they had never met the deceased and weren't given much to work with. He ended with the Lord's Prayer and an announcement that Fox would like everyone to join him for a lunch in Ginger's honor at El Paseo restaurant next door. This sparked some enthusiastic muttering among the crowd; Maggie swore she even heard some muffled applause. Sunny had called it—El Paseo was a popular place.

As the guests trooped over to the restaurant, Maggie made contact with the Texas Fleers and pleaded Tookie's case for their returning to Pelican for Vanessa's wedding. They listened politely, but Maggie got the impression they were humoring her. Tookie would have to come up with another way to maneuver them into ponying up presents. The funeral party reached the restaurant en masse and made a beeline for its banquet room, where a tempting spread had been laid out. A bartender poured pitchers of margaritas, creating a rush for the bar, so Maggie had the lunch line to herself. She filled her plate with fajita fixings and snacked on a tortilla. Once again, Sunny was right; they were fresh and delicious. Bo approached her and motioned to her plate. "Stoking up for the drive home, huh?"

"Yes. I want to avoid stops."

"I'll grab a plate and we can sit somewhere."

"Actually, I'm going to meander through the crowd," Maggie said. "See if I can pick up any useful gossip." This wasn't the time to bring up her fears about Bo's feelings for Whitney, so she opted to retreat before he could sense her discomfort about the situation. She strolled around the room and eavesdropped on snippets of conversation, none of which proved useful. She stopped behind Trent, who was chatting with Ginger's former masseuse. "You'll be hearing from me," he told the woman. "Bibi's going to run the Baton Rouge office, and I'm going to rebrand us here in Houston. I'm going to work the kinks out of the business, and you can work 'em out of my body." He laughed heartily at his own joke. Maggie marveled at how Trent had turned his boss-lover's death into a golden career opportunity.

Maggie realized that she'd emptied her plate and got on the buffet line for seconds. She found herself behind Fox, who was chatting with some men who looked like fellow executives. "My secretary has the file from the Monday meeting," one of them said to Fox. "I'll have her e-mail it to you."

"I appreciate you covering for me," Fox said. "With what all was going on, I just couldn't get home."

Maggie stopped short, causing a Fleer relative on the line to bump into her. "Sorry," she apologized. She went through the motions of refilling her plate, but her mind wasn't on tortillas. When Fox had confronted Ginger in the parking lot during Van and Rufus's shower, she clearly remembered him telling his wife that he was going back to Houston. And after the fight with Trent, he'd mentioned that he'd only come back to Pelican to get Ginger's things. Yet he had just told his coworker that he never made it home. *Why did he change his plans?* Maggie wondered. *And if he didn't drive back to Houston . . . where was he?*

Chapter Fifteen

Maggie scanned the crowd and found Bo surrounded by a quartet of Texas belles, all of whom looked like they'd recently freshened their makeup. She motioned to him.

"Thanks for rescuing me," he told her. "Those gals would not take a hint. I had to go to my fallback position and put this on." Bo held up his left hand, which now sported a thick gold wedding band. Maggie understood that the ring came in handy when he needed to tamp down any unwanted flirtations. Still, she winced at the sight of it.

"Maybe you could palm them off on Johnny. He seems in the market for whatever they're selling."

"That horndog doesn't need any help from me. So, did you get any leads?"

"Maybe." Maggie shared what she'd learned about Fox's mysterious whereabouts during the period before and after his wife's murder.

"Interesting," Bo said. "That would fit the case profile. On average, more than three women in this country are murdered by their husbands or boyfriends every day."

"Ugh, what a horrible statistic."

"I'll pass this lead on to Johnny. There could be a logical explanation. It's a long drive between Houston and Pelican, especially if it's late and you're angry because you just found out your wife's cheating on you. He may have spent the night somewhere. Johnny can check his credit card activity."

"Sounds good." Maggie hesitated, not sure which way the conversation should go next. After a long pause, she finally said, "Well . . . see you in Pelican."

It seemed the safest choice.

*

The first thing Maggie did when she got home was check on the pups and kittens. She found her mother and Gran' already tending to them. "Their mamas are nursing, but we've worked out a system where someone checks on them every couple of hours," Ninette explained. "And a certain someone has been showing up on a regular basis to help out your Gran'."

Ninette flashed an impish grin at Gran', who rolled her eyes. "That's your mother's cutesy way of saying that Stevens has come by a few times. And she believes it's not solely out of concern for the well-being of our charges."

"Gran', he's obviously courting you," Maggie said, with a wink at her mother.

"You don't have to use some nineteenth-century term just because I'm a few years older than you," Gran' said. "And I saw that wink. This would be the ideal time to tell you that as much as I like Stevens, I am very much on the fence about a relationship at my age. I've seen what happens with my friends. If you're lucky, you get a few good months with your new significant other, then one of you goes south physically or mentally, and the rest of the time is spent calling around to find a decent nursing home. Besides, I could never have again what I had with your grandfather. Some people like the drama of saying 'he was the love of my life.' For me, that sentiment is real."

"Of course, Charlotte," Ninette said, her voice gentle. "Still, wouldn't it be nice to have some companionship with a peer?"

"That's a nice way of saying 'an old fart.' You know, there's someone here who's yet to go around the horn once." Gran' pointed at Maggie. "I wouldn't mind having a great-grandchild pop out while I still have the mental acuity to know what it is. Let's turn the focus on her."

"Oh please, let's not."

Maggie darted out of the room and almost collided with Trent in the hallway. She was startled to see him. "Hello," he greeted her cheerfully. "You made it back in good time."

"As did you," Maggie said. "Although I'm a little confused as to why you're back. I assumed you'd be staying in Houston to tend to business."

"Doing some eavesdropping at the funeral, huh?"

Maggie had read people described as "sneering" in books, but she'd never been sure what a sneer looked like. Thanks to the expression on Trent's face, now she knew. "Bibi mentioned your new business arrangement to me," she said, covering the fact that she had actually picked up the specifics of Trent's plan through snooping. "Basically, she gets Baton Rouge, you get Houston."

"True. Bibi's already setting up the office in Baton Rouge. But there's still a lot to do to get it going, and it makes sense for me to be closer to BR than Houston for a little while. It also makes sense to stay here since it's convenient to both cities, as well as New Orleans, another market ready for some tapping by Starke-Socher." Trent pulled a credit card out of the back pocket of his navy designer slacks. "I don't know if Ginger's bill is still outstanding, but you can put our stays on the business credit card. Ginger had the good sense to make us both signatories."

Trent followed Maggie into the B and B office. She swiped his credit card and handed it back to him. "Not to speak ill of the dead, but Ginger seemed a bit self-involved. It's hard to imagine her doing something as magnanimous as sharing her credit card, even if it was for business."

"That's a pretty snide thing to say about someone you didn't know very well. It happens to have been her idea. Maybe I should take *my* business elsewhere."

While Maggie found it obvious that Trent was lying, she didn't want to risk chasing off the possible suspect. "You're right," she said. "That was nasty, and I'm sorry. I'm going to take ten percent off your stay as an apology."

This instantly assuaged Trent's animosity. "I appreciate that. It's very generous."

"Anything to dodge a bad online review," Maggie said, and they both faked laughter at her limp joke.

*

Maggie had to lead several school tours at Doucet the next morning, so she didn't have a chance to catch up with Gaynell and Ione until late afternoon. It was Vanessa's day off, which gave Maggie a brief respite from being badgered about maid of honor duties. She filled her two friends in on what she'd learned about Fox as they all changed into their street clothes after work.

"I hope it's not Fox," Gaynell said as she pulled on a Gator Girls T-shirt. She'd taken to wearing them as often as possible to spread the word about her band. "I feel sorry for him."

"My money's on that snake, Trent," Ione declared.

"He's so slimy that he's almost too obvious a choice," Maggie said.

The three women stepped outside, where the early evening air had picked up a chill. Maggie's phone pinged and she checked it. "Aww. My mother texted me a picture of the puppies and kittens sleeping together. Look." She showed the photo to the other women, who echoed her "aww."

"So no one's claimed them yet?" Ione asked.

Maggie shook her head. "I'm kind of glad. I'm really enjoying having them around. It's a nice distraction from the hell that is being Vanessa's maid of honor."

"I'd love one of those kittens," Gaynell said. Seeing Maggie hesitate, she asked, "What? Is there a problem?"

"It's just . . . I mean, I know that you're saving up so that you can quit Doucet and focus on your music. And when it happens—*it will* happen, Gay, because you are so talented— I'm sure you'll be touring a lot and . . . I just wonder if you'll be home enough for a pet."

"Thank you for the vote of confidence in my music, but that kind of tour is far in my future," Gaynell said, slightly insulted. She sensed that for whatever reason, Maggie was giving her the runaround. "I certainly think I'm home enough for a cat."

"I have my eye on one of those pups," Ione said. "My grandkids would love it."

"I forgot," Maggie said. "How old are your grandkids again?"

Ione gave her a stern look. "Old enough for me to be offended that you think they can't handle a puppy. That is what you're implying, isn't it?"

Maggie was spared having to answer Ione by the unexpected arrival of Chret Bertrand. The young mechanic looked distraught; his skin was pale, and shadows under his eyes indicated a lack of sleep. "I hope I'm not disturbing anything," he said after they had all exchanged greetings. "It's just . . . something's happened. I needed to talk and I don't have too many friends and y'all seem so nice, so I drove over and . . ."

Chret trailed off. Gaynell, concerned, went to his side. "Chret, are you okay? You don't look good."

"I quit early today," he said, balling up his hands and sticking them deep into his pockets. "Uncle Lee understands." The women, confused, waited for him to continue. He looked down at the ground. "I got a call from a man named Lester Robbins. He's a lawyer in Texas."

He paused, a pained look crossing his face. Gaynell took his hand. "Chret, talk to us, please. Whatever's going on, don't worry about it. We're here for you."

Chret lifted his head. "The lawyer called to tell me something. Ginger Starke left me two hundred thousand dollars in her will."

All three women gasped. "Two hundred thousand dollars?!" Ione said. "That is some tip for service. I'm gonna start bringing my car around to you."

"It's not that," Chret said.

A memory came flooding back to Maggie: Ginger and Trent pointing at Chret and whispering when they brought her car in for repair. Maggie having to tear Ginger away from staring at the ex-Marine. It dawned on her that Ginger using the vehicle to scam the Crozats was a side trip from her real agenda. She had wanted to see Chretien Bertrand. To meet him.

Maggie focused on Chret's face, drawing the line of his jaw in her mind, adding a shading of subtle cheekbones. And the similarity to another face became obvious to her artist's eye. "I know why Ginger left you the money," she said. "You're her son."

Chapter Sixteen

Maggie's revelation elicited a gasp from Gaynell and a skeptical look from Ione, followed by a "Girl, that is crazy talk." But Chret confirmed it with a slight nod.

"Mind if I sit down?" he asked.

"Of course not," Gaynell said, then guided him to a seat on the bench. Ione offered him her water bottle and he took it gratefully. "Thank you, ma'am." Chret gulped down the water.

"So . . ." Maggie said after a moment. "Do you want to talk about it?"

Chret gave another slight nod. "Y'all know I was adopted. I was born at Frances Xavier Medical Center, and my parents—the people who raised me—brought me home a few days later. I never knew my adoptive dad. He died about a year after I was born. But Mom was totally cool, and she encouraged me to register with an adoption reunion registry in case my birth parents ever looked for me or I wanted to look for them. I registered, but I never did anything about it cuz I didn't care. I loved my mama. She was the best."

Chret grimaced and covered his face with his hands, but not before Maggie noticed a tear stranded in his lower lashes. "I guess Ginger checked the registration and found me. She never said anything. I only saw her that one time, and all I thought was, *What a rhymes-with-witch.* And now I know I was thinking that about my own mother."

Gaynell couldn't control herself. She threw her arms around Chret and hugged him tightly. He resisted briefly, then put both arms around the young musician and held her. They clung to each a moment before Chret pulled away. He reached into the front pocket of his mechanic's jumpsuit and took out a high-quality piece of ecru stationery. He unfolded it, unleashing the scent of a citrusy perfume. "The lawyer forwarded me this letter. From her. Ginger." Chret cleared his throat and read, "'Dear Chretien: Some people are born to be a parent. I wasn't. I'm sorry.'"

The women waited, but Chret folded up the note and put it back in his pocket. "That's it?" Ione said. "She didn't even sign it? Wow. Cold."

"No, she was trying," Maggie said somberly. "But that's all she was able to give of herself. I'd written Ginger off as pure evil. But maybe she was just a deeply disturbed and emotionally tortured woman. I think that note is heartbreaking."

"Whatever it is," Chret said, "inheriting a bunch of money pretty much makes me suspect number one. Pelican

PD 'asked' me to come down for an interview. Uncle Lee says they probably think that I found out I was in the will." He gave a desperate laugh. "Which is crazy. I didn't know anything about anything until that lawyer called, I swear. Anyway, I'm on my way to the police station." Chret looked straight at Gaynell. "I just needed to talk," he repeated.

"Well, you're obviously innocent," she declared.

Maggie agreed that the shy, vulnerable ex-soldier seemed an unlikely murderer. It was hard to imagine him being devious enough to uncover his true parentage, access his birth mother's will, and then kill her for his inheritance. But the situation required more than faith in Chret's noble character. "Do you have an alibi?" she asked as gently as possible.

Chret shrugged. "I was having a late lunch at the shop. Lee knows I was there, but he was working a big job on a seafood delivery truck that needed a new transmission. He can't swear he saw me there the whole time."

"Then I'll just say I was with you," Gaynell said.

"No way," Chret said, shaking his head vigorously. "I am not letting you lie for me."

"It's good that Lee can verify a good portion of the time you were there," Maggie said. "He can also testify to your mood, that you seemed like your normal self. That's important because if you were behaving any differently, the police might jump on it."

Chret looked down at the ground again to avoid eye contact. "I wasn't totally myself. I'd had the nightmares I get sometimes the night before. So I was, I don't know, fidgety. Cranky."

That wasn't good, so Maggie searched for a way around it. "But were you the same as you usually are after you have the nightmares? Could Lee say that it was your usual behavior, given the circumstances?"

Chret looked up. For the first time, Maggie saw hope in his eyes. "Yeah. I think he could."

"There you go," Maggie said.

"Did Ginger leave anyone else money in her will?" Ione asked. "If she did, it could be one of them."

"Good point," Maggie said. "Do you know about any other beneficiaries?" she asked Chret.

"No. I didn't hear much after the lawyer said I was Ginger's son."

"Did he say anything about who your father might be?"

"No. I've got zero information on him. Either he doesn't know about me or he doesn't want to know. Anyway, I gotta get to the police station."

"I'm going too," Gaynell announced. "If they wanna give you any grief, they're gonna have to go through me. I'll follow in my car."

"Yes, ma'am," Chret said. And for the first time since he'd shown up at Doucet, Chret smiled.

*

As soon as Maggie was done for the day, she got in her car and called Bo to report this new development. "Wow, that's huge," he responded. "I want to know more about this will. I'll get in touch with Johnny. He should be able to get a copy."

Maggie heard a loud cheer in the background. "Where are you?"

"Pelican High football game," Bo said. "I'm on security detail." Bo's voice bristled with resentment.

"Oh. I guess it beats traffic control."

"Not by much. We suck. Our team's down by thirty and we're not even at halftime." Maggie heard muffled voices in the background. "Hey, thanks. Sorry, Maggie, that wasn't to you."

"Is someone working with you?"

"No. Whitney brought Xander here, and they just bought me a hot dog. Okay, I'll see you guys after the game. They're gone now. Whit's trying to get him interested in sports, but he's way more into mixing colors with you."

"That's nice." Why did Maggie feel like Bo had just thrown her a pity compliment? "Let me know what you find out about the will."

She ended the call and felt a sudden need for sugary comfort. It was time for a pit stop at Bon Bon. As she drove toward town, she took in the late-fall scene around her. Some trees had shed all their leaves, others still bore brown ones, and some would never lose their rich green. If she was still in New York, the world would have gone gray by now, a gray that cast a pall on the city except when it was rendered invisible by a fresh, white snowfall. But not Cajun Country. The weather, like the people, refused to completely surrender its optimism.

It was dark by the time she parked in front of Bon Bon, but a warm light emanated from the store. Maggie stepped into the shop and, after saying hello to Lia behind the counter, sniffed the dense air. "Popcorn and sugar," she guessed. "Are you making kettle corn?"

"I'm putting it on sticks so it's like cake pops." Lia showed Maggie a row of what looked like snowball lollipops. "Then I dip them in rainbow jimmies for the kids. Want to help?"

"Sure." Maggie went behind the counter, took the apron Lia offered, and began dipping the pops into a big container of colorful sprinkles. It was an easy, relaxing task and allowed her the freedom to glance around the store. She saw that her artwork still made its home on Bon Bon's walls. "I wonder if I'll ever sell a painting," she sighed as she dipped. "Maybe I should fake my own death. That would make me way more desirable as an artist."

"Stop that," Lia admonished her. "Your art is fantastic. Customers rave about it. But honestly, I'm not sure this is the right place to sell paintings—yours or anyone's. People come in here for a sweet or a souvenir. That's why your mugs and mousepads and other small items do well. When I price anything over twenty or twenty-five dollars, I see customers almost recoil. You need a better venue for your work."

"I'll add 'find a gallery' to the list of things I need to do. It'll go right after 'find a murderer' and 'find an actual boyfriend.'" Lia looked at her quizzically. She was the one person Maggie felt she could confide in about her nebulous relationship with Bo, so she shared her fear that Whitney was manipulating her way back into his romantic life.

"You have pretty accurate instincts about people, so you might be right," Lia said. "But are you picking up on whether or not Bo is interested in rekindling whatever he had with Whitney? That's what's important here."

"That's very muddy. And I can't talk to him about it. It's just intuition, so how do I bring that up without looking kind of psychotic? And our relationship is so amorphous anyway. Ugh, it's incredibly frustrating." Maggie shoved a pop into the sprinkles and it fell apart. "Oops. I'll have to eat this one."

"Just keep an eye out for any overt action on Whitney's part. Then you'd be within your rights to talk to Bo." Maggie, whose mouth was too full of kettle corn to voice a response, nodded to acknowledge her cousin's advice. "On a completely different topic, Kyle and I were talking and we'd love to take a puppy and a kitten when they're ready to go."

"That's great. I'm just a little concerned about the timing," Maggie said. "You're in the middle of a remodel. And even when it's done, there are leftover fumes and sawdust in the air."

"You mean all the stuff that Kyle and I are breathing in, which has never seemed to bother you? And it shouldn't. Our remodel is totally green."

"I know. But it's different with animals. They're more vulnerable."

Lia burst out laughing. "Oh my gosh. You're a helicopter pet parent."

"What?!"

"You know, one of those parents who worries too much about their kids and hovers over them. That's exactly what you're doing with those pups and kitties. Honey, you need a boyfriend *and* a baby."

"No! At least not for a while. A good long while."

The bell alerting Lia to customers chimed, and Bibi came into the store. She was dressed in a bright tie-dyed top and loose black jersey pants; once again, Maggie marveled at the change in the designer. She seemed to be aging backward; it was as if Ginger's death was the equivalent of Dorian Gray's portrait for Bibi. The women all greeted each other. "I thought you were in Baton Rouge," Maggie said.

"I am, but you'll be seeing a lot of me as long as Trent is staying here. We have tons to do before we open the BR location. I was craving some chocolate and saw you were open." Bibi looked around. "This place is wonderful. I haven't been in before." She stopped in front of a painting. It was one of Maggie's personal favorites. She was proud of how she'd captured the twilight colors of a river sunset. "I *love* this," said Bibi.

"It's for sale," Maggie replied, ever hopeful. "They all are."

"Really?" Bibi studied the painting, scrunching her eyes to read Maggie's signature in the lower right-hand corner. "Oh, they're yours. Even better. Would you be interested in having me display them in our Baton Rouge studio? I'm sure I could sell some to clients."

Maggie was ecstatic. Not only was this a chance to showcase her work; it gave her a legitimate reason to further insinuate herself into Bibi and Trent's world. "I would love that, Bibi. I can consign these paintings to you, and you're welcome to anything in my studio."

"Perfect." Bibi switched her attention to Lia's display of handmade candies and ordered a half-pound assortment.

"When you have the time, I wonder if you could take a look at some design drawings my boyfriend and I have been working on for our new home," Lia said as she rang up Bibi's order. "I'd love your input."

"Absolutely," Bibi said. She and Lia landed on a time for Bibi to pick up Maggie's artwork, and then Bibi left with her chocolate, a free six-pack of kettle corn pops, and Lia's renderings under her arm.

Lia and Maggie were silent for a minute. Then Lia said sheepishly, "I kind of hope she's not the murderer."

"Oh, I totally hope she's not," Maggie quickly agreed. She hugged her cousin good-bye and then stepped into Fais Dough Dough, where she picked up some croissants for the family's morning breakfast. She left the store and was about to get in her car when she was accosted by Little Earlie Waddell. He seemed unfazed by his previous run-in with Maggie and Bo's subsequent fist to his stomach. "What now?" she asked, exasperated.

"I heard how Chret Bertrand is really Ginger Fleer's son, and I'm all over the story."

"You heard that already?"

"Seriously? It's Pelican. We've barely got anything to do *except* gossip."

"Right. Anyway . . ." Maggie opened her car door and slid into the driver's seat. "No comment."

Little Earlie, per usual, ignored her. "You have to agree that this moves him to the front of the line as a suspect in Ginger's murder."

Furious, Maggie jumped back out of her car. She'd had it with the intrusive reporter. "No, I do not 'have to' agree. Chret Bertrand is a kind man and a hero who fought for our country. You're always looking for quotes, Little Earlie, so I'm going to give you one. You can put in that stupid paper of yours that if PPD even thinks of charging Chret with Ginger's murder, I'll do whatever I can to prove them wrong and find the real killer."

Earlie took a small step back. "I'm not gonna quote you on that, Maggie." His voice was low, his tone serious. "If you're right and it's not Chret, then whoever it is probably wouldn't be too happy about someone announcing to the world that they were gonna do whatever it took to expose them. In fact, there's a real good chance it would create another murder target—you."

Chapter Seventeen

Maggie stood there, stunned. "You're absolutely right, Little Earlie," she said. "I just blurted without thinking. I do that sometimes. Not a good habit. Thanks for the wake-up call."

The reporter shrugged. "No problem. It's one thing to write about a person that you only met once being murdered. But I'd hate to be writing about a friend."

This touched Maggie. Little Earlie might be as annoying as a tick on a dog, but he was still part of her community, which she and others usually forgot. "I appreciate you looking out for me. And I'll give you quotes when I can. But try not to push so hard."

"Message sent and received," he said. "And I sincerely hope it's not Chret. Nobody can add years to the life of my PT Cruiser like he can."

He headed off while Maggie debated her next move. She was shaken by the revelation that her arrogance could have had fatal consequences. And why was she so adamant that Chret, a young man she barely knew, was innocent? Simply relying on her intuition was hardly a fail-safe position in a murder investigation. The news was littered with stories of wounded warriors suffering from PTSD who had snapped. *I need a drink,* she thought. She looked over to where the neon sign of Junie's beckoned and then made a beeline for the hangout, heading straight for the bar. Old Shari eyeballed her, then poured a shot of whiskey and placed it on the bar with a thump. A small bit splashed out of the glass and onto the bar. "You might want to lick that up," Shari said. "Looks like you need every last drop."

Maggie downed the shot and held out the glass. "I think I'll take a refill instead."

Old Shari obliged, and Maggie swallowed the second round. She noticed JJ listening patiently as Tookie Fleer yammered at him, alternating between pointing to a list on a notepad and then pointing at him. Maggie looked away, hoping to avoid eye contact with the woman, but it was too late. Tookie had locked on to her. "Maggie, get over here," she ordered, skipping the niceties of a greeting as usual. Maggie grimaced, then slunk over to Vanessa's mother. "We didn't want any break in the party planning for Van's bachelorette party, so I've been going over some details with JJ myself. I'll let him fill you in on the décor—" Tookie hit that last word hard, obviously proud that she could fit it into a conversation—"but I did want to let you know that we've decided to save Van's baby shower until after she gives birth. So you don't have to worry about that this week."

Baby shower?! What the . . . Maggie took a deep breath to prevent herself from screaming. "Actually, I don't have to worry about it at all. Maid of honor duties end when the wedding's over. They don't throw baby showers, too."

"Maybe not, but best friends do," Tookie retorted.

"Well, when you find Vanessa's, wish her good luck for me," Maggie, who'd had it with the pushy woman, shot back.

Tookie chuckled. "Magnolia, I love your cheeky sense of humor." She ripped the top page off her pad and handed it to JJ. "Here. My airboat's getting inspected first thing, so I gotta get up early. You and Maggie can go over the list and make sure we're good to go."

With that, she bounced off her barstool and strode out the door. Maggie sighed. She motioned to the piece of paper Tookie had deposited with JJ. "Hit me with what I have to do, JJ."

"Let's start here," JJ said. He crumpled up the list, dropped it in a bucket, and put a match to it. He and Maggie watched with great satisfaction as the paper burned. "They get purple-and-gold balloons because I happen to have a bunch left from the LSU-Ole Miss game. And that's it. I must say, I find Miss Vanessa's LSU obsession hilarious. I'm not sure she even finished high school."

"Yeah, that's not something I'd put money on." Maggie's head was starting to pound. "I need a big glass of water to chase the whiskey."

"Smart choice. You got it."

JJ filled a tanker mug with water and passed it to Maggie. She drank slowly. There was something soothing about the cool, flavorless liquid. "JJ, I'm getting nowhere with finding out who killed Ginger. Maybe it's time to pass the search on to someone else. Like Helene Brevelle."

JJ shook his head. "No voodoo needed. I have total faith in you. But you need to clear your mind, just wipe it clean like it's a blackboard. Then fill that board with everything you remember about Ginger—everything she said, every move she made. You'll get to where you need to go."

"You're right." Maggie pointed to her head. "I've got too much clutter up here. It's time for a little mental housecleaning." She drained her glass and set it on the table, along with cash to cover her tab. Then she reached over the bar and hugged JJ. "Thanks. You're a great friend."

JJ returned the hug. "With you, it's a pleasure. With others"—he motioned to the door that Tookie had marched out of—"it's my job. And a *hard* one at that."

As soon as Maggie got home, she parked in her family's gravel lot and practically ran into the shotgun house. She threw herself on her bed and closed her eyes. She pictured the mix of thoughts and feelings in her mind—concern about Bo and Whitney's relationship, confusion about murder suspects, frustration with the always-frustrating Fleers—as words on an old-fashioned blackboard. Then she visualized erasing every word until the blackboard was black and empty. She focused on her rhythmic breathing, and a feeling of calm soon enveloped her. Maggie let her mind drift, but every time it wandered over to something that might trouble her, she erased the thought. Instead, she focused on Ginger. She relived her every interaction with the woman and followed every step she'd seen her take. And finally her mind landed on a potential clue. She grabbed her phone and tapped out a text to her friends.

*

Daybreak found an energized Maggie gathered with her Yes We PeliCAN! fundraiser walking team in the Crozat parking lot. They'd all responded yes, albeit reluctantly, to her text asking for an early morning rendezvous. Gaynell and Ninette didn't bother to cover their yawns, while Ione drank coffee from a Big Gulp–sized travel mug. "I'm gonna have to power up for this power walk," Ione grumbled as she took a hearty swig. She chomped on a croissant from a box of French pastries that Lia had brought.

"Maggie, sweetie, I appreciate your enthusiasm for the walkathon, but we really don't have to train at dawn," her mother said.

"Today's less about training and more about following a trail," Maggie said. The others forgot their weariness and looked at her with interest. "I wanted to do it as early as possible, before anyone could see where we're going."

"Then what are we standing around for?" Ione put her travel mug on the hood of her car. "Let's make tracks."

Maggie led the women down the country road that ran alongside the B and B. But instead of going straight, she made a left and followed Ginger's jogging route down the old, overgrown dirt road. The foliage had grown thick from lack of attention, and the women batted away cobwebs and dodged low-hanging branches. "Where exactly are we going?" Gaynell asked, nursing a scratch on her arm from a branch that she'd missed.

"This leads to the Callette family's old lodge," Ninette said. "But that was abandoned years ago. Why would Ginger want to go there?"

No one had an answer, so the women continued on in silence. The road disintegrated into a path as foliage closed in on it. Some trees had lost their leaves, but the shrubs and pines hadn't, so very little sun made its way through the forest's canopy. The air was warm and musty, but every so often the group would find themselves walking through an inexplicably cold spot. "Am I the only one who finds this creepy?" Lia asked, gazing around nervously, shivering as she walked.

"No," Gaynell and Ione chorused. Maggie didn't disagree. It *was* creepy, and she prayed that she hadn't assembled the group at dawn's early light for nothing. They trekked on a few more yards and then Maggie stopped.

"Whoa," she exclaimed.

"What, what?!" Gaynell cried as she clutched Ione's arm. Ione clutched her back.

"This," Maggie said, gesturing at the sight in front of them. A handful of decaying wooden cabins formed a horseshoe around a weedy green. At the head of the horseshoe stood what was left of a two-story building that had once been a lodge. Its wood siding was a faded, peeling red. Half of a second-story balcony still remained; the other half, and the building with it, had collapsed into rubble. Still, it managed to convey a bit of grandeur that the rudimentary cabins lacked. The ground around all the buildings was littered with the shattered glass of their windows.

"What *is* this?" Ione asked.

"There was a family called the Callettes; sometime in the twenties, they built this as a kind of rustic resort," Ninette said. "They thought it would be a good summer escape for people from New Orleans, but then the Depression happened and the place foundered. It's been closed for seventy or more years. I had no idea any of it was still standing."

"I remember some big kids bringing me here when I was really little," Maggie said. "It scared me so much that I ran home and never came back. I put it out of my mind until I saw Ginger make her turn onto the old road."

Ninette nodded. "Kids used to play here, but after a few broke legs or arms by jumping from a roof or tripping on something, the 'No Trespassing' signs got posted and everyone pretty much forgot about the place."

"It's a good piece of property," Ione said as she sized the place up. "There's already plumbing and electricity. I'm surprised it hasn't been developed."

Maggie walked along the rutted path that ran in front of the cottages, careful to avoid the shards of glass. She noticed a scrap of paper staple-gunned to a wall of a cabin and looked down at the ground below it. A flyer lay there, wet and wrinkled by the dew. She picked it up and showed the others. "The parish took over the property. The auction was just last week—when Ginger came to town. She was interested in getting into real estate. I think the real reason she came to Pelican wasn't to attend Vanessa's wedding festivities. It was to check out this property."

It was Ninette's turn to shiver. "I don't know about anyone else, but I'm chilly and a bit spooked right now."

"I'm sorry," Maggie said. "Let's go back."

Relieved, Ninette and the others reversed course back to the plantation. But Maggie lingered a moment, staring at the encampment enshrouded by decades of nature reclaiming its turf. Her instincts had awakened, and the message they sent was that the secret to Ginger's death lay somewhere in the weeds and history of the Callettes' abandoned lodge.

Chapter Eighteen

The women made small talk as they strode back to Crozat—all except Maggie, who kept silent as she mulled over the link between Ginger and the land auction. When they reached the manor, the women said their good-byes and went their separate ways. Maggie took a quick shower and threw on a pair of jeans. She was way behind on her laundry, so the only shirt she could dig up was a bedazzled tee that read "Good Girls Go to Church, Bad Girls Go to Mardi Gras," which Gran' had given to her as a joke birthday present. She was eager to research the Callette property at the Pelican Hall of Records, a grandiose name for a couple of rooms behind the town's senior center. She called to find out when it opened, and a recording told her that it wouldn't be for a few hours. She scrambled some eggs, made a cup of tea, and sat down at the kitchen table with a notepad.

Gran' came out of her bedroom, clipping on a pair of gold knot earrings as she strolled into the kitchen. She was dressed in a navy linen pantsuit and a pale-blue silk blouse with a bow at the neck. "You look nice," Maggie told her. "Are you wearing your sorority colors?"

Gran' modeled her outfit. "The blue-and-blue, the golden key, the fleur-de-lis, all that's for me," she sang. "Rah rah for KKG!" She finished with a flourish. "Yes, I'm meeting a few of my remaining Kappa girlfriends for brunch at Commander's Palace. Stevens is being very noble and driving me down to New Orleans. He'll wait for me at the bar and then we're going to walk the Quarter."

"Really?"

"Don't grin at me like that. We're just a couple of old folks keeping company. Oh my goodness, you're going out in public in that T-shirt?"

Maggie accepted her grandmother's obvious change of subject. "I need to do laundry. Gran', do you know anything about that those abandoned cabins in the woods?"

"You mean the old Callette property? That's been returning to dust for years."

"What do you know about the family?"

"About as much as anyone around here, which isn't much. I remember the last two Callettes, a brother and sister. They only spoke French and walked around in their slippers. That is, when they left their home, which was rare. They were recluses. Neither ever married, and they died within a day of each other, both in their nineties. There wasn't a will, so their house, which was on the outskirts of town, sat empty until the parish eventually laid claim to it. The place was a wreck, so they tore it down and now use the land to store service equipment."

Maggie thought for a moment. "Is there any chance Ginger Fleer was related to them?"

Gran' shook her head no with vigor. "Absolutely not. She was American, not Cajun, on both sides. The Fleers came to this part of the country from Kentucky, and only about fifty years ago. She's an Abbott on her mother's side; they came over from North Carolina sometime after the Civil War."

"You know everything about everyone, don't you?" Maggie gave her grandmother an affectionate grin.

Gran' shrugged. "It's a small town, so there's not a whole lot else to do besides poke around other people's business. That's why I love the Internet so much. Lets me poke around the whole world's business."

There was a "shave and a haircut, two bits" knock at the door. "That's my ride," Gran' said. She picked up her purse and kissed her granddaughter on the top of her head. "Stay safe, dearest. Poking too far into people's business can be dangerous."

"I'll be careful. And I won't tell anyone that you bought this shirt for me."

"I'd appreciate that."

Gran' left, and Maggie returned to her notepad. She jotted down a list of things to look for in the town records. Were there any surviving Callette heirs? Who owned the property now? What was its value? She checked the clock on the microwave and saw that the Hall of Records would open in fifteen minutes, so she grabbed her wallet and car keys. She was about to head out when there was a persistent rapping on the door.

"Maggie! Hey! It's Van. Me and Ru are here for our session."

Maggie groaned. She'd completely forgotten that she'd scheduled the couple for what she prayed would be their last sitting. "Right. I'll meet you at the studio."

"Bring coffee so's I can stay awake this time," Rufus ordered through the door. Maggie heard them tromp off, then gritted her teeth and went back into the kitchen where the remnants of a pot of coffee sat moldering. She heated it up in the microwave, took a couple of mugs, and slowly made her way from the shotgun to her studio.

*

Maggie endured a very long hour of Vanessa and Rufus alternating between flirting and fighting. "Time's up," she told the couple at the hour's blessed end and then put down her brush. She stepped back to examine the portrait. It was a miracle—somehow she'd created a balance of flattering and realistic. Vanessa or Ru would find something to complain about, but Maggie didn't care. She was proud of her work.

"I guess that's as good as it's gonna get," Rufus said as he peered at the painting over her shoulder.

Vanessa was even less enthusiastic. "It doesn't have enough SA. You know—sex appeal."

"It's a portrait, not a boudoir photo," Maggie responded.

"We already got plenty of those, don't we, babe?" Ru said, nudging his wife-to-be in the ribs. He leered, Vanessa simpered, and Maggie suppressed the urge to take a hand to each of their throats.

"Alrighty, time to book," Ru said. "I need to get some decent coffee. No offense, but yours stinks."

"You're welcome," Maggie said dryly. Her sarcasm sailed by Rufus. "By the way, have you heard anything new about Ginger's case?"

"I could be asking you the same question," Vanessa said, wagging a finger at Maggie. "I expected more from you, Maggie."

"Are you serious?" Maggie yelped. "Vanessa, I couldn't give you more if I opened a vein."

Vanessa dismissed her with a wave of a hand. "It's probably Fox anyway. It's always the husband."

"He had a big-ass insurance policy on her, that's for sure," Ru said. "Cal told me."

This was a new development. "Was it unusually high?" Maggie asked.

"Maybe, maybe not. About a million. But what is unusual is that he upped it from five hundred grand just a few months ago, about when Ginger decided to expand her business to Baton Rouge. Could be that he had a lot of faith in his wife's talent. Or could be that he had his own business plan, which included offing her."

Ru walked out the door and Vanessa followed. "Byeee!" she called back to Maggie. "I'm putting together a spreadsheet for my baby shower. I'll e-mail it to you later."

"No!" Maggie exclaimed as the door slammed shut behind Van. Her cell phone rang and she answered it without ID'ing the caller. "What?" she snapped.

"Well, hello to you, too," Gran' responded. "I called to ask if you would make sure our fur-babies have fresh water before you go out, but it sounds like you're ready to chew nails and spit spikes."

"Oh, I am." Maggie railed about Vanessa's latest unreasonable expectation. "I've had it with that woman. I'm telling her she can find another maid of honor, because I am done, finished, finito."

"Well now, you made a promise, didn't you?"

"Yes, but—"

"And do we Crozats ever renege on our promises simply because they no longer suit us?"

"No, but—"

"Would you like to be the first Crozat to break with that storied tradition?"

Maggie paused. "No," she said.

"Then you'll just have to accept you made a commitment and see it through, chère. Don't forget about the fresh water."

Gran' ended the call. Maggie groaned and sank into an old club chair that she'd pulled from the attic and placed in the studio. Then she pulled herself to her feet, picked up Ru's coffee cup, and took it to the sink for a wash. She got some satisfaction from serving him vile coffee but needed a way to channel the vitriol she still felt toward Vanessa.

She dried the mug, pulled out a large pad and black charcoal pencil, and started drawing. Five minutes later, she sat back and admired what she had produced—a spot-on caricature of a hugely pregnant Vanessa in a horned headdress on an opera stage singing, "Me, me, me, me, me, me, me." It was ridiculous and nonsensical and made Maggie feel much better.

She put the pad away and locked up the studio. She'd freshen Brooke and Jolie's water and then pay the Hall of Records a visit. And after that, she'd delve into the questionable insurance policy Fox had taken out on his wife.

*

"Magnolia Marie Crozat, what a treat to see you!"

Village Clerk Eula Banks beamed at Maggie. Given the isolated location of the H of R, as some in Pelican called the place, Maggie had a feeling that it would be a treat for Eula to see anyone. "It's very nice to see you too, Mrs. Banks," she responded politely. The niceties were followed by ten minutes of grandbaby stories and photos. Maggie nodded and voiced a few "awws" when appropriate; she suppressed an acerbic response when Eula tsk-tsked over Maggie's still-single status, reminding herself that Mrs. Banks was in her late sixties and thus from a different generation.

"So what brings you to the H of R?" Eula finally said.

"I heard the old Callette property went up for auction last week," Maggie said. "I'm interested in learning what happened to it."

"Really." Eula eyes brightened. She'd picked up the scent of new gossip. "Is the Crozat family thinking of expanding its operation? I've always said y'all should think about adding a spa. New Orleans folks'd lap that up."

"Shhh," Maggie cautioned, putting a finger to her lips. The last thing she needed was Eula bringing attention to her interest in the Callettes' land. "We don't want anyone to know we're even thinking about that."

"Of course," Eula said. She pretended to zip her lips. "But I'm afraid you're out of luck on that particular parcel. It sold."

"Oh." Maggie feigned disappointment. "Any chance I can look up the sale? I'd like to know who our new neighbors might be."

"That information is public record, so that's not a problem. We're doing everything on the computer now, so I can open a file and set you up at the computer." Eula gestured for Maggie to follow her to an old computer that sat on what looked like a discarded school desk. "The independent auditor that Mayor Beaufils hired to go through old town records found unclaimed properties like the Callettes all over the place. Fortunately, the mayor isn't one of those development-crazy types who'd sell his mama's house from under her if he thought it'd fill our coffers. But he did see how that particular piece had potential since it already has lines for utilities." Eula reached down for the reading glasses that dangled around her neck on an old-fashioned chain and then parked them on the bridge of her nose. "Let me call up that file." She chuckled. "Listen to me, I sound like one of those Silicone Valley smarty-pants."

"You sure do," Maggie said, not wanting to hurt the woman's feelings by pointing out that it was actually Sili*con* Valley.

Eula tapped a few keys. "Got it. There you go. If you need anything else, just let me know."

The clerk returned to her station, and Maggie perused the dense document on the screen in front of her. It was a real estate sales contract between the representatives of Pelican and a limited liability corporation with the innocuous name of Sunset LLC. She paged through the hefty document until she found how much the property had sold for: $125,000, which seemed perfectly reasonable. Hoping to learn more about the LLC, she entered a search for it, but nothing came up. It seemed to be a company created solely for the purpose of acquiring this particular piece of property.

"Mrs. Banks, would it be okay if I made a copy of this? I'll pay for it."

"Of course, honey. But don't worry about paying for it. It's not like anyone's counting the paper we use." Mrs. Banks winked at her.

Maggie thanked her and sent the document to a wheezy old printer that seemed close to expiring with each piece of paper it slowly spit out. As she waited for the print job to end, she endured ten minutes of Mrs. Banks running through a list of potential mates for her, including the woman's own son, Wiley, who Maggie knew had just moved into a French Quarter apartment with his boyfriend. When the print job finally completed, she grabbed it, said her good-byes, and fled the H of R.

169

As Maggie walked back to her car, she put in a call to Bo and shared what she'd learned about the sale of the property to Sunset LLC. "I didn't find anything particularly suspicious, but I just don't have a good feeling about it," she said.

"That's the basis of a lot of detective work," Bo said. "Feelings and hunches. I'll see if I can find out anything else. Perske has me on desk duty, which is a bore but a good cover for some computer snooping. By the way, Johnny checked out Fox Starke's phone and credit card statements but didn't find anything to indicate where he was the night before Ginger was murdered. No motel charges, no gas charges . . . nothing to incriminate or exonerate him."

"Where was he that night?" Maggie wondered. She reached her car and got inside. "Maybe he got tired on the drive back to Houston and pulled off the road to sleep somewhere."

"Could be. I wish we could find something that could cement him as a suspect. Perske tried to find a way to hold Chret Bernard and couldn't come up with anything, so we let him go. But the chief's on a mission to find any evidence he can to bring a murder charge against the kid."

"Oh, that's not good. I still have trouble seeing Chret doing something this cold-blooded."

"Unfortunately for Chret, the chief doesn't have the same problem. I better go. I have to try and find a limo for Ru's bachelor party tonight. He's assuming we'll all be too drunk to drive home. He's probably right. I know I'll have to knock back a few just to get through it."

Maggie smiled. "You won't get any sympathy from me. All you had to do was book a car and a table at a strip club. You wouldn't believe what Van's put me through. And at the last minute, she decided to make the party co-ed, which pretty much doubles the guest list. Whoever heard of a co-ed bachelorette party? Isn't that an oxymoron?"

"I believe so," Bo said with a laugh.

"She's lucky that Rufus kept his guest list short, otherwise there wouldn't even be guys to invite."

"Yeah, I'm not sure if that was intentional or a result of guys he's ticked off over the years enjoying the opportunity to RSVP a big, fat no. Anyway, I hope you have some kind of fun tonight. I'm sorry I won't be there."

"Me too." Maggie felt a pang of loneliness. "And I hope you *don't* have much fun tonight."

"Don't worry, I won't. I've never been one for strip clubs." Bo dropped his voice so that it was low and sexy. "I'll be thinking of you the whole time."

The pang inside Maggie turned into something else, and she ended the call before it got any more heated. She leaned back against the car seat, closed her eyes, and took a deep breath to regain control of her emotions. Bo was still interested in her. Still attracted. *Shame on me for feeling threatened by Whitney,* she thought.

Maggie was brought back to earth by the sound of her cell phone ringing. It was Lia.

"I saw your car," her cousin said. "Kyle's going to watch the store so I can go up to Baton Rouge to see Bibi. She already has some sketches and swatches to show me. Want to come?"

"Sounds great. We can go to a party supply store while we're there. I need to pick up some stuff for the bachelorette party. And a backup helium tank in case JJ's runs out. Van wants the balloons to cover the whole 'tacky' ceiling."

"You mean 'tacky' as in the beautifully handcrafted, historic tin ceiling tiles?" Lia said, her tone dry.

"Do *not* get me started. I'll drive. It's warm today—I'll put the top down."

Moments later, Lia appeared and hopped in Maggie's Falcon convertible. She tucked her mess of brown curls under a blue bandana, Maggie put the car's top down, and the women took off. The balmy air whipped around them as they drove along the interstate, singing along to whatever tunes Maggie was able to drum up on the car's fifty-plus-year-old AM radio. Maggie couldn't remember the last time she'd felt so free—just her and her dearest friend enjoying an in-the-moment outing devoid of drama and murder. At least until they got to Socher-Starke Design, where Maggie hoped to glean any new information she could on Bibi's complex relationships with Fox and Trent.

They followed Bibi's directions and found themselves driving down a tree-lined boulevard in the city's Garden District. Maggie located the address, and they parked in front of a charming gray-and-white Creole-style bungalow. Banana plants lined a stone walkway that led to a bright-red door. The women walked up the steps to the home's portico and were about to ring the bell when Bibi opened the door. She was dressed in jeans and a paint-smeared T-shirt.

"I saw you pull up," she greeted them. "Come on in. Pardon the smell; I've been painting the back bedroom."

They followed Bibi inside, and she led them on a tour of the small home, pointing out the eventual function of each room. The tour ended in Bibi's office, where Maggie was thrilled to see her paintings on display. She was even more excited to see a red dot on one of them, indicating that it had been sold. "I'm designing the interior of a new tea shop in the neighborhood, and the owner loved that painting," Bibi said in response to Maggie's obvious excitement. "She's got an eye on a couple of others too. I don't know if you've ever done any textile design, but I was thinking that if you're interested, maybe you could design a fabric for the tablecloths and chairs that complements your artwork."

"I *love* you," Maggie said, overwhelmed.

Bibi laughed. "Just doing my job. Speaking of which, here are some of my thoughts for Grove Hall, Lia. I only had time to do the front parlor and dining room, but you'll get the general direction I'd like to go in." Bibi opened a file on her computer and a stunning 3-D design of a living room filled the large screen. "My goal is to make sure every historical detail of the home is highlighted, like that gorgeous carved-cypress rosette around the chandelier. I'd also like to do a bit of architectural archeology to see if we can figure out the original paint colors and then let that determine the palette for each room."

Lia analyzed the rendering. "Oh, this is spectacular. I love you, too! Draw up a contract. You're hired."

"That's wonderful!" Bibi clapped her hands gleefully. "Let's celebrate. I have a bottle of champagne in the kitchen. It's cheap, but who cares?"

"We don't!" Maggie and Lia chorused as they followed Bibi into the bungalow's compact, old-fashioned kitchen.

Bibi poured them each a glass and then led them to a backyard patio, where they toasted, sipped, and chatted. Maggie was debating how to steer the conversation toward Ginger's murder when Bibi saved her the trouble. "So I heard about that guy Ginger left a bunch of money to," she said. "Who knew she had a child?"

"She never said anything to you or Trent?" Maggie asked.

Bibi shook her head. "Certainly not to me, and judging by Trent's anger when he heard about it, not to him either."

Maggie picked up the satisfaction in Bibi's voice as she shared the news of Trent's unhappiness. "I heard that Ginger's husband was blown away by the news, too," she said, adopting a gossipy tone. "*And* I also heard that the police caught him in a lie about where he was the night before Ginger was killed. He said he went back to Houston, but he didn't. So they're very suspicious about where he was."

Bibi stiffened. She looked down at the worn bricks of the bungalow patio. "Fox is a really good guy. If he lied, he had his reasons."

Maggie sensed the woman was hiding something. She took a chance and pushed a little harder. "I don't know. I mean, this is a murder investigation. A lie could send him to the electric chair."

Bibi's head snapped up. "He was trying to protect someone." Bibi's hand shook, and champagne splashed from her glass onto the ground.

"Maybe he just told you that to cover where he really was." Maggie said. She knew she was being ruthless in pressing the designer, but she also sensed that she was close to getting the truth from her.

"No," Bibi said. "It wasn't a cover. It's true. Fox didn't drive back to Houston because he was with me. We spent the night together at Crozat."

Chapter Nineteen

Maggie's surprise at Bibi's revelation lasted less than a second. A man cuckolded by his wife. A younger woman desperately infatuated with him. When she thought about it, the liaison seemed inevitable.

"He didn't want anyone to know, so we hid his car on a back road and I drove him to it in the morning," Bibi said. "He hasn't told the police because he's trying to protect me. He's afraid they might suspect me of . . . of trying to get Ginger out of the way."

"That sounds very noble, but he's also protecting himself," Maggie pointed out. "The police could see it as a classic case of a husband with a mistress who wants to get rid of his wife."

"No," Bibi responded. "I was never his mistress. It only happened that once. Fox felt terrible about it, so we agreed to keep it a secret. Fox swore there was still good in Ginger and was determined to help reclaim that part of her."

Bibi wiped her eyes with her hand. Lia handed her a tissue, which she accepted gratefully. She might be lying to cover for Fox's whereabouts that evening, but the pain of a woman dismissed after a one-night stand was too obvious. Maggie had been there herself a few times in New York; she knew there was no faking it.

Bibi's cell rang, and she checked the screen. "It's Trent," she said. "I better take it." She answered the call as she walked back into the house.

As soon as she was gone, Lia turned to Maggie. "Talk about blinded by love. She doesn't even see that Fox used her."

"Yes," Maggie said. "And no. He took advantage of her attraction to him, for sure. But I don't think he used her to establish an alibi. I think Fox was devastated by Ginger's betrayal, and Bibi offered him comfort. And it didn't hurt that it was a way to get back at Ginger for her own affair, although he seemed to have second thoughts about throwing that in her face."

Their conversation was disrupted by a stream of foul language that came from inside the bungalow. Bibi stormed out a moment later, her face flaming with anger. "Um . . . everything okay?" Maggie asked, although it obviously wasn't.

"That lying, manipulative, useless . . ." Bibi spewed venom at her business partner. "He agreed with me that we shouldn't use Ginger's name in our company name anymore, especially in Baton Rouge. If anyone here knows her at all, it's as a murder victim, which isn't exactly the best advertising. He promised to include my name instead, but do you know what he did? He went and ordered a sign and stationery and everything with the name 'Trent Socher Design Group.' I do all the work and he gets all the credit. And what do I get? I'm 'Group'!"

Bibi collapsed into a chair. Maggie took what was left of her champagne and poured it into Bibi's glass. "Here. You need this more than I do."

"Thank you." Bibi gulped down the contents of the glass. "How did I ever get involved with that snake? He's a cheat and a user and not fit to walk this earth."

The women made the appropriate sympathetic noises, and then Lia subtly showed Maggie the time on her phone. "We should go," Maggie said.

She and Lia stood, then Bibi jumped up. "I am so sorry. I shouldn't have gone on like that. It was totally unprofessional of me."

"Don't worry about it," Lia said as she gave Bibi a hug. "We completely understand."

Bibi relaxed. "I'll see you at the bachelorette party tonight. It was nice of Vanessa to invite me. I promise I'll be in a better mood."

"Don't worry about it. Just come and enjoy yourself." Maggie chose not to mention that Vanessa's invitation to this virtual stranger was motivated by the bride-to-be's panic that her regular crowd had wearied of buying presents for her battery of wedding-related celebrations. To allay her fears,

Van had fattened her guest list with new potential gift-givers like Bibi.

The designer walked Maggie and Lia to their car and waved them off. "Well, that was something," Lia said as they drove out of Bibi's neighborhood and made their way back to the interstate.

"Oh, it was very much something," Maggie agreed. "And I'll tell you one thing for sure: as much as Bibi is in love with Fox, it's half as much as she hates Trent."

*

Maggie and Lia stopped at a party store for supplies on their way out of town and used the car ride home to go over the last-minute details of Vanessa's bachelorette party. Kyle and Lia's gift to the bride was picking up the tab for the photo booth the Bridezilla had demanded. Originally Vanessa envisioned it for her wedding reception, but Maggie put the brakes on that idea by declaring, "You're getting married, not throwing a bat mitzvah." Once Maggie explained to the woman what a bat mitzvah was, Vanessa agreed that the photo booth was better suited to a more casual event.

Maggie dropped Lia off at Fais Dough Dough and headed for Crozat. Having decided she'd earned some downtime before the bachelorette party, she parked and made her way to the Crozat library, where she searched the centuries-old bookcases until she landed on an ancient photo album. She carefully removed the album from its home on the shelf and then traipsed home to the shotgun house. There, she sat on the couch with the album on her lap, carefully turning its delicate pages filled with photos of Newcomb Pottery, the storied clayware created by Newcomb College students in the early years of the twentieth century. Maggie and Lia's great-great-aunt Sylvie Doucet had been one of those students, and now Maggie turned to her ancestor for design inspiration. Within minutes, her mind was brimming with potential fabric patterns, so she pulled out her battered container of colored pencils and quickly sketched a few. When she was done, Maggie felt a peace within her that she hadn't experienced in weeks. Whether she was painting a landscape, creating plantation souvenirs, or experimenting with fabric designs, art grounded her in a way that nothing else did.

She put away her art supplies and treated herself to a long, luxurious bath, then dressed for the evening's festivities. She opted for a stretchy, purple halter minidress that she'd splurged on in New York and paired it with strappy, black high-heeled sandals and minimalist jewelry—gold hoop earrings and a gold chain sporting a crawdaddy charm that Tug and Ninette had given her when she moved back home. She was surprised to find herself looking forward to the party.

Maggie had just finished her makeup when there was a tentative knock on the front door. "Be right there," she called.

"Take your time," Whitney Durand Evans called back. Maggie got the sinking feeling in the pit of her stomach that she'd come to associate with any mention or sighting of Bo's ex-wife, but she fought it back and welcomed Whitney into the shotgun.

"I know you're getting ready for that party, so I'll keep it short," Whitney said, "but I needed to talk to you."

Go away, tummy feeling! Maggie told herself.

"I think it would be great for Xander to have a pet. When the time comes, I wondered if you might be willing to give us either a pup or a kitty."

That's it? Phew! "Oh, yes." Then Maggie backtracked. "My only concern is Xander going back and forth between houses like he does might be traumatic for a pet. And, of course, for him separating from the pet."

"That is something to think about. But I'm sure Bo and I could find a way to make it work."

"They're still weeks away from going anywhere, so we have time to figure it out." Maggie made a point of looking at a clock on the mantle above the fireplace, but Whitney didn't take the hint.

"There is one other thing." Whitney spoke slowly. She sat down on the living room couch. "I need to talk to someone, and you're the only person I feel like I know well enough here in Pelican."

Maggie instinctively clutched her stomach. She sat in a chair across from Whitney. "Okay," she said tentatively.

"Zach and I are having . . . problems," Whitney began. "He's gone so much. It puts a strain on our relationship. I see Bo with Xander, how gentle he is and how caring and . . . sometimes I think I made a mistake ending the marriage. Maybe I got it right the first time and I was just too dumb to know it." Whitney paused. She looked down, and her red-gold hair fell in soft tufts around her angelic face. Even in the midst of emotional trauma, she was dazzling. "I know you and Bo are good friends. Has he ever said anything about me? Like regrets that we broke up?"

Maggie didn't rush to answer. The landscape was littered with potential emotional landmines—Whitney's, Bo's, hers . . . even Xander's. "Bo's a very private person," she said, picking her words with precision. "I think he respects you and what you shared too much to talk about it with someone else."

Whitney chose to read what she wanted to into Maggie's words. "So he does care about me. Couples who get divorced do remarry sometimes. I've read articles about it."

Oh, dear God, Maggie thought. *This woman is on a mission.* "Whitney, here's what I think's going on," Maggie said, channeling her best lay therapist. "You miss Zach and you know he has to do what he has to do, but you're also angry at him for his absence. You have a fantasy of what it would be like rekindle a relationship with Bo. Before you give in to that and find out the hard way that it may be just that—a fantasy—I think you need to work on your marriage. I'm sure he's a good guy. Bo's only said positive things about how he is with Xander, and that's important. You need to reconnect with the reasons why you fell in love with and married Zach. And you need to *talk* to him, even if it is long-distance. I think you both need to commit to doing whatever it takes to make your marriage work before you do anything rash."

"That's really good advice, Maggie. Thank you." Whitney sighed. So did Maggie—with relief. It *was* good advice, even if self-serving. "I just wish I'd followed it with Bo. We might still be married."

And the sinking feeling in the pit of Maggie's stomach returned.

Chapter Twenty

Maggie could hardly focus on the road as she drove to JJ's. Her party mood had evaporated the minute she opened the door to Whitney. Now she was in a quandary. Should she alert Bo to Whitney's dream of reviving their relationship? Was it even her place to share a conversation that Whitney considered confidential? If so, how could she do it without sounding catty or like a jealous girlfriend? And when *would* she officially be Bo's girlfriend—if ever, given the current complications?

Maggie found a parking spot in front of Junie's and entered the restaurant. The minute she walked in, she was overwhelmed by the scent of a rich blend of oregano, pepper, tomatoes, chicken, and Andouille sausage. And bread— freshly baked and buttered. She saw that JJ had set up a buffet table whose centerpiece was a giant, steaming pot of jambalaya. "JJ, the smell in here gives me a reason to live," she told her friend. "But how much is it going to set me back?"

"Nothing, darlin'." JJ embraced her with his meaty arms. He'd decided to take Vanessa's purple-and-gold color theme to a comedic level. He'd sprayed his hair gold and was attired in gold lamé harem pants and a purple silk blouse that he'd inherited from his mother. "This feast isn't for Vanessa. It's my present to you. I got the sense that somebody needed a little Cajun comfort food."

"Oh, JJ, you have no idea." Maggie buried her face in her friend's chest and forced herself not to cry, knowing the tears and mascara would stain his blouse. She kissed him on the cheek, then looked up and scanned the room. Party prep fairies in the shape of Lia, Gaynell, and Ione had arrived early. The ceiling was already covered with purple and gold balloons. Crepe paper in the same colors decorated the bar and, just as at Vanessa and Ru's shower, vases filled with irises adorned each table. Maggie hurried over to her friends. "Sorry I'm late. Thanks for getting started without me."

"We're pretty much done," Ione said. "Did you see the theme of the photo booth?"

"No."

Ione turned to the other women. "She hasn't seen it yet. I get to show her."

"Nuh-uh, you don't get to have all the fun," Gaynell retorted. "We'll all go."

"Oh dear," Maggie said. "This can't be good."

Ione, Gaynell, and Lia led Maggie to the photo booth. A large box of hats, glasses, boas, and other props stood ready for use. Maggie looked at the booth and gasped. There, displayed in all its tasteless glory, was a mug shot backdrop. "And you get to hold this when you pose," Lia said. She picked up an ID slate that read, "Perp at Vanessa's Bachelorette Party, Property of Fleer-Durand PD." "Or this," she continued, pulling out a frame that read, "You've been framed!"

"I . . . I don't know what to say," Maggie sputtered. She gasped again. "Oh no! What if people think this was *my* idea?"

"You can relax on that score," Ione said. She pointed to a large bow attached to a corner of the booth. Under it was an equally large card that read, "You're about to get 'mugged' courtesy of Rufus Durand."

"He insisted the card stay on the booth during the party," Lia said. "It's in the paperwork."

"Amen to that for me," Maggie said. She collapsed onto a chair. "If one of the guests tonight proves to be Ginger's murderer, it'll save the PPD some trouble. They'll already have the mug shot."

"Considering some of the crowd Van invited, I think a lot of those mug shots are already on file." Ione motioned for the others to follow her to the bar. "I'll buy the first round. We can't start soon enough tonight."

"Kyle's at Ru's bachelor party," Lia said as she lifted herself onto a barstool. "I know I'll need a lot of liquor in me to listen to God-knows-what stories he brings home."

As Old Shari was depositing drinks in front of the women, the front door flew open and Tookie strode in, followed by the guestess-of-honor, Vanessa. She wore a floor-length rayon caftan in a variety of pastel ombré colors. Stick-thin Tookie wore a hot-pink shift and looked like the swizzle stick to Vanessa's Tequila Sunrise.

Tookie did a quick check of the room. "Not bad," she said.

"High praise indeed," Maggie responded dryly.

Vanessa threw her purse on the bar. "I'm so mad at Rufus I'd like to knock him hard enough to see tomorrow today."

"What did he do now, Vanessa?" Ione accompanied her question with an eye roll.

"I thought before our parties would be a good time to exchange wedding presents. I found this supernice leather wallet for Ru, and they gave me a real good price on it at the St. Gabriel pawn shop. I figured it would remind him of me when he pulls out those dollar bills to tip the lap dancers tonight. Anyhoo, he loved it, of course. And then it's his turn. And you know what he gives me? This."

Vanessa reached into her bag and pulled out a tiny silver pistol. The other women instinctively stepped back. "Relax, it ain't loaded. At least I don't think it is. But can you believe that? A lady pistol. I swear, he's taking this whole police theme way too far. He wanted to start his vows with 'Vanessa, you're under arrest for stealing my heart.'"

Vanessa tossed the gun back in her purse and hailed Old Shari. "Whiskey, neat."

Ellen Byron

Old Shari shook her head no and pointed to Vanessa's protruding stomach. "Near beer or nuthin'."

Vanessa gave an exasperated groan. "What*ever*, you old witch."

"It's not the worst gift in the world," Gaynell said, looking for a way to justify the odd present. "It shows Rufus worries about your safety. That's . . . kind of romantic."

"Oh, puh-leeze." Vanessa knocked back her near beer. "You know what would be romantic? A bracelet with diamonds, or rubies, or any kinda stone. There's gotta be some jewelry hanging around the PPD evidence room. Which of course he couldn't get near anyway, what with his suspension. Hey, Shari, I'll take another." She looked at her empty beer bottle. "Maybe if I drink enough of these suckers, I'll get some kinda buzz."

Tookie patted her daughter on the shoulder. "Never you worry, dear girl. I got a surprise coming that'll make your night."

Tookie flashed a broad wink at the others. "Cue male strippers," Maggie muttered to Lia.

Vanessa noticed the buffet spread and instantly cheered up. "Yay, food! I'm starving. I better get to it before the guests do. Come on, Mama. Time to tie on the feedbag."

The bride-to-be hopped off her stool with surprising agility for a woman due in weeks and pulled her mother toward the buffet. Maggie watched both women make a dent in the jambalaya. "Shari, can you get us another round?" she asked the bartender. "And this one's on me."

188

*

The guests came—first in a trickle, then in a flood. The room soon filled with the white noise of a hundred conversations. Maggie and her friends were kept busy replenishing the buffet and bussing dirty plates and cups off the tables. Bibi brought a mini tablet with her and pulled Lia aside to show her a few new sketches that, judging from Lia jumping up and down as she clapped her hands, the candy and patisserie proprietress loved. Lee Bertrand brought Chret, who stayed by his great-uncle's side even as his eyes followed Gaynell longingly wherever she went. Tug and Ninette came by to drop off a large bowl of crawfish dip along with loaves of French bread and then stayed to help out. Stevens brought Gran', and Maggie found them a table that first required relocating the couple that had claimed it as their make-out station. "Thank goodness this is as far away from Vanessa as we can get," Gran' said as Stevens pulled out a chair for her. "The instant we walked in, all she did was gripe about Rufus's present. If I had to listen for another minute, I was going to borrow that pistol and use it on myself."

Father Prit arrived and was greeted warmly by all. The eager, ingenuous priest was beloved in the community despite the fact that few parishioners could navigate his thick Indian accent. Maggie, whose ear had been trained by having to communicate with many a New York cab driver, had no problem conversing with the good father. She waved to him, and he immediately came to her side. "What a lovely event," he told her as he flashed a large, happy grin. "I am so pleased to be included."

Ellen Byron

"Of course, Father." Maggie smiled back at the kind-hearted, friendly man. "I wanted to tell you how grateful we all are that you're allowing Rufus and Vanessa to marry in the church." In keeping with Vanessa's philosophy that more is more, she had tried to worm her way into being wed at one of the more grandiose churches in the area but was instantly dismissed due to her "condition." She'd slunk back to Father Prit, who said a prayer for her, then agreed to perform the ceremony.

"Thank you, Magnolia Marie," Father Prit said. "In a situation like Rufus and Vanessa's, I ask myself, 'WWPFD?' What would Pope Francis do?" The priest was a besotted fanboy of the pontiff. "I believe he would say that with so many people today abandoning their faith, Vanessa's desire to be wed in a house of worship under the eyes of God should be embraced. It is not ours to judge. It is ours to show mercy." JJ walked by carrying a fresh pot of jambalaya, and Father Prit's eyes followed its path to the buffet table. "Now there's a heavenly scent," he said, inhaling the aroma left in the jambalaya's wake.

"Please, go enjoy the buffet," Maggie said.

"Thank you, I believe I will," Father Prit replied, then hurried over to the food.

Maggie did a circle around the room, bumping into a variety of friends and townspeople—literally. The dozens of balloons that covered the ceiling and lighting made the room, never bright to begin with, even darker. "It's like bumper cars with people," Gaynell told Maggie after colliding with the same woman for the third time.

"I know." Maggie deposited an armful of dirty paper goods in the trash and then glanced up at the TV that JJ always kept on over the bar. She was annoyed to see Little Earlie looking smug as a reporter interviewed him. A caption below the two read, 'Little Earlie Waddell, journalist and expert on Fleer Case.' The goodwill Maggie felt toward the overeager reporter vanished. "I do not want to know what that twerp is blathering on about." She picked up a remote and switched to Pelican's public access channel, where a city council meeting appeared to be in progress. "Now if anyone gets bored, they can drunk-dial the city council."

Gaynell directed Maggie's attention toward the front door. "There's someone I didn't expect to see." Trent Socher had sauntered in, checking his phone as he walked. He bumped into a partygoer but didn't look up to see the dirty look that the guest cast his way.

"Do you think he's here by accident or by *design?*" JJ, who had put an apron over his ensemble so he could wash glasses, chuckled at his pun.

"Okay, I'll let you get away with that because of all the free jambalaya," Maggie responded.

Trent approached the bar and tore himself away from his mobile long enough to order a drink. "Gin and tonic," he ordered Old Shari, neglecting to add a "please."

Maggie sidled up to the interior designer. "Hi, Trent. I didn't know you'd be here."

Trent looked around the room with distaste. "I'm not sure why I'm here myself. But Vanessa and her mother pretty much insisted I come."

llen Byron

His eyes connected with Tookie, who waved and darted over. "Hey there," she cooed as she threw an arm over his shoulder. "We are *so* honored you made it. Lemme introduce you to some of Pelican's *playas*." Tookie made a rapper move, which was disconcerting coming from a white woman with an AARP card. But Trent obliged and let her lead him into the crowd. "Be extra nice to that guy," Tookie whispered to Maggie as she went by. "We want him to forget that bill Ginger sent us for her crappy decorating ideas."

Tookie took off after Trent. JJ grinned. "So . . . he is here by *design*."

Maggie wagged a finger at him. "No! Free food only bought you one round of that joke."

There was the faint sound of a spoon rapping against a glass. The sound grew louder as guests echoed it by tapping spoons against their own glasses, and the party quieted down. Vanessa helped her mother stand on a chair, which made Tookie only slightly taller than her daughter. "Thank you all so much for coming tonight," Tookie told the crowd. "I'm sure you heard that we lost our dear cousin Ginger this week. I would like to ask you all to observe a moment of silence in her memory." People barely had time to drop their heads down before Tookie piped up again. "Now, let's party the way Ginger would have wanted us to—hard!"

"Whoo-hoo!" Vanessa called out as she fist-pumped the air.

Gaynell and the Gator Girls took the stage and launched into an infectious zydeco number. Dancers filled the floor. Maggie was less than thrilled to see Little Earlie wander in

92

and try to ape the casual attitude of an invited guest. She stopped helping JJ put away clean glasses and strode over to the newsman. "Junie's is closed tonight for a private party," she told him.

"Yes, and I received an invitation, which I don't have at the moment. Now if you'll excuse me, I gotta interact with some guests if I'm gonna write this up for our social column." Little Earlie zipped away from Maggie before she could ask, "What social column?"

Maggie was about to follow the journalist when she heard a loud argument erupt. She looked around, saw Bibi yelling at Trent, and hurried over to the warring duo. "You can't take rent out of my salary when we're running the business together!" Bibi screamed at her partner.

"Technically, I'm still your boss," Trent replied, unfazed by her anger.

"That's not what you said when you were desperate to keep me," Bibi shot back at him.

"Hey, guys, maybe tonight's not the time to—" Maggie tried to interject, but Bibi ignored her.

"What changed?" Bibi challenged Trent. "Did you find a new sugar mama in Houston?" Trent's lack of response affirmed the answer. "You did, didn't you? You're such a liar and a jerk, and since I'm doing all the work in Baton Rouge, I think I'm just going to spin off my own design firm."

This inflamed Trent. He got so close to Bibi that she flinched as if afraid he might hit her. Maggie tried pulling him back, but he shook her off. "You even think of doing that," Trent hissed at Bibi, "and I will put you out of business so fast that the only thing you'll be decorating is the box you live in under a bridge."

"Hey, that's—" Maggie began, but Trent disappeared back into the crowd before she could complete her sentence. Bibi burst into tears and ran in the opposite direction.

Maggie gave up her attempts at mediation and went to check on her grandmother, who was still parked at the same table with Stevens. "I'm trying to get this one to dance, but he won't oblige," Gran' said as she gave her date a playful poke in the ribs.

Maggie noticed that Stevens had taken off his jacket; beads of perspiration inched down his face. "I'm not much of a dancer," he confessed with a weak smile.

"I keep telling him we should go out and get some air, but he's too stubborn to admit he's uncomfortable," Gran' said. She picked up a purple paper napkin and gently swabbed the sweat from his face. Lee Bertrand, who was bouncing in rhythm to music, caught Gran's attention and waved for her to join him on the dance floor.

"Go," Stevens said, smiling at her. "I'll be fine."

Gran' hesitated, but Maggie said, "Yes, go, Gran'. I'll get Stevens some water and make sure he's okay."

"Alrighty then, I'll put on my dancin' shoes. But only for one number. Or maybe two." Gran' got up, straightened her skirt, and went to join Lee, who swept her onto the dance floor.

Maggie was on her way to get Stevens some water when she heard someone yelling. She saw a cluster of

Vanessa's cousins pointing and giggling. "What's happening?" she asked.

One of the girls pointed, and Maggie saw Vanessa tearing into Trent, backed up by her mother. "You are the worst person on this planet," Vanessa yelled at him. "You don't deserve to live."

"What she said!" Tookie chorused. "You tell him, baby girl."

Maggie started toward the three to intervene in their argument, but suddenly there was a loud popping sound. People screamed and ducked. "What the—?!" she cried out. There was another pop, and then another. Something light fell on Maggie from the ceiling. She reached down and picked up the remnants of a balloon. "It's okay!" she yelled to the crowd. "It's just the balloons; they're getting too hot and exploding."

Gaynell realized what was going on and stopped her band. "Hey, everyone," she announced into her mic. "I guess the balloons are getting a little overexcited and popping themselves. No worries. Just keep dancing."

The band picked up where they left off, and the crowd relaxed. Maggie looked for the fighting threesome, but Trent, Vanessa, and Tookie seemed to have gone their separate ways. Ione approached her and held out a balloon shred. "We can't get them down because Van wouldn't let us put strings on them—'it wouldn't be *pretty*.' This is gonna go on all night."

"Maybe we should borrow her gun and shoot them out," Maggie said wryly. She noticed Chret by the bar; his arms were wrapped around his upper body. Maggie could see that he was trying to keep himself from shaking. Concerned, she went to him. "Are you okay?"

"Yeah. Sure." He gave her a pleading look. "It's the popping. The sound. It reminds me of . . . you know . . ."

"Afghanistan?"

Chret nodded. Maggie's heart broke for him. "It's just these stupid balloons. Now, if they'd been in Tulane colors instead of LSU, this wouldn't be happening." Chret forced a smile at Maggie's attempt at a joke. "Maybe you should go outside for a bit. Get some fresh air and get away from the sound."

"Yes, ma'am. That's a good idea. I'll do that."

Chret started for the door, and Maggie followed to make sure he was alright. They passed Trent, who was holding court with a group of besotted single friends of Vanessa's. "Hey, Chret," he called to him. "Just an FYI that I'll be contesting that will. No way is Ginger's money going to some bastard."

Without warning, Chret threw a punch that sent the designer flying. Maggie grabbed the former soldier and pulled him toward the door as Trent staggered to his feet. "Assault!" he screamed at Trent. "I'm gonna get you arrested, then sue you!"

Maggie pushed Chret outside and stomped back to Trent. "Shut up, you big wuss," she snapped. "And you leave Chret alone or you're gonna be assaulted again, this time by me."

Trent glared at her, but then backed down. "I've got to tend to my wound."

"The only thing wounded was your pride, and it was about time that got knocked down a peg," Maggie said, walking away before he could come up with a rejoinder. She reached the bar, where Vanessa was guzzling another near beer. "Maggie, did you see that?" she said, her tone vicious. "Did you see how Chret took down that SOB?"

"I saw you and Trent going at it before. I'm guessing he's not going to forgive your design bill."

"Oh, it's way, way worse," Vanessa said. "He's tacking on a late payment fee. I wish he'd hit his head on his way down from that punch and never got up again. And I wish I was the one what done it."

Maggie went behind the bar and pulled out another near beer. She handed it to Vanessa. "Nessa, this is your party. How about you forget about Trent and go enjoy yourself?"

Vanessa made a face. "I guess." She got off her barstool and wandered off into the crowd clutching her beer.

Maggie poured Stevens a tall glass of water but was way-laid by guests clamoring for drink refills. It took a good ten minutes, but she finally extricated herself from the bar and went to deliver the water. While Stevens's jacket was draped over the back of his chair, he wasn't at the table. Maggie glanced around the room and didn't see Stevens anywhere, so she left the water at his place and headed toward the back door, accompanied by a loud chorus of balloon pops. Her head pounded, as did her heart; the stress of the chaotic evening had gotten to her. "I'm taking a break," she called to JJ.

"No problem, chère," he called back. "You earned one."

Maggie stepped outside. She leaned against one of the restaurant's century-old brick walls and allowed herself to enjoy the crisp, cool air. She breathed in the fragrance of a late-blooming sweet olive tree, but the delicate scent was overwhelmed by the smell of rotting refuse coming from the restaurant's dumpster. Maggie grimaced and went to close the dumpster. She glanced inside and reeled backward. She opened her mouth to scream, but no sound came out.

On top of the garbage lay Trent Socher. A small bloodstain grew as the red liquid leaked through a small, perfect hole in his shirt.

The interior designer had been shot.

Chapter
Twenty-One

Maggie stood for a moment, trying to quell her panic. Then she reached into the dumpster, gently lifted Trent's wrist, and felt for a pulse. After the deaths at the B and B, Maggie had taken an intensive CPR and first aid class so that she would be prepared if any guests ever needed emergency medical attention. But there would be no opportunity to apply that training to Trent. The designer had no pulse. He was dead. Maggie pulled out her cell phone.

"Nine-one-one, what is your emergency?" an operator asked.

"I need to be connected directly to Pelican PD," Maggie said.

"Maggie Crozat, is that you *again?*" Delphine Arnaud, the recipient of Maggie's 9-1-1 call after she found Ginger's body, happened to be the operator on duty. "Oh, dear. I'll put you right through."

There was a brief pause, and then Maggie heard Artie Belloise's voice say, "Pelican Police Department." She could tell by the sound of his voice that he was, per usual, eating.

"Artie, it's Maggie Crozat. I'm at Junie's, and we have a situation." She explained about Trent. As soon as she was done, she heard Artie swallow.

"We'll be over fast as we can. In the meantime, keep this on the down low. We don't want the guests to go all crazy and run outta there before we can talk to them. And do not let anyone into that alley. Block it off as safely as possible."

"Will do. Thanks, Artie."

Maggie ended the call and hurried back into the restaurant. The air felt sticky and smelled like a combination of sweat, beer, and jambalaya. She leaned against the end of the bar to stave off a wave of dizziness that she feared might end in a faint. JJ saw her and hurried over.

"You okay, darlin'?" he asked, reaching out to steady her. "You look like you've seen a ghost, which around here wouldn't surprise me at all. I can name a few right off the top of my head."

She shook her head. "No ghost. More like a ghost-to-be." She let out a hysterical giggle that turned into a sob.

"I'm getting your parents."

JJ started to go, but Maggie grabbed his arm. "No!" She told him about finding Trent's body and then relayed Artie's instructions. "Lord have mercy," JJ muttered as he crossed himself. "I can't lock the door because it's a fire exit, but I'll hang by it and make sure people don't go out there for a smoke," he said. He took off his apron, hung it on a hook, and strode toward the back door. Maggie then punched in Bo's cell number on her phone. He answered on the second ring.

"Hey. What's up?" He had to shout to be heard over the background noise of music and catcalls at the strip club.

"I found Trent Socher dead in the dumpster. It looks like he's been shot."

"What?! Sonuva—"

"Can you tell Rufus? He should probably be here for Vanessa. She's going to have a breakdown when she hears about this. PPD is on its way."

"We'll get there as fast as we can . . . no, thank you. Seriously, no, I'm good."

"What?"

"Sorry, I wasn't talking to you."

"Bo Durand, are you getting a lap dance?"

"No! I'm trying *not* to get one. Be there soon."

Bo ended the call, and Maggie was about to go wait for Pelican PD in the alley when Gran' approached her. "Dearest, have you seen Stevens?" she asked. She pulled a monogrammed handkerchief out of her purse and dabbed at the slight sheen on her forehead. "Lee and I were dancing, but when we came back to the table, Stevens was gone. I thought he might be visiting the men's room, but Lee checked and he's not there."

"I wouldn't worry, Gran'. I'm sure he just stepped outside for some air."

"I looked out front and he's not there. I'll check the back."

Gran' started for the back door, but Maggie grabbed her arm. "I'll do it." She gestured to Old Shari. "Shari, can you get my Gran' a drink? Bill it to me." Gran's look of confusion over Maggie's odd behavior transformed into one of anticipation, and Maggie took advantage of the moment to escape. She hurried to the back door, and JJ opened it just wide enough for her to slip through.

Since Junie's was a mere blocks from the Pelican police and fire departments, the alley was already swarming with PPD's finest. An officer was taping off the area while two EMTs, Cody Pugh and Regine Armitage, laid Trent Socher on a gurney. They covered him with a sheet and wheeled the gurney toward the street as a van from the coroner's office pulled up. Acting Chief Perske saw Maggie and motioned to her with his index finger. She swallowed her resentment and joined him. "So," he said, "another day, another body."

"I don't go looking for them, you know," Maggie defended herself. "They seem to find me."

"Yes, they do," Perske said. Maggie couldn't tell from his expression whether she was ruled out as a suspect or should extend her hands to be cuffed. "Walk me through what happened."

Maggie recounted her discovery of Trent, making sure not to leave out a single detail.

"Did you notice anything unusual about the victim's behavior prior to the discovery? Any altercations with other guests at the party?"

Maggie hesitated. She knew she should share Bibi's fury at her business partner as well as the story of Chret's clocking the man but hated putting either of them in Perske's crosshairs. There was also Vanessa's incensed reaction to Trent's refusal to forgive her bill. Maggie was saved from having to implicate any of the three by Artie Belloise. "Chief, come here," he yelled. "We may have another vic."

Perske made his way to Artie, and Maggie followed. She cried out at what she saw; Stevens Troy lay on the ground, either dead or unconscious. She prayed it was the latter. The EMTs raced over and began triage. "He's breathing," Regine announced.

"Oh, thank God," Maggie murmured.

"Pulse and heartbeat are weak," Cody told his partner. They maneuvered Stevens onto a gurney, placed an oxygen mask over his face, and raced him to their ambulance.

"I need to tell my grandmother what's happened," Maggie said to the police officers. "He was her date tonight."

"It'll have to wait until we alert the guests to the situation," Perske said. "I don't want rumors to start flying around and cause a panic."

"My grandmother isn't some low-rent gossip," Maggie said defensively. "If you're going to be our acting chief, you might want to get to know the locals a little better so you don't insult them."

Perske ignored her and turned to Artie. "Track down every officer you can and get them over here. We've got a party full of potential witnesses to interview."

Artie went back to his squad car to put out the word, and Perske followed Maggie back into Junie's. Perske nimbly climbed onto the stage and indicated to a perplexed Gaynell that she should stop playing.

"If that's the male stripper, Tookie should ask for her money back," Maggie overheard one guest mutter to another, who nodded in agreement.

Perske explained to the partygoers that there had been an "incident," as he euphemistically described it, and then gave orders that no one was to leave until everyone's statements had been taken. A few other officers appeared and began dividing up the crowd. Pelican being the kind of small town where gossip traveled fast, news of Trent's murder somehow leaked out and rapidly spread through the room. Annoyance at being inconvenienced turned to fear that some kind of madman had set up shop in the town. Meanwhile, Maggie pulled Gran' and her parents aside and revealed Stevens' crisis.

"Oh, no," Gran' said, holding a hand to her heart. "Was he attacked by whoever murdered Trent? Is he going to be alright?"

"I don't know anything else," Maggie said. "I'll talk to Artie and make sure the police take your statements next. Then you can go to the hospital."

Artie, who'd been tasked with handling a distraught Vanessa, grabbed the opportunity to interview the Crozats and led them to a private corner of the dance hall. A weeping Vanessa clung to Maggie. "How could this happen *again*?" she cried. Maggie didn't know what to say. The Internet was rife with stories of bridal catastrophes. There were brides whose weddings were disrupted by a natural disaster and brides whose nuptials were thrown into disarray when their reception location was shuttered due to a business's bankruptcy. But Maggie had yet to hear of a bride whose impending marriage went off the rails because of not one, but two murders.

As she searched for platitudes that Vanessa might buy, she was relieved to hear a familiar voice calling to her. "Over here, Bo," she called back, waving to him. He wended his way toward her, with Rufus right behind him. "Rufus, I am so glad you're here." Maggie pushed him toward his fiancée, who fell into his arms.

"It's gonna be okay, baby," Rufus comforted Vanessa. "Let's get you some air."

Bo's phone pinged, and he read the new text message. "Interesting. Perske wants me back on duty. He's out in the alley."

Bo headed for the alley, and the others followed him out the back door. As soon as Perske saw Bo, he motioned him over. Rufus tended to Vanessa while trying to eavesdrop on Bo and Perske's conversation. Maggie scanned the scene and noticed that Cal Vichet, clad in crime scene investigation gear, had been tasked with searching the dumpster for clues. She walked over to the edge of the police tape and then recoiled from the dumpster's putrid bouquet. "It stinks in here," Cal grumbled. "I better get overtime for this."

Bo finished his tête-à-tête with Perske and found Maggie. "Chief needs me to analyze whatever forensics digs up.

Artie'll take your statement and then you can go. I'll give you a call later. Or in the morning."

"Okay."

"Anyone who isn't with PPD needs to leave the area," Chief Perske declared. He glared at Rufus. "That means you, Durand."

Rufus sucked in his gut and stood up tall. "I *am* with PPD."

"Not right now you're not," Perske shot back. "So move it on out."

"Yeah, that ain't happenin'."

Perske took a step toward Rufus. "You and your fiancée need to leave or—"

"I found something!" Cal Vichet called out from the dumpster. The officer stood up and shook off some vegetable parings that clung to his protective covering. A tiny pistol dangled from the pinky of his gloved hand. A pistol that Maggie recognized as Rufus Durand's wedding present to his bride.

Chapter
Twenty-Two

Once the gun was discovered, Maggie discerned a not-so-subtle shift of focus in the investigation. Under the guise of gossip, she did a casual polling of guests as they left Junie's; those who'd overheard Bibi's altercation with Trent or seen Chret deck him were interviewed briefly and dismissed. But those who'd witnessed Vanessa's dustup with the designer were grilled by the PPD. No one claimed to have heard the gunshot. The popping balloons had masked the sound.

Vanessa didn't help her case by at first vehemently denying the gun was hers, even after she checked her purse and saw that it was missing. The best she could do was eventually declare, "Someone stole it. So now there's two victims here: Trent and me."

"That's right," her mother parroted. Unlike her daughter, Tookie had been pounding back real beers, not near beers, and the alcohol had kicked up her usual orneriness to just shy of red alert. She got in Chief Perske's face, or rather his chest, since even in six-inch heels, the top of her head fit under his chin. "You best leave my child alone," Tookie ordered, jabbing at the chief with her finger, "and find what villain stole her brand-new, pretty pistol, or there will be hell to pay, mister."

Maggie had to give Perske credit for not tossing Tookie straight into a police car. Instead, he showed restraint and replied, "We're working on assembling all the facts, ma'am. We won't do anything without having a good reason for it."

"Humph," Tookie said. "I'm thinking I better cancel the male stripper. But I'll lose the deposit."

Considering the circumstances, Maggie marveled at the gall of Tookie fishing for a way not to lose that deposit. Perske gave the woman a cold stare. "Cancel the stripper," he said.

As the night wore on, Gaynell, Lia, and Ione helped Maggie clean up. Kyle had escaped from Ru's raucous bachelor party with Bo, so he pitched in as well. "Look at this," he said, holding up one of the party's souvenir pictures from the photo booth. It was a shot of Vanessa and a friend goofing off as they pretended to be in a police lineup. "You've been framed," the tagline beneath the photo read. Maggie found the picture disturbingly prescient.

Midnight passed, and the last group of guests was released. Bibi was among them. "Did this really happen?" she asked Maggie as she paused on her way out. The rhetorical question didn't beg a reply, so Maggie just gave a slight nod. "What do I do?" Bibi continued, her voice shaking. "Trent signs the checks. I'm not authorized. I can't conduct business. I can't pay the bills or the rent or—"

Maggie put her hands on Bibi's shoulders. "None of this is important right now. Go home and get whatever sleep you can. Then call Lia in the morning. She and Kyle will pay a retainer that will float you until you work things out with Trent's estate."

"His estate," Bibi repeated. "Oh my God, this is so strange. I don't know anything about him. I don't even know where he's from. He has—had—people. Family. I'm a horrible person."

Maggie suddenly heard a screech from Vanessa and squawking from Tookie. She looked over and saw Vanessa bawling as Tookie chewed out Perske. Rufus was doing his best to calm both women down. Maggie ran over to Bo, who answered her question before she asked it. "Perske wants to continue their 'conversation' at the station," he said.

A lock of his dark hair had slipped onto his forehead, and Maggie suppressed the urge to gently put it back in place. *Don't engage,* she told herself. *You could wind up hurt.* She forced her attention back to the conversation.

"You better call Quentin MacIlhoney," Bo was saying.

Quentin MacIlhoney was one of the premiere defense attorneys in Louisiana. The only thing bigger than his colorful personality was the bill he handed clients at the conclusion of their case. "If the Fleers need MacIlhoney, Vanessa must be in serious trouble," Maggie said.

"If she's not there, she's on her way to it," Bo said. "Make the call."

*

The last place Maggie expected to be post–bachelorette party was the Pelican PD lobby. Yet there she was, in the all-too-familiar setting. Quentin MacIlhoney's service had alerted her that he was on his way, and she didn't want to leave until she'd explained Vanessa's dilemma in person.

It occurred to Maggie that she hadn't touched base with her family. She speed-dialed her father, who answered on the second ring. "Hey, Dad. Are you still at the hospital?"

"Yes. We've been waiting on a diagnosis for Stevens. Turns out he's got a cardiac arrhythmia. They're giving him a pacemaker."

"I guess you could call that good news. I was afraid he'd been attacked by whoever killed Trent."

"Your grandmother asked him about that when he recovered consciousness. He was in the alley because he wasn't feeling well and had to step outside for some air. Then he passed out and didn't hear or see anything."

Maggie was relieved that Stevens would be okay but disappointed he hadn't witnessed something that would target another suspect besides Vanessa. Every instinct she had screamed that the pregnant drama queen was not Trent's murderer. "That's too bad, for Van's sake."

"Huh?"

She updated her father on the recent developments, ending with, "So basically, Van is a 'person of interest.'"

"That's ridiculous," Tug said, his voice incredulous. "I can see Vanessa complaining a person to death, but no way can I see her as a murderer."

"I know." Maggie heard the roar of a high-powered engine and glanced out the window. A gleaming, gold Bentley with a vanity plate that read "LWYR UP" had pulled into the parking lot. Purple-and-green tracer lights framed the plate. "I have to go. Quentin MacIlhoney just got here. Give Mom and Gran' kisses for me, and tell Stevens to feel better."

Maggie stepped outside and waited for Quentin on the steps of the nondescript building. He came toward her with a jaunty step that belied the late hour. He wore his usual pressed jeans and pricey Italian loafers, although he'd deigned to don socks on the chilly night. A black turtleneck peeked out from under a beige cashmere V-neck sweater. She was surprised to see that the sixty-something lawyer had shaved his white beard, transforming his look from fit Santa Claus to 1970s TV star who looked great for his age. "Evening, Miss Magnolia," he greeted her with a flourish. Maggie half-expected him to bow and kiss her hand.

"Hi, Quentin. You're looking good."

"I do what I can."

Maggie gestured to the Bentley, which sparkled like real gold under the parking lot lights. "I thought your Bentley was purple."

"Yeah, that car ran out of gas, so I got a new one."

Maggie assumed Quentin was kidding, although she could never be too sure with him. This was one of many attributes that made him a great defense attorney. He had a showman's ability to entertain a jury and the legal ability to confuse them, thus creating a scenario of doubt that more often than not got his clients off the hook.

"Bodies sure have been piling up in this tiny town lately," Quentin said as they walked into the police station. "I can't complain. Where there's a sketchy death, there's a suspect in need of one Quentin MacIlhoney. So, what ya putting on my plate tonight, Magnolia?" Maggie gave him a detailed explanation of the evening's events. When she was done, Quentin chortled with glee. "A pregnant bride-to-be as a potential suspect," he said. "Thank you for this early Christmas present, my dear. I should have Miss Fleer out of the station and on her way home in fifteen minutes." The lawyer took off a gold watch with diamonds instead of numbers and handed it to Maggie. "Time me."

Quentin marched ahead of Maggie into the station, where he was greeted like a long-lost fraternity brother. The defense attorney might eviscerate a police officer on the witness stand, but every station in the parish knew who was behind the "anonymous" donations to their charitable organizations or the occasional bushel of fresh crawfish that showed up in their break lounge. He caught up with Artie Belloise, who was manning the lobby desk, and insisted on seeing school photos of Artie's four kids. Maggie texted Bo, alerting him to their presence, and then checked the watch Quentin had given her to hold. Four minutes had elapsed already, and the big hand was heading toward another diamond. She was beginning to wonder if Quentin would meet his self-imposed deadline when he asked Artie, "So, Artie, my friend, you ever delivered a baby?"

"No, sir, and to be honest, the only reason I even watched the wife pop out ours is that it seems to be what guys do these days," Artie confessed. "Wouldn't want anyone calling me a wuss cuz I passed on that."

"Well, if we don't get my client, Miss Fleer, out of here fast, there's a chance you won't just be watching her give birth, you'll be pulling that baby out of her lady business." Artie couldn't keep himself from recoiling. "So," Quentin continued, "let whoever's interviewing her know that her lawyer is here and it's quittin' time."

"Yessir. In fact, I'll take you back there myself. Lemme just call someone up to watch the desk." Artie lifted the phone but was interrupted by shouting and what sounded like furniture being thrown coming from the back rooms. "What the hey?"

Artie started for the back, almost colliding with Bo as he threw open the door between the offices and the lobby. "Give the chief a hand," Bo instructed the officer. "I'll watch the desk and take care of Maggie and Mr. MacIlhoney."

Artie nodded and ran down the hall. The door slammed shut behind him. "What's going on back there?" Maggie asked.

"Rufus got a bug up his butt about how Perske was treating Vanessa like a suspect and went after him. Tookie piled on, so Perske tossed both of them in a holding cell, and Vanessa lost it."

"Three potential clients in one night," Quentin said as he rubbed his hands together with gusto. "You're a dang cash register for me, Miss Maggie. May I?"

Quentin gestured to the door, and Bo held it open for him. "They're all yours," Bo said.

"Wait," Maggie said. "Here's your watch."

She went to hand it to him, but Quentin pressed the watch back into her hand. "Think of it as a finder's fee," he said.

The lawyer disappeared down the hallway, leaving Maggie and Bo alone in the lobby. Maggie didn't know what to say. It certainly wasn't the time to examine her and Bo's relationship, and she was tired of talking about murder and murder suspects. She held up Quentin's watch. "You want a ridiculously expensive watch?" she asked.

Bo burst out laughing, breaking the tension between them. "No. You want a cheap domestic beer?"

"Yes."

Bo bent down behind the desk and emerged with two ice-cold bottles of beer. He twisted off the bottle tops and handed one to Maggie. "You've got a cooler back there?" she asked.

"Minifridge. For emergency supplies, like ice packs. And these."

He tapped her bottle with his and took a swallow. Maggie did the same. "So does Perske really think he has a case against Vanessa?" she asked.

"She had personal and financial issues with her late cousin Ginger, and that carried over to Trent," Bo pointed out. "They had a fight at the party and everyone seems to have heard her tell him he didn't deserve to live—words that get thrown around in a lot of fights without actually resulting in murder, I know. But if ballistics matches her gun to the bullet that killed Trent . . ."

Bo trailed off. But he didn't need to finish the sentence for Maggie. She could see how it ended. She heard voices coming from the hallway. The door opened, and Quentin emerged, followed by Rufus, Tookie, and Vanessa, who seemed to be in a semicatatonic state.

"Who do they think they are, treating us like that?" Tookie fumed to Quentin. "You tell those a-holes that they'll be hearing from our lawyer."

"He is our lawyer, you old bat," Rufus snapped at his future mother-in-law.

"Oh, shut up," she snapped back. "We wouldn't need a lawyer if you hadn't gone at that chief like you had rabies."

"Vanessa would still've needed one," was Rufus's best defense.

"Yeah, because of *your* stupid wedding present. Who gives their beloved a gun?!"

"Someone who cares about her safety, that's who!"

"Will you two be quiet?" Vanessa said in a dull tone that Maggie had never heard her use before. "Please."

Both Rufus and Tookie had the decency to look abashed. Tookie put an arm around her daughter's waist. "I am so sorry, baby. It's been a long night. Let's get you home."

Rufus nudged Tookie out of the way and replaced her arm with his around his bride-to-be's waist. "Yes, let's. This lawyer guy said he'd drop us there." He grimaced and said to Quentin, "I hope you don't charge by the mile."

Quentin flashed a big, wide grin. "Of course not. I charge by the hour. But I drive real slow."

Rufus gave him a suspicious look and then ushered the Fleer women out the station's front door. Quentin lingered for a moment to speak to Maggie and Bo. "I talked that new chief of yours into releasing those stooges with just a warning. I also asked him to rush ballistics, and he agreed. He may have a stick up his you-know-what, but he's not eager about stressing out a woman with child." He clapped Maggie on the shoulder. "Thanks again for the referral. But you best slow down, or people around here are gonna be thinking that you're setting up these murders just to get me business."

Maggie managed a small smile. "I feel bad for Vanessa. I hope she makes it to her wedding without falling apart."

Quentin hesitated. "Yeah . . . you might want to put a pin in that wedding. I'll be talking to her tomorrow about what she can scrape together for bail, should the need arise. I take great pride in my track record for getting it lowered, but even so, it's dang high for a murder charge." With that, Quentin strode out of the station.

Maggie added "Help bride beat a murder rap" to her ever-growing list of maid of honor duties.

Chapter
Twenty-Three

Maggie crawled into bed at two in the morning. As she drifted off to sleep, she said a silent thank-you to Vanessa for putting a day between the bachelor and bachelorette parties and the wedding so that "Rufus could sober up his sorry butt before we get hitched," as the bride-to-be put it.

A few hours later, Maggie roused herself and showered, then threw on jeans and a T-shirt. She stepped outside and shivered. Clouds hid the sun, graying the day. The weather was getting a head start on the winter season with a twenty-degree drop in temperature. Louisiana's famous mugginess usually turned to clamminess in the cooler months, adding to the air's chill.

Maggie hurried to the main house, welcoming its warmth as she stepped inside. She went into the office. Gran' had beaten her there and was seeing to the comfort of their animal guests. Gopher roused himself from the foot of the playpen to give a proprietary bark. He sniffed Maggie and then resumed his prone position, approving her approach to the pups and kittens.

Maggie gave her grandmother a kiss on the cheek and then peered inside the playpen. Two puppies were nursing while another squeaked and rolled away from his siblings. The kittens, having finished breakfast, slept, letting out an occasional contented mew. "They grow a little more every day," Maggie said, reaching in to pet a sleeping kitty.

"I know," Gran' replied. "Watching them gives me such joy. Sweet, sweet babies. All of them. Even the mamas."

"How's Stevens?"

"Good. Better than good, actually. It's as if the pacemaker revived the poor man. Those little things are miracle workers. He's being released today." Gran' gazed into the playpen. "He's taken a shine to Jolie. I think having a pet would be good for him."

Maggie frowned. "I don't know. It might be too much for a man who has heart issues."

Gran' sighed and shook her head. "Oh, my darling girl. Someday you will have children. And your life will revolve around them to the point where you have only vague memories of what it was like before they entered the world. And then you will have to let them go. You won't know what to do with yourself at first. But eventually you'll find the life you had before, or even a better one, if such a thing is possible. And your children will always be part of that in some way. You will not lose them." She put her arms on Maggie's shoulders and looked straight into her granddaughter's eyes. "But you must let your babies go, chère. Let them go."

Maggie's eyes filled with tears. Gran' had touched the nerve that connected to the part of Maggie that longed for a soulmate and family someday and feared she might never know either. She bit her lower lip to keep it from quivering. "I will," she choked out. "I'll start thinking about good homes for all of them."

Gran' enveloped her in a hug, and the two women held each other. Then Maggie pulled away and examined her grandmother. "Are you okay? I feel like you're not completely yourself."

Gran' sat down on an antique wingback chair and leaned back. "Perceptive as usual. No, I am not myself. And I wish I could tell you why."

Maggie parked herself on the arm of her grandmother's chair. "Could it have something to do with Stevens? It's been a long time since you had romance in your life. Maybe you're not comfortable with it."

Gran' waved a hand dismissively. "Oh, that isn't a romance—it's a flirtation. Romance is what I had with your grandfather. I don't expect that to come around again."

"I don't know, Gran'. Stevens seems to really care for you."

"We enjoy passing time together, that's all."

"I think it's more than that," Maggie said. "And I'll make a deal with you. I'll give up my attachment to our fur-babies if you give up your resistance to finding love again."

"Those seem like two very different things."

"They're not. They just sound like they are. You're being stubborn. Which you passed down to me, thanks very much."

Gran' gave a mischievous grin. "I did, didn't I? Well if you can fight your stubborn streak, so can I. You have a deal."

She extended her hand. Maggie shook it and then stood up. "Now, time for me to have a very ugly conversation with Vanessa and Rufus."

"About what?"

"About how they're going to scrape together bail if Chief Perske brings a murder charge against Vanessa."

*

Despite the chill outside, the living area of Vanessa and Ru's small trailer felt stuffy. Through the trailer's largest window, Maggie could see the wooden skeleton of one wall of La Plus Belle, the couple's future dream home. It remained exactly that—a dream.

"Again, I am not saying that any charges will be brought," Maggie repeated for what felt like the umpteenth time. "I'm just suggesting you have a bail plan for the *very* remote possibility that they are."

"Bo put you up to this, didn't he?" Rufus demanded.

Maggie groaned and dropped her head into her hands.

"He'd just love to see me lose everything. He's always been jealous of my success."

"I am not giving birth in ja—" Vanessa stopped herself. "I can't even say it. I can't say the j-word."

"Nobody wants to see that happen, Van," Maggie said. "That's why Quentin's on board. He's going to have the same conversation with you. I just thought I'd have it first, so you can have an answer and save some time with him."

"Time with that shyster is money, so I do appreciate that," Rufus said.

Vanessa gave a slight nod. "I guess if worse came to absolute worse, we could put up La Plus Belle."

"What?!" Rufus barked. "Nuh-uh, no way. Not our baby."

Vanessa pointed to her stomach. "This is our baby, you dumb cluck! You'd rather see it born in the j-word than put up that pile of wood to make the b-word?!"

"You mean bail? I'm just saying, let's explore all our options," Rufus responded. "We could always put up my pension for bail. Or my life insurance policy."

"I'd like to start collecting on that right now!"

"It's you making threats like that what got us into this mess in the first place!"

"No, it was your stupid wedding present! Who buys their fiancée a gun?!"

"Stop saying that! It's a useful gift!"

Maggie held up her hands. "Whoa. Everyone take a breath. Let's focus on the positive—worst-case scenario, you at least have assets." She looked at her wrist. "I have to go or I'll be late to work. Vanessa, I'll check in with you later."

Maggie practically ran from the trailer to her car. She hoped that neither Rufus nor Vanessa had noticed that she wasn't wearing a watch.

*

Maggie was on autopilot as she led morning tours at Doucet. The events of the week—*had it only been a week? It felt so much longer*—had drained her. Aside from being upset about Ginger and Trent's murders, Maggie felt as if her whole life was in flux. She longed to lock herself in her studio and paint away her stress for a couple of hours but didn't see how that would fit into a schedule crammed with maid of honor chores, working at two plantations, relationship problems, and trying to track down a killer.

She walked her small group of visitors through the wide center hall of Doucet into its front parlor. "In the mid-nineteenth century, the Mississippi could be seen through these large windows, which also served as French doors that welcomed any breeze off the river," she told the visitors. She lacked her usual desire to riff on the prepared text, so she delivered it by rote. "These days the river's view is blocked by that high, grassy berm you see, which serves as a levee. It's not as scenic, but it's prevented Doucet from being swallowed up by the Mighty Mississip, unlike Uncle Sam Plantation and so many others."

A teen girl stopped texting and looked up at a portrait of Maggie's ancestor, Magnolia Marie Doucet, which hung above the room's fireplace. "Who's she?" the girl asked. "She's pretty in an old-timey way."

Maggie gazed at the painting. Magnolia Marie had been an iconoclast in her day. In fact, if not for the venerated Doucet name, the locals would have labeled her a nutjob. She was a widowed mother of two by the time she was twenty-three and ran Doucet on her own until she horrified neighbors by marrying a former Union officer after the Civil War. While Maggie would never lose the guilt that came with having ancestors who owned slaves, she took comfort in Magnolia's reputation as a kind, generous woman who actually freed the enslaved Doucet workers before the war began and offered them homes and jobs when it ended. Magnolia Marie died at age 101 in 1941, knowing that she'd helped Doucet and its employees survive three wars and the Great Depression. If Magnolia Marie could triumph over such great losses and traumas, Maggie could certainly power through the lesser obstacles that currently challenged her. "That," Maggie told the teen, "is the woman I was named after."

The girl grinned. "Awesome."

"Yes," Maggie said. "It is."

Maggie led the group into the Doucet gift shop, marking the tour's end. She was happy to see several tourists pick up the souvenirs she had designed—a mug, a mousepad, and yes, the thimbles she had resisted making for so long. "Ione, do you have paper and a pen back there?" she asked her boss, who was working the register.

"Here you go." Ione handed her both. "Look how some talented artist made a lightly-colored rendition of Doucet as the background on the pad's paper. I am *so* impressed." Ione winked as she handed over a pad of Maggie's own design.

"Thanks. How are they selling?"

"Surprisingly well, considering people mostly jot down notes on their phones these days. It's your paintings and drawings, honey. They pull people in."

Maggie was surprised at how good this made her feel. Being validated for her artwork meant something, even if it was just that a tourist would be drinking their morning brew from one of Maggie's coffee cups.

She headed to the break area and parked herself under the big magnolia tree. It was time to stop brooding and resolve some outstanding issues in her life. First up was who killed Ginger and Trent. She felt safe in assuming that the murders of the interior designer and her lover were related. Maggie started the list of potential suspects with Fox's name. The adage "start with the husband" seemed appropriate in this case, given Ginger's terrible reputation and predilection for cheating on him. Next, she wrote Bibi's name. Much as she hated adding her possible patron to the list, Bibi had undeniable motives for both murders; she desired Ginger's husband and despised Trent. Maggie then reluctantly added Chret to the list. Did discovering Ginger was his mother push the emotionally damaged ex-soldier over the edge? There was also the possibility that he'd secretly learned he was in her will and was motivated to murder by the hefty inheritance his birth mother left him.

Ione wandered over to where Maggie sat writing and dropped onto a bench, stretching her legs and hoop skirt out in front of her. "It's my favorite time of day here," she said as she pulled off her wig. "The 'whoo-hoo-this-place-is-empty-for-two-minutes' time. Whatcha doing?"

"Making a list of suspects and motives."

Ione pulled her legs in and sat up straight. "And?"

Maggie ran through the names she'd already written down. "I'm putting Rufus on the list because of his hot temper. Tookie for the same reason," she explained as she continued adding names to her list. "Either of them could have snapped out of a desire to protect Vanessa, although Tookie seems more likely on that score. And I'm putting Stevens down just because he's from Houston, although it's hard to believe that poor guy has the strength to do in two people. I'm also leaving a blank space for any potential suspects that Bo uncovers in Texas."

Maggie perused the list to see if she'd left anyone out. She thought for a moment and then wrote down one more name. "Who'd you add?" Ione asked.

"Lee Bertrand," Maggie said without enthusiasm. She was fond of the garrulous repair shop owner.

"I can see that," Ione said. "On the surface, he seems like a good ol' boy, but he's superprotective of Chret."

"Lee's from a very close family, too. What if one of his siblings knew the identity of Chret's mother and revealed it to him when Ginger came to town? With Trent vowing to break Ginger's will on top of that, he might have fallen into a fury so bad that it led to murder."

Maggie's cell rang. "Go ahead and take it," Ione said as she stood up. "I need a mirror to help me put my wig back on. A busload of tourists from New Orleans is due in ten."

Ione headed off, and Maggie checked her phone. She saw a Texas number that didn't look familiar. "Hello?" she asked, her voice tentative as she answered the call.

"You still as pretty as you were in Houston?"

Maggie recognized the Texas twang of detective Johnny Tucker. "Hi, Johnny. I don't remember giving you my cell phone number."

"You didn't. But my job is tracking people down. Especially when they're 'of interest.'"

Maggie rolled her eyes. "Next you're going to say I'm under arrest for stealing your heart."

Johnny roared. "I like that."

"As did half the construction workers in Manhattan. And Rufus Durand, who wanted to put it in his vows." While Maggie had to admit she enjoyed Johnny's mild flirtation, she wanted to know the real reason for his unexpected call. "What's up? Do you have any new information, I hope?"

"Bo let me know about Trent Socher's murder. And I tracked down a cell call between Bibi and Fox that took place at 11:48 PM, after Trent's body was discovered."

Maggie digested this revelation. "Who called whom?"

"Nice grammar. She called him."

"To either share the news of Trent's death. Or . . ."

"Let a partner in crime know, 'mission accomplished.'"

Maggie had one more question for Johnny. "Why are you telling me this? Shouldn't you be telling Bo?"

"I will. Right after I ask you out to dinner."

Chapter
Twenty-Four

Maggie debated her response to Johnny's bold move. Instinct told her that the good-looking detective was what Gran' would call "a bad bet" and what her own friends would label "a playa." Guys like him were great for a fling, something Maggie might have gone for in her twenties. But she was in her early thirties now, and flings were like cheap candy— briefly delicious, but with an unpleasant, lingering aftertaste. "Thanks for the invitation, Johnny," she said. "But I don't think it's a good idea."

"It's just a meal," Johnny persisted. "Only a three-hour drive to Pelican from here."

"It's three and a half hours."

"Not the way I drive, baby."

Maggie had to laugh. "Sorry, but I don't consider excessive speed a turn-on."

"I can do slow. Think about it, okay? But I'll tell you one thing. Don't let whatever's going on between you and Bo get in the way of anything. Between us, I don't know if he's ever truly gotten Whitney out of his system."

All Maggie wanted to do was end the call before Johnny realized what a punch to her gut he had just delivered. "Okay, I'll think about it. But now I have to get back to work."

"Bye, Cajun girl. Talk to you soon."

The call over, Maggie tucked her phone into her dress décolletage. She felt a bit guilty, knowing it was a bad habit that upset her mother, who'd read an alarmist online article about how too close contact with a cell phone might have a detrimental effect on a woman's fertility. But at this point, worrying about her ability to bear a child seemed a moot point. She leaned on the picnic table and dropped her head onto her crossed arms. Then she felt a gentle hand on her shoulder and looked up to see Gaynell. She was the only tour guide whose natural ringlets negated the need for a wig. With her pale-pink ball gown and blonde curls that formed a cloud around her face, she seemed like an angelic apparition.

"Did I startle you?" Gaynell asked.

"No. But for a minute, I almost thought you were a ghost."

"Sometimes I wish I were." Gaynell sat sidesaddle next to Maggie on the bench. "Ghosts don't have feelings."

"I think they do. Otherwise they wouldn't have to come back."

"Good point." Gaynell scrunched her nose. "I believe in them. Do you think that's silly?"

"No. I don't believe in actual ghosts, although there are nights when I'm in charge of closing up here that I swear I feel Magnolia Marie Doucet's presence—like she's almost haunting me. I'm sure that's just my overactive imagination, but I do think there's a lot in this world and beyond it that we don't know anything about." Gaynell sighed, and Maggie put an arm around her shoulder. "Is it Chret?"

Her friend nodded. "We were starting to have something between us, but now he's pushing me away. Between the murders and finding out Ginger is his mother, he's gone to a dark place, and I don't know how to help him."

Maggie felt for her. "I'm so sorry. I think if anyone's haunted around here, it's poor Chret. All you can do is be patient and let him know that you're there if he needs you. The murders have created a bad energy in Pelican, and I think that's affecting everyone in different ways. But eventually the killer—or killers—will be caught, and that will restore the town's equilibrium."

"I sure hope you're right." Gaynell stood up and patted a wrinkle out of her gown. "I've got a school group in five. Fourth graders doing state history, so they actually have to listen to me. You coming?"

"In a few. I have to make a call first."

Gaynell hugged Maggie. "Thank you. I feel much better." Then she took off for the main house.

Maggie pulled her phone out of her décolletage and called Lia. The call went to voicemail, so Maggie left a message. "Hi, it's me. Are you free in a couple of hours? I want to pay Bibi a visit."

*

"So what's your plan?" Lia asked her cousin as they zipped up I-10 toward Baton Rouge.

"I want Bibi to think we're there on business and then make sure the conversation segues toward Trent's death. I'm hoping if I ask the right questions in the right way, I can pick up what's going on between her and Fox."

"Do you think they might have planned the murders together?"

"It's possible." Maggie had filled Lia in on her conversation with Johnny, leaving out his dinner invitation, which she decided to ignore. "Anyway, I whipped up a couple of fabric sketches to show Bibi, and I figured you could say that you were so excited about her initial ideas for Grove Hall that you insisted on coming with me to see if she'd come up with any new designs."

"All of which could have been done over the phone or online, so we look like a couple of impulsive airheads," Lia commented as she examined Maggie's sketches.

"Exactly. We don't want her to get suspicious."

"Uh-huh. Mags, these sketches are wonderful." Lia held up a drawing that Maggie had created. It was a muted green-and-dark-blue pattern of the evening moon framed by tree branches dripping with Spanish moss. "I would totally buy this fabric. I can see it covering dining room chairs, or even a room's walls."

"I was inspired by some of the patterns of Newcomb Pottery," Maggie explained. "Remember the pictures of the bowls and vases Great-Great-Aunt Sylvie made when she was an art student there? I found the photo album and let my imagination go."

"She'd be very impressed."

"Thanks. I wish we still had at least one of her pieces. Nobody took the pottery seriously back then. They'd give it away. People even sold it at garage sales. I check online auctions sometimes, but the prices are too high for a tour-guide-slash-B-and-B-employee-slash-struggling-artist. Oh, here's our exit."

Maggie got off the interstate and followed her phone's GPS directions to Socher-Starke Design. She parked, but both women hesitated before getting out of the car.

"I'm a little nervous," Lia confessed.

"Me too. But let's remember. My suspicion that she and Fox might be involved in the murders could be something . . . or nothing."

Maggie took a deep breath and then opened her car door. Lia did the same. They walked up the front path onto the bungalow's porch, and Maggie rang the doorbell. They waited, but Bibi didn't answer. After a minute, Maggie rang the bell again. Lia looked through one of the home's large front windows.

"I don't see anyone."

"Maybe she's in the back and doesn't hear the bell. I'll see if one of the side gates is open."

Maggie scampered off the front porch and checked the wooden gate on the left side of the house. It was locked, and there was no way to climb over it. She crossed the front lawn and went to the gate on the right side of the bungalow.

This one was loose enough to create a small space where Maggie could fit her hand. She endured a few scratches as she maneuvered her fingers behind the gate and lifted the latch. The gate creaked open, and Maggie walked down the narrow side path. She stepped on a decorative rock in the flowerbed next to the house, placed her hands on the windowsill, and pulled herself up to look through the window. There was no sign of life.

"Hey! What'd you think you're doing?" an angry voice yelled.

"Ah!" Maggie lost her balance and tumbled into the flowerbed. She looked up and saw the top half of the face of an older man; the rest was hidden by the high fence separating the properties. She also noticed what appeared to be the tip of a gun.

"I'm s-s-sorry," she stammered. "I'm just trying to see if my friend is home."

"Ever hear of a doorbell?"

"We tried, but there was no answer."

The man's eyes narrowed as he evaluated Maggie. She stayed frozen in the bushes, afraid that any sudden movement might reveal the rest of his gun. "Come to the front yard," he instructed her.

She pulled herself to her feet and followed the man's instructions. When she got to the front lawn, she found herself face to face with a beefy man in his late sixties wearing a security guard uniform. He was holding a rifle. Lia saw what was happening and called from the porch, "It's okay, sir. We're together."

"So were Bonnie and Clyde," he responded. "ID."

"I've got our purses," Lia said. She literally tiptoed down the front steps to where Maggie stood with the surly stranger. Lia handed Maggie her purse, and the women pulled out their driver's licenses to show the man. He studied the licenses carefully, handed them back, and leaned his rifle against his leg.

"Crozat, huh?" he said, addressing Maggie. "This have anything to do with the murder at that B and B?"

"I'm Maggie Crozat and this is my cousin, Lia Tienne. Crozat Plantation B and B is my family's home and business. And we don't know if this is related to the murder. Maybe."

"I'm Don Wertz," he said without extending his hand for a shake. "Retired Baton Rouge PD. And you don't have to sneak around to find out where your friend is. I can tell you. She's gone."

Chapter
Twenty-Five

"Gone?" Maggie repeated. "Bibi's gone?"

"That's what I said. I was closing up late last night when I heard a car screech up here. I looked out and saw your friend run into the house. I could tell something was up, so I maintained surveillance. Not ten minutes later, she came running out with a big suitcase. She threw it in the back of the car and took off. Last I seen of her."

Don picked up his rifle and motioned toward his house with it. "Let's finish this conversation sitting down. In just a bit, I'm gonna be on my feet for hours working security at the mall."

Maggie and Lia followed Don into his home, which was a dustier, bachelor pad version of Socher-Starke Design's bungalow. Don nodded at a couch, and the women sat down, or rather sank into the lumpy mass. Maggie grimaced as a broken coil stuck her in the rump.

"You want coffee?" Don asked. Both women shook their heads, and Don, looking relieved, sat on a worn club chair across from them. He leaned his ever-present rifle against the arm of the chair. "I'm sure your friend was a nice girl," Don said, "but I got a bad feeling about what might be going on over there. Heard a lot of phone conversations filled with yelling, followed by cursing. She was polite enough and had a hello when I saw her but always seemed nervous. I picked up pretty clearly that something was wrong. At first I thought maybe she was a victim of domestic abuse who'd made a run for it. But she didn't have that haunted quality so many of those poor women and kids have. She just seemed . . . jittery."

"Those are really valuable observations," Maggie said. "Thank you."

"You can retire from the force, but you never retire your instincts. If the mall paid me for every shoplifter I sussed out, I'd be selling this dump and moving to Vegas." Don noticed Maggie glance at a faded family photo of a much younger Don with a smiling woman and two sulking adolescents. The woman's poufy hair and mauve outfit placed the photo somewhere in the 1980s. "My kids and my ex. I worked Vice. Job takes a toll on a marriage. All law enforcement jobs do, if you're not careful."

"Yes," Maggie said. "I have a . . . friend who's a detective."

"If he's homicide, watch out. Those guys can go dark."

Maggie didn't need to hear this on top of her other concerns about her relationship with Bo. She stood up and the others followed suit. "Thank you so much for your help, Mr. Wertz," she said, extending her hand. Don shook it, his grip firm and slightly painful. "If you hear anything next door, or if Bibi comes back, would you call me?" She rummaged through her purse and finally dug up an old business card from her years running an art gallery in New York with her ex-boyfriend. She drew a line through the outdated information and wrote her cell number, plus the phone number at Crozat, then handed it to him.

"Yes, ma'am," Don said, and raised his hand to his forehead in a salute. "Hope things work out with you and that 'friend' of yours."

Don winked and opened the front door for the two women. Not sure what else to do, Maggie winked back and then she and Lia headed out to her car. "I have to call Bo right away and let him know Bibi's gone," Maggie told Lia as they got into the Falcon. She put on her Bluetooth and pressed a button, then began driving. After a couple of rings, Bo answered.

"Hey, what's up?" he asked.

Maggie shared what she'd learned from Don Wertz. "Interesting," Bo responded in his laconic way. "We'll put out an APB for her here, and Johnny can do the same in Texas. He found a cell call between Bibi and Fox, right after Trent's murder."

"A call between Bibi and Fox?" Maggie repeated, feigning ignorance. "It sounds like they're in collusion. I almost feel sorry for Trent. To be so hated and have people conspire against you, and then end up dead and lying in a morgue, unwanted."

"His wife claimed his body."

"His wife?!" Maggie squawked, almost losing control of the car. "He had a wife?"

"Yes, and his catting around with Ginger was news to her."

"Or was it? She could be another suspect."

"That was my first thought, but she was so furious when she learned about Ginger that it made it pretty clear she knew nothing about her hubby's extracurricular activities. I was with her when she claimed the body, and let me tell you, I have never seen anyone go ballistic on a corpse like that. I wouldn't be surprised if we got a call saying someone found old Trent dumped in a ditch on the side of the interstate."

"I wouldn't blame her one bit."

"Me neither. Anyway, thanks for the intel. Call me when you get back to town."

The call over, Maggie turned off her Bluetooth. She could feel Lia staring at her. "What?"

"You pretended you didn't know about the call between Bibi and Fox. You didn't tell Bo that Johnny already called you with that information."

"It didn't seem relevant to the conversation," Maggie said. She caught her cousin's skeptical look from the corner of her eye. "Okay, fine. When Johnny called, he asked me out. I didn't know what Bo's reaction would be if I told him. And if he had no reaction . . . that would have been worse. So I took the coward's way out and didn't even mention the call."

"Got it." Lia gave Maggie a sympathetic smile.

"I hate when relationships get complicated. And why does every law enforcement official assume Bo and I have something going just because I mention him? They're like middle school teens."

"They react that way because when you mention him, you make a face like you have digestive issues." Lia made a facial expression that was half weak smile and half grimace.

"What? No," Maggie protested. Then she sheepishly added, "I do?"

Lia nodded. "You don't have to be a detective to pick up on that clue."

Maggie took one hand off the wheel to smack herself on the forehead. "Ugh, I am such an idiot."

"No, you're not. You just have more questions than answers right now, and that's always disconcerting in a relationship."

Maggie's cell phone lit up and blared a few notes of a Trombone Shorty song, signaling an incoming call. She pressed a button on her Bluetooth to answer it.

"Tookie here. Just a reminder that you and the bridesmaids need to pick up your gowns by three PM today."

"We know," lied Maggie. She'd blocked the purple-and-gold monstrosity from her mind, but now its image returned like a recovered memory.

"And my Van had a supergreat idea. Y'all are gonna wear LSU bows in your hair and carry pom-poms instead of flowers! How adorable is that?"

"It isn't, it's awful," Maggie exploded. "This is where I draw the line, Tookie. If this wedding even takes place—"

"Oh, it's gonna take place."

"If it does and you insist on this insanity, you'll have to find another bridal party because neither I nor any of the bridesmaids are marching down the aisle carrying pom-poms and wearing LSU bows in our hair."

Lia's eyes widened. "What she said!" she yelled into Maggie's ear and Bluetooth.

"Oh yes, you will. What my baby wants, my baby gets, so it's bows and pom-poms. Go, Tigers!" Tookie disconnected the call, ending the argument.

"*Nooooo*," Lia said, a look of horror on her face.

"Yes," Maggie replied. She let out a loud groan. "I hate my life."

*

Fifteen minutes later, Maggie pulled up in front of Lia's shops and the women hopped out of the car. "I need chocolate," Maggie said as they made a beeline for Bon Bon.

"You and me both," Lia responded. She held the door open for her cousin and then followed her inside. Kyle was manning the shop, and as the women helped themselves to restorative sweets, they shared the details of their adventure—from Bibi's mysterious disappearance to Tookie's terrible sartorial news. The latter had Kyle laughing until tears streamed down his face.

"Stop that," Lia ordered her fiancé. She gave him a light punch in the arm.

"Sorry, it's just . . ." Kyle was so consumed by laughter that he couldn't finish his sentence.

Maggie held up her cell phone. "I just got a text from Ione. I'm guessing she heard about the bows and pom-poms."

"What does her text say?"

"'Stop the madness,' all caps, followed by a ton of exclamation marks and frownie faces."

"There's nothing to be done," Lia said with a sigh. "I just pray I don't log on to the Internet postwedding and see a picture of us above the caption, 'World's Most Embarrassing Wedding Photos.'"

"Oh, honey, I can't see that *not* happening," Kyle said as he wiped tears of laughter from his eyes.

"You won't be laughing so hard when you find out what Rufus has planned for you ushers," Maggie said, a vengeful glint in her eye. "You're supposed to match us in some way. LSU bowties, anyone?"

Kyle immediately stopped laughing. "Maybe we could make people check their phones and cameras at the door, like celebrities do."

"You know, when you think about it, it's kind of sweet," Lia mused. "Vanessa never went to college, so in a weird way, this is making up for something she missed in her life."

"Maybe," Maggie said. "But I think she also just likes the colors." She spread her fingers and circled her hands in a jazzy move like a Broadway dancer. "Purple! Gold! They're flashy. You don't see her picking Tulane's boring colors, olive green and blue."

"True," Lia said. "Anyway, I know you've got a lot going on, so I'll pick up our gowns and . . . accessories."

"That would be great," Maggie said. "Thank you."

She put a few more chocolates into her bag and returned to her car. As she drove, Maggie pondered where Bibi might have gone. Was she calling Fox to say good-bye? Was she making plans to rendezvous with him so they could escape together? Maggie noticed her folder of fabric sketches lying on the floor in front of the passenger seat. She may have thrown them together as part of a ruse, but they were good and deserved a home. But it didn't look like it would be at Socher-Starke Whatever-Bibi-Would-Have-Renamed-It Design Group.

Maggie pulled into the graveled family parking area and was surprised to see Bo there standing next to his car. She parked the Falcon and got out. "Hi," she greeted him. "Is everything okay?"

"Yes, didn't mean to scare you," he said. "I have a huge favor to ask, and I didn't want to call or text it."

"Okay," she replied, a little wary.

"Johnny Tucker found Bibi at Fox's house. According to her, she was terrified that one of Ginger's disgruntled former customers had taken to killing off Starke Design employees, so she ran to Fox."

"Ah. That's actually not so farfetched, considering that two of the three members of the company have been murdered."

"I know. Anyway, Chief Perske wants me to go to Houston to interview both of them. It's my day with Xander, and

Whitney went up to Shreveport to visit her mom. Is there any way you could keep Xander for the night? I know he loves you, which is why I'm even asking. I'd tell Perske I can't take the assignment, but my relationship with him is so dicey that I'm sure he'd find a way to punish me for saying no."

"Of course," Maggie said. "I'll make it an adventure for him. We can paint and spend some time with the kittens and puppies. I'll let him choose where he wants to sleep and keep him company, even if it's under a fort made from sheets."

Bo flashed a smile of relief, a smile so wide that dimples appeared under his chiseled cheekbones. "Thank you. I'm aiming for a fast turnaround. I'll be back in the morning as early as possible. I better let Xander know what's going on. He's in the kitchen with your parents."

Bo pulled Maggie into his arms and gave her a quick peck on the lips. "I can always count on you."

"That's me," Maggie said with a tight smile. "Old Reliable."

*

After Bo said good-bye to his son and took off for Houston, Maggie and Xander enjoyed leftovers of Ninette's oyster soup—always as good and sometimes even better on day two—and then retreated to Maggie's studio, where they painted side by side in happy silence. She was close to finishing her portrait of Rufus and Vanessa. All she had left to do was remove the laugh lines around Vanessa's eyes. They might be authentic and charming, but the tour guide would rather have a "Real Housewives of Pelican" look than have anything she considered a flaw represented.

Maggie snuck a peek at her young companion's painting. He had returned to his rendering of the Crozat chickens, which somehow managed to look both two- and three-dimensional. She marveled at the detail Xander tendered on each feather and counted at least five shades of yellow in the birds' bodies. The boy yawned, snapping Maggie out of her artistic reverie. She checked her phone. "Oooh, it's almost nine. We need to get you to bed, buddy. We'll go back to the house, and you can pick any room you want."

Xander nodded. He helped Maggie clean up, handing her one paintbrush at a time and then thoroughly examining each to make sure it was completely clean before being put away. When they were done, Maggie led them out of the studio and to the manor house, carefully negotiating the dirt path in the dark. She saw her parents waiting at the back door of the house.

"We were about to come get you," Tug said. "We're a little concerned about Jasmine."

Maggie hurried into the house with Xander right behind her. They found Gran' in the office with a lethargic Jasmine on her lap. The pup gave a tiny sneeze. Maggie felt its nose. "It's dry," she said. "She's got something for sure."

"We talked to Dr. Waguespack, and she said it sounded like a mild upper respiratory infection," Ninette shared. "She told us it doesn't sound like an emergency but messengered over some antibiotics. We have to make sure Jasmine stays hydrated and isolate her from the other animals. Doctor Wags said to let her know the instant there's any change in the pup's condition and if there isn't, to bring her in first thing in the morning."

"Her breathing is a bit raspy, but not terribly so," Gran' said.

"Still, one of us should stay with her to make sure she's okay," Maggie said. "I'll do it. Let me just get Xander to bed."

She reached for the boy's hand, but he pulled away. "No," he said.

The others stared at him. They were aware of Xander's selective mutism. "No," he repeated. He walked over to Gran', gently picked up Jasmine, and sat on the floor with the pup on his lap.

The two "nos" that he uttered were the first words the Crozats had ever heard him speak. Maggie suppressed the urge to burst into tears and throw her arms around the boy. Instead, she asked in a calm, even tone, "Dad, will you get me two sleeping bags?" The family kept a tent and a handful of sleeping bags on hand for families that wanted the experience of sleeping outside for a night during their stay. Tug nodded and left the room. Maggie sat on the floor with Xander. "Okay, buddy," she told the boy. "We're spending the night with Jasmine. But how about I hold her while my mom takes you to wash up and get ready for bed?"

Xander thought for a moment. He stroked Jasmine on her head a few times and then handed the pup to Maggie. Ninette smiled at him. "Come with me, sweetie. I promise we'll do everything real fast so you can get back to your little friend."

She led Xander out of the room, crossing paths with Tug as he returned with the sleeping bags. He set them up while Maggie fed Jasmine some puppy formula.

"He *talked*. Did you hear that?! He said *words*." With Xander out of the room, Maggie felt free to shed a few happy tears.

"It's truly a breakthrough for him," Tug said. "Are you going to call Bo?"

"I'll tell him in the morning. If I call him now, he'll just drop everything and drive home. For one thing, I don't want him on I-10 all sleep-deprived. For another, if he just rushes in here, it might startle Xander back into silence. We shouldn't make a big deal out of it, even though it *so* is one. If we act like it's normal, then Xander will be more relaxed and hopefully start talking more."

Gran' watched them both from her comfortable roost on the room's settee. "Anything I can do?" the senior asked. "I doubt it, but it would be rude not to at least ask."

"How about you make us a couple of nightcaps?" Tug said as he put air in one of the two air mattresses he'd pulled out of the room's closet.

"Sir, yes sir." Gran' responded. "Whiskey neat for you, son. Maggie, what can I whip up for you tonight?"

"Nothing. I want to be alert for Jasmine. And for Xander."

Gran' got up, went to Maggie, and deposited a kiss on her head. "I am so proud of my darlin' girl."

"For what?" Maggie laughed. "I'm basically a tour guide and hotel housekeeper."

"You are so much more, and never, ever forget that. Tug, your drink will be waiting for you in the front parlor. My age gives me the liberty to start without you. I could pop off at any minute, and I'd hate for the last thing I see to be an untouched Sazerac."

Gran' sauntered out the door. Tug put air in the second mattress and then placed a sleeping bag on top of each one. "There, that should be pretty comfortable."

"Thanks, Dad."

Tug wiped a trickle of sweat from his forehead. "If I haven't said it lately, I want you to know that your mama and I are real proud of you too, sweetheart."

Maggie cast her gaze down at the puppy in her lap. "I wish y'all would stop saying that. You're going to make me cry." She looked up at her father. "I honestly don't feel I've earned all this pride. But I will, I swear. I'm going to do something someday that will *really* make you proud."

"Maggie, it's never about what you do," her dad said. "It's about who you are." He leaned down and hugged his daughter.

Ninette returned with Xander, who was wearing the pajamas from his overnight bag. They were light blue and decorated with a pattern of orange and yellow aliens. "Let Dad and me know if you need us," Ninette told Maggie. She kissed her daughter good-night and then left the room with Tug.

Xander got into one of the sleeping bags. He held his hands out to Maggie. She got up, carried Jasmine over to the boy, and tucked the pup in next to him. "I'll be right here next to you," she said. "And I'm going to check on Jasmine every couple of hours to make sure she's doing okay."

Xander nodded and closed his eyes. He fell asleep, and his steady breathing seemed to have a soporific effect on Jasmine, because soon she was also sound asleep with her tiny head resting on his chest. It was such a sweet sight that Maggie snapped a few photos to send Bo in the morning. She checked on the other animals and was relieved to see that none seemed to have any symptoms. Maggie set the alarm on her phone, then climbed into the other sleeping bag and fell asleep.

*

Waking up every couple of hours was not easy on Maggie's constitution, but she was relieved to find Jasmine sleeping relatively comfortably each time she checked. She fell back asleep after the four AM pup exam and dreamed she was wandering through the abandoned property that Ginger visited on her morning jogs. In the dream, Maggie climbed over fallen beams and broken glass, not sure what she was looking for. Then she stopped short. "I found it!" she called out to someone. There were footsteps, and Maggie turned. A face was hidden by a shadow, but Maggie knew it was not the person she expected. They came toward her and she ran, tripping over broken furniture and rotting wood. She heard a voice calling to her—the voice of salvation. "Maggie," it called out. "Maggie, where are you?" The stranger gained on her. "Help!" she screamed. She managed to get out of the broken building and began running out of the woods. She heard her name called again and looked around to see where the voice was coming from. She didn't see the fat tree root in her path and tripped on it, slamming to the ground. She lay there in pain. A hand reached out and grabbed her arm. The stranger yanked her up and Maggie found herself face to face with—

"Maggie, wake up. Maggie?"

Maggie started out of her disturbing dream and bolted up. Her rapid move startled Bo, who was kneeling next to her, and he almost lost his balance. "Way to give me a heart attack," he said as he righted himself.

"I'm sorry. I was having a nightmare."

"I could tell. I've been trying to snap you out of it. What's going on? Why are you and Xander sleeping in here on the floor?"

Maggie rubbed her eyes, which were dry and itchy. Her body ached from a lack of rest, and her mouth felt dryer than her eyes. She swallowed a couple of times to wet it. "I need coffee before I give you any details." She checked on Xander, who was sleeping the sound sleep of children who were able to shut out the world. Then she leaned down to feel Jasmine's nose, which was cold and wet, and listen to her breathing, which had only the slightest hint of raspiness. The puppy was on the mend.

Maggie looked at her phone and saw that it was six AM. She stood up and stretched. "The most important thing," she told Bo, "is that Xander talked."

He stared at her. "He what?"

"He talked. He said 'no.' Twice."

"He did?"

"Yes."

Bo sat back on his haunches. "Sonuva . . ." He got up, went to his son, and gently laid a hand on the boy's cheek. Xander sighed in his sleep, and Jasmine burrowed her tiny head under his chin.

"You stay with him so he sees you when he wakes up," Maggie said. "I need to get ready for Van's big day."

Bo nodded but didn't take his eyes off his son. "He talked, Maggie." His voice was thick with emotion. "My boy talked."

*

Maggie fought off fatigue with a bracing cold shower. She checked her phone afterward and saw a text from Bo: "Xander woke up. And said 'hi.'" Maggie shared Bo's joy over that one small syllable. The joy dissipated when she saw that there were six texts from Vanessa. It was seven fifteen AM. Maggie counted to ten to calm herself and then scrolled through the stream of messages. There was nothing that couldn't wait until a couple of hours before the wedding, so she texted back "I'm busy!" and turned off her cell's text alert. She drove over to Fais Dough Dough to retrieve her maid of honor dress from Lia and found her cousin in the kitchen pulling a pan of sticky buns out of the oven. The air was warm and so rich with the scent of butter and sugar that Maggie had to stop herself from drooling. Lia saw the look in her cousin's eyes and extricated a gooey bun from the pan. She plated the tempting treat and handed it to Maggie. "You'll burn it off running around for Vanessa," Lia said.

"I'd like to say you're wrong, but you're not." Maggie waved her hand over the bun to cool it off and then bit into it. The rich pastry melted in her mouth. She saw a bright-purple gown embellished with gold lace hanging from the store's bathroom door. The dress beamed like a neon casino sign through the plastic that covered it. "That's the finished product?"

"Yes, and believe it or not, it's flattering, in a Vegas showgirl way."

"I never heard of a Vegas showgirl wearing LSU bows in her hair."

"Yes, well . . . there's that," Lia said. Maggie offered up the last bite of her sticky bun, and Lia took it. "Vanessa was in the middle of her last fitting, and Tookie was all over her about that baby weight. 'You gain any more weight, girl, and you're gonna need a tentmaker instead of a dressmaker.'"

"Way to show motherly love." Maggie used her finger to retrieve an errant glob of bun on her plate. "I wonder if Vanessa's farther along than she thinks." She placed her empty plate in the store's dishwasher. "I better go. I need to rest up for tonight's festivities."

Maggie hugged her cousin good-bye and took off for home. As she drove past Vanessa and Ru's property, she saw workers erecting a tent next to the one framed wall of their future McMansion. She was relieved that the couple had decided to save money by having a potluck reception on their own land. It was tacky as the day was long, but it beat the terrifying alternative Maggie had envisioned—Vanessa insisting that the event be held at Crozat.

Maggie parked in the family lot and saw her dad walking toward her carrying a large, full plastic bag. "Hey, chère," he greeted her. "We took Jasmine to Dr. Wags. She gave us some more medicine and said the pup'll be fine. And Xander's mom stopped by to pick him up."

"Thanks for letting me know. What's in the bag?"

"Some of Trent's things that were left in his room. I asked his wife what to do with his stuff and she said to burn it. Doesn't seem right, so I'm going through it all to see if there's anything we can donate."

It occurred to Maggie that there might be some clue to Trent's death in his belongings. The police had already gone through everything in the room, but given the limited resources of the PPD and the equally limited experience of Cal and Artie heading up an investigation, there was a good chance they'd missed something. "I'll do that for you, Dad. I'll sort it all for charity. It'll be my good deed for the day. That and everything I do for Van's crazy wedding. All I ask is that if she calls on the home phone, you tell her you don't know where I am, but that I'll be at her place by two. I think three hours of prep time is plenty."

"Sounds good." Tug handed Maggie the plastic bag. "This is just a bunch of papers and stuff that were cluttering his room. PPD's already been at them, but I'm sure you'll be able to dig up some clue that they zoomed right by."

Tug smiled at Maggie. He knew his daughter well.

*

Maggie sat in the middle of the floor of Trent's guest room, surrounded by the ephemera of the murder victim's stay at Crozat. Pelican PD had carted away whatever they thought was of interest to the case, but there was enough left behind to keep her busy. She'd already gone through every scrap of paper and was now focused on clothing pockets. She found nothing in his jackets and moved on to pants pockets. Maggie didn't need price tags to know that Trent's wardrobe was high-end. The man had expensive tastes that would benefit some of Saint Tee's poorest parishioners when the Crozats donated his belongings to the church's outreach program.

She pulled a pair of women's panties out of the back pocket of a pair of slacks and recoiled. Going through a dead man's belongings was a creepy business. But in a low, zipped pocket on the calf of a pair of trendy cargo pants, Maggie finally unearthed something interesting. She pulled out a crumpled business card. It was tattered and faded almost to oblivion, indicating that it had been through a couple of wash cycles. She peered closely at the card. All she could make out were faint letters that spelled out Sunset Properties under what was left of a drawing that appeared to be a housing development. Sunset Properties—the company that bought the old Callette place. Maggie couldn't make out anything else on the front of the card. She turned it over and saw illegible remnants of letters and numbers. But someone had scribbled a number that had managed to survive the laundry: 1147. Maggie pondered the card. What was Trent doing with it? She could hardly see him as the brains behind some big real estate venture. And what did the four digits, 1147, represent? An address? A locker combination? Part of a phone number?

Maggie's cell rang, startling her. She saw the caller was Vanessa. She also noticed the time and realized that she was supposed to be at the bride-to-be's home fifteen minutes ago. She jumped up as she answered the call. "I'm on my way," she said, then disconnected before Vanessa could dump any crazy on her. She ran back to the shotgun and grabbed her wedding prep supplies. Then she sprinted to the Falcon and peeled out of the driveway.

*

Maggie shoved her way into Vanessa and Ru's trailer, which was packed with bridesmaids and the bride's prep team. Lia and Gaynell, already in their bright-purple bridesmaid dresses, were pressed against a wall to stay out of the way, while Ione focused her attention on trying to get one of the trailer's tiny windows open. "I have got to get more air in this shack," she said. She gave the window a hard yank and it finally succumbed.

Tookie, fully made up and clad in a sequined, lavender mother-of-the-bride dress, snapped at Maggie, "About time you showed up. Fix your hair—it looks like crap. Once you put your face on, hand out the bows and pom-poms."

"Mama, I'm not poufy enough," Vanessa whined.

"Gimme that." Tookie yanked a teasing comb out of the hair stylist's hand and teased up Vanessa's thick head of hair. She grabbed a can of hairspray and let loose, cementing the style in place. Everyone in the trailer coughed from the fumes.

"The higher the hair, the closer to God," Maggie muttered to Lia.

"Amen," Lia muttered back.

"Alrighty," Tookie said. "It's time for you put on your dress."

She laid out the bridal gown on the floor, and Vanessa stepped into it. Maggie helped negotiate the dress around Vanessa's baby belly and buttoned what seemed like hundreds of buttons. Vanessa stepped back to strike a model's pose. "What do you think?" she asked.

"You look beautiful," Maggie replied with total sincerity. The white satin gown was gathered under Vanessa's bust line and then flowed out beneath, giving her the look of a medieval lady-in-waiting. The designer had applied lace, rhinestones, and pearls with a heavy hand, but Vanessa had the height and borderline trashy style to carry it off. For the first time since Rufus and Vanessa had trumpeted their engagement, Maggie had a good feeling about the wedding. And an even better feeling about the fact that it would all be over in a matter of hours.

A sharp rap on the trailer door interrupted the oohing and aahing over Vanessa's dress. "Rufus, I told you a million times, you can't come in!" Van yelled at the door.

"This isn't Rufus, ma'am."

Maggie recognized the voice and exchanged a worried look with Lia.

"Is that . . . ?" Lia asked. Maggie nodded. "*Why?* Why are the police here now?"

"I'm praying that it's not my worst fear come true," Maggie said. She opened the door to reveal Pelican PD Chief Perske, flanked by Artie and Cal. All three looked grim. Perske nodded to Cal, who entered the trailer, squeezing through the clutch of women frozen in place by shock.

"Cal, what's going on?" Maggie asked. "Artie? Someone, please talk to us."

Cal shook his head slightly and avoided eye contact with Maggie. Instead, he addressed Vanessa. "I'm afraid I'm gonna have to ask you to put your hands behind your back, Vanessa."

"*What?!*" screeched Tookie. "She ain't putting her hands anywhere."

Tookie made a move toward her daughter, but Cal whipped up a hand to stop her. Vanessa, stunned into complacency, silently followed Cal's order. He clamped handcuffs on her wrists and led her down the short, narrow hall to the trailer's entrance.

"Vanessa Fleer," Chief Perske intoned, "you're under arrest for the murder of Trent Socher."

As the police led her daughter away, Tookie let out a piercing scream and fell to the floor in a dead faint. Vanessa's hair stylist and makeup artist screamed and burst into tears as the other women dropped to the floor to revive Tookie.

"Worst fear?" Lia asked Maggie as the two helped bring the mother of the bride to a sitting position. Tookie moaned as she regained consciousness, then threw up into her own lap.

"Times infinity," Maggie said.

Chapter
Twenty-Six

Maggie helped Tookie change into clean clothes and then called Rufus to alert him to the latest heinous development. His reaction necessitated holding the phone a distance from her ear to prevent deafness. The bridesmaids put on their street clothes and followed Maggie to Crozat, where they spent the next hour calling all of Vanessa's guests to let them know that the wedding was postponed until further notice. They made sure to hang up before having to explain why.

Tug and Ninette kept the women fortified with wine and crawfish étouffée. "Please eat up," Ninette said. "I was donating this to the wedding potluck and I'd hate for it to go to waste."

"People in Pelican will eat well tonight, when you think of all the food that was destined for the wedding," Maggie said as she poured herself a second glass of wine.

"I'm freezing my red beans and rice for when this crazy wedding actually does take place," Ione said. "No one'll know the difference."

"Those beans may be sitting in your freezer for a while," Tug responded. "With Vanessa under arrest, it doesn't look like she and Rufus will be riding off into the sunset any-time soon."

"Sunset," Maggie repeated. The others exchanged confused glances, but she didn't notice. A series of random images were clicking into place in her mind, forming a story. A story that just might have an ending. "I think I know who bought the Callettes' property." She jumped up and ran toward the door. "I'll see y'all later. I have to talk to Bo."

*

Maggie texted Bo to let him know that they needed to talk, then hopped into the Falcon and drove to Pelican PD headquarters. Cell reception in Pelican was quirky and calls occasionally got crossed, so Maggie didn't feel safe sharing her theory over the phone. She pulled into the police department parking lot and found herself next to Quentin MacIlhoney's Bentley. She ran up the steps into the building's lobby, where she found Bo and Rufus deep in conversation. They were both in their wedding attire, and despite the gravity of the situation, Maggie couldn't help but note how hot Bo looked in a tux. Rufus also wore a tux surprisingly well, but the glowering look on his face made him look like the evil villain next to Bo's James Bond. "Rufus, you are not going to lose La Plus Belle," Bo was saying, his patience obviously strained. "It's not like Vanessa's going to jump bail."

"Yeah, I know she's not going anywhere with that big old baby belly," Rufus responded. "The whole thing's just a pain in my behind. How the hell could they think my Van had anything to do with that murder?"

"The fact they're letting her out on bail tells you it's a weak case," Bo said. He laid a comforting hand on his cousin's shoulder. "We'll find the real killer."

Maggie cleared her throat, and the men registered her presence. "Hey, Rufus. I'm so sorry you're going through all this. Bo, can I steal you for a minute? I have a couple of thoughts I need to run by you."

"Sure." Bo walked away from Rufus, who slumped into a chair. "I got your text. Talk to me."

"Ginger Fleer-Starke loved sunsets," Maggie blurted out. "I remember her telling me that it was her favorite time to go for a run. I think she was Sunset Properties. She didn't care about the wedding. She wanted to make sure she had the winning bid on the Callettes' property." Maggie showed Bo the business card that she'd found among Trent's belongings. "Remember that story I told you about the woman in Houston, Nancy Brown Bradley? She's the one who inherited a house from her parents that Ginger tried scamming her into selling for nothing. When that didn't work out, I'm guessing Ginger started looking for other investments. And since she grew up in Ville de Blanc, which is only a half hour from here, it made sense to look in the area. She could build little cabins in the woods near the bayou and market them as vacation retreats. The big question is, if Ginger didn't get the money from Fox or her own business, where did it come from? Maybe whoever financed Ginger ended up killing her. It wouldn't be the first business deal gone horribly wrong."

"No, it wouldn't. My caseload in Shreveport was full of them. I'm going to give Johnny a heads-up about this. He's been stubborn about bringing in the FBI, but nobody can follow a money trail like they can."

The hall door burst open, and Quentin blew into the lobby, leading a bewildered Vanessa by the hand. Her hair had deflated and her makeup was rendered stained and runny by tears, a few of which had dripped onto her bridal gown. Chief Perske followed close behind them. "I'm a fan of keeping the law on my side, so rather than bring a lawsuit for wrongful arrest, we will graciously accept your apology when you realize that you've nailed the wrong suspect," Quentin told the chief. Perske replied with a skeptical grunt.

Rufus hurried to Vanessa and put his arm around her waist. "Let's get you outta this hellhole," he said as he nudged her toward the door.

Quentin took her arm and pulled her away. "Sorry, but that pickup truck of yours is going to bounce the baby right out of her." He gave Vanessa's stomach a small pat. "I can get a lot of mileage out of this situation, so let's keep little him or her in the oven." He addressed Vanessa. "You, my dear, get to ride in the Bentley."

"Okay," she responded in a robotic voice.

The lawyer put his hand around her waist and led his client toward the door, followed by Rufus, who looked as if he'd like to add a third killing to Pelican's roster of recent murders. They were greeted by Little Earlie Waddell and his camera. As the journalist started to photograph the bedraggled, befuddled bride, Rufus made a move toward him, but Quentin held up his hand. "Hello there, young man," he said to Earlie in a jovial tone that also managed to be terrifying. "You take one picture and I'm afraid you'll be having that camera surgically removed from an orifice." Little Earlie instantly retreated into the shadows. "Oh, and Chief Perske," Quentin called back as he steered Vanessa outside, "you might take another look at that Chret Bertrand for these crimes. That boy sure did well by them. Two hundred thousand dollars well." Then the door swung shut, and the odd trio was gone.

"Chret is a really good guy," Maggie jumped in. "And he had no idea Ginger was his mother."

Perske fixed her with his now-familiar glare. "Why are you here?"

"I am here because I'm Vanessa Fleer's maid of honor," Maggie said. "One of my tasks is to hold her bouquet when she says her 'I dos,' and in order for me to do that, I need to make sure she doesn't go to jail for a crime she didn't commit. *Comprenez-vous?*"

"Asking me if I understand isn't any less insulting in French." Perske turned to Bo. "Get her out of here."

"Yessir." Bo strode over to the front door and held it open for Maggie. She marched out of the building, determined to maintain what little dignity she had left.

As soon as she got to her car, her phone pinged. "Sorry about that," Bo texted. "I'll call you later." Perske might think she was an idiot, but at least she hadn't embarrassed herself in front of Bo. That was some small comfort.

*

As Maggie drove home, she noticed angry clouds accumulating in the early evening sky, hastening darkness. The days seemed to be growing shorter by the hour. Her phone sang out. She glanced down and saw a number she didn't recognize. She pressed a button on her earbud. "Hello?" she said tentatively.

"Hi there. I'm calling about the lost dog and cat."

Finally, a response to the fliers and inquiries about Jolie and Brooke. Yet instead of feeling relieved, Maggie's heart sank. She'd become attached to the Crozats' animal guests. "Do you know anything about them?" she asked.

The man chuckled. "We know a lot about them. We're Spunky and Pansy's pet parents. I'm Jerry Baylor. I'm real sorry I didn't get in touch sooner, but my wife, Hallie, just got a new phone and only now figured out that one of our neighbors left us a message that they'd seen your flier."

"Ah. Well . . . nice to phone-meet you, Jerry. I'm Maggie Crozat."

"Your family owns that plantation B and B, right? Sweet."

"Can you describe the animals to me?"

"Sure. Spunky's a real pretty ginger kitty and Pansy's a chi mix. I can give you more details, but if you just call them by their names, they'll come and that'll be proof."

Maggie thought she heard a conch shell blow in the background. "Where *are* you?"

"Honolulu. We're waiting on a luau. My wife's an English professor at University of New Orleans and she's on sabbatical teaching here at U of H. We rented out our house in New Orleans and brought the fur-babies up to our summer place in Pelican. My son was supposed to be taking care of them, but he's a musician and got a gig on a cruise ship, so he found some dumb bunny friend of his to house-sit. Turns out the guy covered up the doggy door, so he accidentally locked out the animals. When they didn't come back, he panicked and took off—double dumb bunny. I guess we're just lucky he didn't turn the place into a meth lab."

"Jolie—I mean, Pansy and Spunky are fine, and so are their babies."

"Babies?" Jerry yelped. "What babies?"

"They both had litters. You didn't know they were pregnant?"

Jerry let out a string of cuss words far less tame than "dumb bunny." "I feel terrible. We couldn't bring Spunky and Pansy with us because of Hawaii's quarantine laws. Spunky's an indoor-outdoor cat, so we were worried she wouldn't pass muster. And she and Pansy are so close to each other that we didn't want to separate them. We thought we were doing what was best."

He sounded so plaintive that Maggie felt sorry for him. "Don't worry, everyone's healthy and happy. And we have lots of possible homes for the pups and kittens."

"That's a relief to hear. We're not due back for a month at least. Can we impose on you to look after them a while longer? We'll pay whatever you want."

"We won't take a dime. It'll be our pleasure." Maggie was feeling magnanimous. "In fact, I'm happy to check on your house, since it's just sitting there empty."

"Really? I hate to bother you."

"It's no bother at all. You can't live that far from us. What's your address?"

"1145 Valcour Lane."

"Valcour Lane? We have a friend who lives on that . . ." Maggie trailed off as her heart started to race. An image flashed before her: the numbers "1147" painted dark green with light green shading. 1147—the same numbers on the business card for Sunset Properties. The numbers that would logically follow the Baylors' street address. She swallowed and then found her voice. "Jerry . . . do you happen to live next door to Stevens Troy?"

"Maybe. Is he the guy who brought the Reeves house? They had a Doberman named Cutie who was best friends with our Pansy. Used to come in and out of each other's doggy doors. Ours was smaller, so once poor Cutie got stuck and . . ."

Jerry continued to talk, but Maggie had stopped listening. Always the artist, she often had moments of clarity appear to her as a scene she might paint. The image that flashed in her mind was of a man crazed by anger. He was in a fierce struggle with a woman who looked frightened yet defiant. The woman was Ginger Fleer-Starke. And the man was Stevens Troy.

Chapter
Twenty-Seven

Maggie hurried Jerry off the phone with a promise to send photos of Jolie/Pansy, Brooke/Spunky, and their respective broods. She took a deep breath to quell the anxiety pumping through her. She knew that it would take more than a psychic flash to convince Pelican PD that Stevens was a killer. She speed-dialed Lia. "You have a magnifying glass at the store, right?" she asked without a second of preamble.

"Yes, we use it to help us make out sloppy, handwritten orders." Lia picked up on the urgency in Maggie's voice. "I'm at Bon Bon."

"Be there ASAP." Maggie's tires squealed as she flipped the car around in a U-turn and raced to Lia. She screeched into a parking space behind the store, leapt out of the car, and ran into the Bon Bon workroom. Lia and Kyle were waiting for her.

"Kyle is a genius at deciphering chicken scratch," Lia said.

"This is different," Maggie said. She handed Kyle the worn business card for Sunset Properties. "There were numbers here that may be the key to Ginger and Trent's murderer. I think I know what the 1147 is. I have to figure out what the others are."

Kyle sat at a work desk, turned on a bright overhead light, and held the card under a magnifying glass. "Luckily, they were written in pen, so they left an indent. And there's a little color left."

Maggie bent over his shoulder. "That could be a three. Or an eight."

Lia wrote both numbers down. "We'll just make a list of whatever numbers we come up with."

"There are indents for dashes," Kyle said, pointing them out. "Two of them. I think this was a telephone number."

It took half an hour, but Maggie, Lia, and Kyle were able to come up with three iterations of telephone numbers. When they tried calling the first number, they learned that it was disconnected. When they called the second number, someone yelled at them in a foreign language and then hung up. Maggie's last hope was the third telephone number.

"I can hear your heart beating," said Lia, who was standing a few feet from Maggie as she punched in the number.

"I know, I—"

"Robbins, Farnham, Connon, and Stern," came a voice from the phone.

"Yes!" Maggie exulted. "I mean, hello. I got this number from someone and I can't explain in detail, but I think it's important. Do you mind telling me what kind of company this is?"

"We're not a company." The woman on the other end of the call sounded perplexed. "We're a law firm."

Robbins, law, Robbins, law . . . why does that—and then Maggie realized the connection. "Would the Robbins in your firm happen to be Lester Robbins?"

"Yes." Now the woman sounded wary.

"Please, I need to ask Mr. Robbins about another lawyer he might know. A Stevens Troy."

"Stevens?" Lia gasped.

Maggie raised a hand to shush her. There was silence on the other end of the telephone. "Hello?" she prayed that the woman hadn't ended the call.

"Mr. Troy used to be a partner here."

"What?" This was a revelation Maggie never expected. "His name isn't in the firm title."

The woman hesitated. "I don't know what I should tell you. I'm just the receptionist."

"This involves a very serious crime," Maggie said. "If you don't tell me, you'll probably have to tell the police." Maggie neglected to mention that if the woman's information proved crucial, she'd be talking to the police anyway. But the quasi threat did the trick. The woman let loose with a flood of shocking information.

"He was let go about five years ago. He had anger issues, what they call an explosive temper. And there were improprieties with some of his client relationships. Anyway, the firm made a deal with Mr. Troy that kept everything quiet. He 'retired' and they even made a big donation to finagle some Lawyer of the Year award for him on his way out. It was all about damage control."

"Thank you," Maggie said, forcing herself to stay calm. "That's very helpful. I just have one more question. Have you ever heard of Sunset Properties?"

"Yes, that's a business one of our clients started."

"Just one of them? Not two? You know that for a fact?"

"Yes. I can't give you any names, of course, but I know because I printed out a file that the client was supposed to pick up. It's sitting right here waiting for her."

Her. As in Ginger. "Thank you so much, Ms. . . ."

"I'd rather not give you my name."

Maggie didn't blame the woman for sounding nervous. "Of course. We'll keep this between us." Maggie ended the call before guilt about the lie she had just told prompted a more honest answer. Because she was about to spend the car ride back to Crozat sharing every detail of the conversation with Bo.

*

Bo was there when Maggie roared into her family's gravel parking lot. He opened her car door and helped her out. The drizzle that had begun on Maggie's ride home had developed into full-blown rain. "It all makes sense if you just think step-by-step," she told Bo as they pulled jackets over their heads to ward off the wetness and ran toward the manor house. "Stevens lied to us. He knew Ginger because she was a client at his firm. Maybe they had an affair, maybe they didn't. But I think they planned to start a real estate development business together—Sunset Properties. Only Ginger cut Stevens out behind his back and bought the Callette property on her own. And when he found out, he snapped."

"It does make sense," Bo said. "Unfortunately, it's all circumstantial. There's not a DA in the country who'd give me a warrant."

The two made it into Crozat's back hallway and shook off their jackets. "Your grandmother's been spending time with Stevens," Bo continued. "Maybe he mentioned some small but illegal thing he's done. I could pick him up on that and hold him until we have concrete evidence of his involvement with Ginger."

"Good idea. Let's ask her. She's probably having dinner with my parents."

They hurried into the kitchen, where they found Tug and Ninette fixing bowls of oyster soup for dinner. "We're looking for Gran'," Maggie said. "No time to explain why."

"She's out, chère," Ninette said. "Stevens invited her over for dinner."

"No!" Maggie exclaimed.

Bo grabbed her hand. "Come on." He pulled her toward the back hallway, and the two ran through the rain to his car. Tug ran after them.

"Hey!" Tug yelled as Bo peeled out of the driveway. "Maggie! What's going on?"

Maggie opened her car window and yelled back, "No time!" Cold rain whipped her face and she closed the window. "Put on your siren. We need to get there fast."

Bo shook his head. "No. And I'm not calling PPD yet either. They'll show up with sirens blaring and guns blazing. The more noise we make, the more we put your grandmother in danger of becoming a hostage. We need to extricate her from the premises in a nonconfrontational way and then move in on Stevens."

"I'll do it," Maggie said. "I'll get her out. It's all my fault, anyway. I encouraged her to date that psychopath."

"That's ridiculous," Bo said. "You had no idea he was dangerous."

They reached Valcour Lane. Bo made a right, drove down to the end of the cul-de-sac, and parked in front of Stevens's house. It emanated such a homey glow that for a moment, Maggie wondered if she was out of her mind for pegging the retired lawyer as a murderer. Then she thought of her beloved grandmother and shook off all doubt. She reached for the car door handle.

"Wait," Bo said. He pulled out his gun. "I'm going to cover you from outside. If I see the smallest, hinkiest thing, I'm coming in."

"Okay. Look, if anything happens to me—"

"Nothing's going to happen to you."

"If anything happens to me," she continued, ignoring him, "I want you to know why I've been kind of weird lately. Whitney confided in me about some problems with her marriage and her conflicted feelings about her relationship with you. I felt like I should step back and let the two of you figure out your future."

"What the—"

"No time!" Maggie jumped out of the car and dashed up Stevens's front steps. She took a deep breath, summoned up her courage, and rang the doorbell. She heard a snippet of muted conversation, then footsteps. Stevens opened the door a crack and then, seeing who was there, opened it wider. "Maggie?"

"Yes, hi." She flashed a wide, fake smile. "I am so sorry to interrupt your dinner, but I need to fetch my grandmother. My mother's not well and we need to get Gran' home."

"Maggie, is that you?" Gran' called from the living room. "Come inside, you're letting the rain in."

"I'll wait for you out here. Just hurry."

"You're being rude," Gran' admonished her. "You can step inside for a minute so I'm not talking to you through a door."

Maggie reluctantly stepped into the living room, where Gran' sat in an easy chair drinking a Sazerac. "Now, what's going on with Ninette?"

"It's her stomach. She's weak and throwing up. It might be food poisoning. Or it might be more serious. We never know with Mom."

"That's not good. Is Tug taking her to the hospital?"

"No." Maggie cursed her innate honesty and backtracked. "Yes. Maybe. We don't know; we just need to get you home."

Gran' stood up. "Of course. I'll use the little girl's room and then we'll be on our way."

"Can it wait?"

Gran' gave her granddaughter an affronted look. "No, it cannot. I assure you I'll be quick."

Gran' briskly walked down the hall, leaving Maggie and Stevens in awkward silence. "I'm sorry about your mother," he said.

"Thank you," Maggie replied, feeling guilty for lying to him. *Stop that!* she told herself. *He's a murderer.*

Stevens lifted a curtain and glanced outside. "Rain's coming down harder."

"Yes. Yes it is."

He continued to stare out the window. "That's not your car."

Nerves set Maggie's heart thumping. "I got a ride with a friend. My convertible sometimes leaks in the rain." She congratulated herself for coming up with a plausible excuse.

"All ready," Gran' announced as she emerged from the bathroom.

"Great, let's go." Just a few more minutes and Gran' would be safe.

Stevens retrieved Gran's coat and helped her slip it on. He put an arm around her shoulder and gave her a squeeze. "Too bad the evening has to end early. I have a delicious tarte Tatin from Fais Dough Dough."

"Sorry about that," Maggie said. "Another night. Come on, Gran'."

Gran' took a step, but Stevens didn't let go of her. "You're a wonderful artist, Maggie."

"Thank you." Maggie tried to keep the anxiety she felt out of her voice.

"But you're a terrible liar." Stevens moved his arm from Gran's shoulder to her neck.

"Stevens, what are you doing? That hurts." Gran's eyes were colored with fear.

"Here's what going to happen," Stevens said, ignoring her. "I'm going to get in my car with your grandmother and I'm going to drive. You and your 'friend' will not follow me. At some point, I will deposit your grandmother somewhere. Whether she's alive or dead will depend on how well you've followed my directions."

"What?!" Gran' struggled to pull away, but Stevens tightened his grip. "Stevens, you're talking like a madman!"

"Leave her here," Maggie said. "Take me instead."

"Of course you'd say that," Stevens said. "You're *so* predictable."

Maggie was desperate to keep the conversation going. She didn't dare glance toward the back of the house to see if Bo had made his way inside for fear of alerting Stevens to his presence. "You don't have to do this," was the best she could come up with.

"Again, predictable. Out of my way."

Stevens pulled his arm even tighter around Gran's neck and shoved her forward. She choked and flailed her arms. As the deranged man tried to control her, Gran' managed to grab the waist of his pants and yank them up. Stevens yelped in pain and let go of Gran' as his hands flew to his most sensitive parts. Gran' fell to the floor, where she lay still. Something in Maggie snapped. She let out a roar and drove her head into Stevens's stomach. Taken by surprise, he flew backward. Maggie pulled herself up and grabbed Stevens's Lawyer of the Year award, but she slipped in a puddle of rainwater that she'd dripped onto the floor earlier. Her legs shot out from under her, and she fell on her back, dropping the heavy award as she went down. Stevens was on top of her in a split second, his hands around her throat. She tried to fight him off, but insanity gave him a terrifying boost of adrenaline. As she began to succumb to Stevens's strength, she heard Bo yell, "Maggie!" He'd made it inside.

Maggie felt herself starting to pass out when her attacker grunted. His eyes closed, and he slumped on top of her, unconscious. Maggie pushed him off and staggered to her feet. She expected to find Bo standing over Stevens with his gun drawn, but instead she saw the detective maneuvering himself through the doggy door. "Then who . . . ?"

"Are you all right, chère?"

She turned around to see Gran' holding Stevens's Lawyer of the Year award. It was edged with blood where it had made contact with Stevens's skull.

"And you wonder why I don't date," Gran' sighed.

Chapter
Twenty-Eight

Pelican PD screeched into the cul-de-sac as Bo was cuffing Stevens. They were followed by three unmarked cars from a different branch of law enforcement—the FBI. Bringing up the rear was a familiar, slightly battered minivan sporting a magnetic placard that read, "Crozat Family Bed and Breakfast, Offering Homey Historic Hospitality." The van parked halfway into the street, and Tug leaped out, followed by Ninette. They ran up to Gran' and Maggie, who were giving their statements to Chief Perske. The chief was showing off for the FBI by flexing his territorial muscle, which only seemed to amuse the agents. "Feel free to pee on this hydrant," one of them told him with a shrug, then loped into the house to retrieve Stevens.

"Thank God you're all right," Tug said.

"We've been sick with fear that something happened to you," Ninette added. She threw her arms around Maggie as Tug hugged his mother tightly.

"I didn't know what was going on, but I figured it was a good idea to bring in some heavy artillery," Tug said. "So I called PPD *and* the FBI. Turns out Bo had already alerted them to the situation, and they were on their way."

"Thanks, Dad," Maggie said. "We'll tell you the whole story, I promise. But right now, I just want to get home and clean up."

"As do I," Gran' said. "It's been a less-than-pleasant evening in every possible way, and I'd like to wash away any connection to it."

Still clinging to each other, the family walked down the street to the Crozat minivan. They passed Cal Vichet and Artie Belloise, who were lounging against a squad car, watching the action. Artie was munching on a bag of Zapp's Potato Chips. "Can you believe this?" he said, gesturing to the scene at Stevens's house. "FBI and everything. I gotta say, Maggie, you sure brought a higher class of crime with you when you moved back home." He winked before Maggie could protest, and she followed her grandmother into the family van.

*

"Stevens Troy seemed like such a nice old man," Gaynell said. "How could we all have been so wrong about him?"

It had been three days since Stevens's arrest and Vanessa's release, and Maggie and her fellow bridesmaids were readying themselves for Vanessa's hastily rescheduled wedding.

This time they were utilizing St. Tee's powder room instead of Vanessa and Rufus's trailer. Vanessa, still shaky from her false arrest, had opted to have only her mother Tookie help her prep for the big day. Since she and Rufus couldn't afford to keep up their party tent for the wedding reception, the Crozat facilities had once again been called into service. When Maggie checked the Crozat tent before leaving for the church, she'd seen that Ione wasn't the only guest who'd decided to freeze her potluck donation from the previous postwedding dinner. The buffet table was lined with defrosting casseroles.

"We cut Stevens slack for a lot of reasons," Maggie said as she pulled her hair back into a ponytail and clipped it in place with the LSU bow that Vanessa had insisted they all wear. "He was a widower, so we felt sorry for him. And he seemed successful, so we never thought of him being involved in some shady real estate scheme." Maggie finished her eye makeup, then got up and walked over to Ione. "Where do you want your bow?"

"In the garbage, but since that's not possible, stick it somewhere at the back of my head and try to hide it under my hair."

Maggie did as instructed. "Anyway, as soon as they brought Stevens in, he tripped over himself trying to justify why he was 'forced to take care of' Ginger. Quentin was all ready to step in as his attorney, but Stevens refused. I think he thought it would somehow get him off the hook."

"So he's gone mental," Ione commented.

"I think if you murder someone, you're already there," Lia said as she parted her thick, curly hair and pulled one side of it behind an ear. She affixed her LSU bow in this inconspicuous location.

"Anyway, the FBI traced seventy-five thousand dollars of the money Ginger used to buy the Callette property back to a Swiss bank account that they were able to connect to Stevens. She seems to have gotten the other fifty grand through blackmail. Houston PD interviewed several high-profile former 'clients' who admitted paying Ginger a lot of money to keep her from going public about their assignations. Anyway, it was just as I thought. Ginger cut Stevens out of the deal by forming Sunset Properties on her own. He confronted her, she blew him off, and he went into a rage and killed her."

"But why did he kill Trent too?" Gaynell asked as she clipped her LSU bow into her blonde curls. "Y'all are so lucky you have brown hair. There's no way I can hide this thing in mine."

"Don't fret, chère. I think I can shape some of your hair over at least part of it," Lia said. She picked up a comb and brush and started experimenting with styles that might lessen the damage of the bright purple-and-gold hair accessory.

"Stevens had no idea that Ginger had shared her scheme with Trent, but as soon as Ginger died, Trent let Stevens know that he'd be happy to keep his mouth shut for the right price. Stevens stalled for time by agreeing to pay him and then grabbed the opportunity to both kill Trent *and* frame

Vanessa at her bachelorette party when he heard her griping about her wedding present gun from Rufus."

"And then he kicked the whole thing up a notch by faking that heart condition." Ione shook her head. "What a loon."

"No, that was real," Maggie said. She circled her eyes with a thin line of purple and then mascaraed her lashes. "I guess a double murder can be rough on a seventy-something's heart. Horrible as this whole story is, what really chilled my bones was why he pursued Gran'. He was upset that his arrest ruined their 'romance.' He pretty much admitted that his game plan was to marry Gran', then get her to change her will and leave him Crozat."

"He had a lot of faith in his own longevity, because that plan would only work if she died before him," Lia said. Then she gasped. "No."

Maggie nodded grimly. "He didn't come out and admit that he'd planned to murder her to get what he wanted, of course. But it turns out that the money he passed on to Ginger came from his late wife's estate. She supposedly passed from natural causes, but Houston PD is taking another look at that."

Gaynell shuddered. "Thank goodness it's all over." She examined herself in the mirror and smiled. "You can hardly see that ugly thing. Thanks, Lia."

"Of course. I think we all look as lovely as possible, given the circumstances."

"A Wednesday wedding." Ione rolled her eyes. "Crazy on top of crazy."

"I think at this point it's just 'get 'er done,'" Maggie said.

"I don't want my staff partying too hard tonight." Ione wagged a finger at Maggie and Gaynell. "You both still need to be at Doucet bright and early in the morning, and no dragging hangovers to work with you."

"Yes, ma'am," the two tour guides chorused.

There was a tentative rap on the door. Maggie opened it a crack and peered out. She was surprised to see Fox standing there. "Hey there. I wasn't expecting to see you here tonight."

"I know. But I decided to come out of respect for the Fleers. I feel at least a little responsible for what they went through. Can we talk for a minute?"

"Sure." Maggie stepped into the hallway.

"You look very—"

"Purple," Maggie said. "It's okay; it's only for a few hours. So, what's up?"

"I wanted to thank you for helping to find Ginger's killer. And let you know that Bibi's going to continue the design business. I'm helping her out financially. And . . ."

"Personally?"

"We're taking it very slow, but yes." Fox sat down on a worn bench. "I also had to let you know something. Ginger wasn't always . . . the way she became. That's why I stayed with her. I remembered who she was and thought maybe I could rekindle that. Every time I was ready to give up, I'd see a glimmer of the girl I fell in love with. I wonder now if she was just playing me."

Maggie took a seat next to Fox on the bench. The man needed to talk, and since the wedding party was still bride-free, she had some time to give him. "How long were you two together?"

"We first went out right after high school, when she moved to Houston. She was so smart and enthusiastic about life. And fun. She was always ambitious. We broke up for about a year because she felt like she was putting too much attention on her relationship and not enough on her career. That's when she moved back to Louisiana for a while. But then out of nowhere she was back in my life with only one condition—no kids. I regret that now."

Maggie noticed that his eyes were damp. And a unique shade of grey-green that she'd only seen once before. "Fox . . . the year you broke up. How long ago was that?"

"About twenty-two, twenty-three years ago."

She searched for a delicate way to ask an indelicate question. "This may sound a little off the wall, but has it occurred to you that Chret might be your son?"

"What?" He gave Maggie a blank look. "Chret? The mechanic?"

He seemed unable to process the possibility, but Maggie pressed on. "The timeline of when you and Ginger broke up seems to fit. There are physical similarities. I'm not saying it's for sure. But it's something to think about."

"I don't . . . But . . . How . . . but . . . she'd give up our son?"

Maggie didn't say anything. She let the reality sink in. Fox rubbed his forehead. "Wow. I've been kidding myself all these years, thinking I knew her."

"The important thing is to talk to Chret. And figure things out for sure."

"Yes. Right." Fox stood up, and Maggie followed his lead. "Thank you. Again. For everything."

Fox headed down the hall and disappeared into the church. Gaynell stuck her head out of the dressing room door. "We got a text from Tookie. They just got here. It's show time."

*

The bridesmaids lined up behind Vanessa outside Saint Tee's carved wooden doors, pom-poms in hand. "Please tell me we're not marching down the aisle to the LSU fight song," Ione muttered to Maggie.

"I'd love to say, 'No, that would be insane,' but I can't," Maggie replied. Something bumped her lightly on the head, and she turned to see that a giant bouquet of red balloons shaped like hearts had been delivered. They strained to be freed from the weights that held them in place. "Rice and butterflies are so last century," Tookie told the wedding party. "Instead we're gonna have our guests release heart balloons. Pretty smart, huh? I'll be sending that idea in to the bridal magazines."

While Tookie babbled on, it occurred to Maggie that Vanessa had yet to utter a word since her arrival. *Must be nerves,* she thought to herself.

"Excuse me, sorry, we're running a bit late." Maggie recognized the voice and turned to discover Grand-mère being escorted up the church steps by Lee Bertrand. She moved over to let the couple pass, and Gran' stopped briefly. "Like I promised, I'm allowing love into my life," she whispered to her granddaughter. Then she went into the church with her date.

The ushers, having finished seating the smattering of guests that had shown up for a Wednesday late-afternoon wedding, came out and took their places next to the bridesmaids. Maggie slipped her arm through Bo's and was about to head into the church when Vanessa declared, "Wait." She grabbed Maggie by an arm and gripped it tightly. "I'll never forget what you've done for me."

"Of course," Maggie said. "I wouldn't be much of a maid of honor if I let you spend your wedding day in jail for a crime you didn't commit."

"Thank you for that. And for everything." Vanessa released Maggie and returned to her place. As the organist launched into Mendelssohn's "Wedding March," the bridal party began its procession into the church and down the aisle, parting to the left and right as they reached the altar. The organist played a flourish that indicated the bride's arrival, and the guests stood up as Tookie led her daughter down the aisle and delivered her to Rufus. Father Prit led his usual unintelligible service, but the guests, trained by years of Catholicism, stood and kneeled by rote. Father Prit invited the bride and groom to share their own vows, and

Rufus delivered a short speech that he'd found on the Internet. Then it was Vanessa's turn.

"Rufus," she said, taking his hands in hers, "if there's anything that this last week has taught me, it's that life is short and things happen that you don't expect."

"Ain't that the truth," Rufus said from the side of his mouth. The guests chuckled.

"We must be grateful for the gifts God gives us," Vanessa continued.

"I'm looking forward to the ones our *guests* give us," Rufus wisecracked, to more chuckles. He was on a roll.

"And we must live a pure, honest life," Vanessa paused. "Which is why I can't marry you."

The guests gasped. Rufus dropped Vanessa's hands. "*What?!*"

"I'm sorry. I thought I could go through with this, but I can't. It wouldn't be fair to you. Not when I'm in love with someone else."

"*What?!*" Rufus repeated. "*Who?!*"

The guests leaned forward.

"The man that saved my life. Quentin MacIlhoney."

There was another gasp from the guests, followed by dead silence. Then Rufus let out a roar. "I'll kill him!"

The jilted groom took off on a tear down the aisle. "It's the Crozat Curse!" he yelled at Maggie as he stormed by her. "I blame you!" He burst out of the church. The bridal party ran after him, followed by the guests, who pushed and shoved each other as they stumbled outside onto the church steps, eager to witness the next turn of events. They were rewarded when Vanessa let out a scream.

"Help! My water just broke!"

Tookie sprinted to her daughter's side. She jostled Maggie, who bumped into the balloon bouquet. It broke free from its weighted moorings, and as the wedding descended into total chaos, Maggie watched the heart balloons waft up into the sky and float away.

Chapter
Twenty-Nine

Maggie had long ago realized that Pelican was the kind of place where it seemed like nothing happened for a very long time or everything happened all at once. The week after Rufus and Vanessa's 'Wedding That Wasn't' turned out to be one of the latter times.

Despite being three weeks early, Vanessa's infant girl weighed in at ten pounds, four ounces, leaving many in Pelican to wonder how much the infant would have weighed had she been full-term. Vanessa decamped from the trailer she shared with Rufus to Quentin's Baton Rouge McMansion, bringing along baby Charlotte Elizabeth Diana, a little Cajun princess who would forever share a name with England's real princess. Pelican phones blew up with news of the scandalous pairing, which fazed neither Vanessa nor Quentin. "What can I say, I've always had a soft spot for a damsel in criminal distress," the defense attorney told Maggie. "At least she's innocent. My last two wives were guilty as hell." As an engagement present for his future wife, Quentin paid Maggie to paint Rufus out of the ill-fated portrait she'd spent months working on and paint him in instead.

Rufus dealt with the blow to his marital status and ego by turning his trailer into party central for Pelican's resident miscreants. When Maggie heard that he'd refused to visit his newborn daughter, she decided to risk being subjected to the verbal abuse he might heap on her and join Bo in entreating the new dad to be in his child's life. Fortunately for her, Ru was so drunk when they showed up that she wasn't sure he even recognized her. "Who cares anyway, it's a girl," he slurred. "I wanted a dang son. At least I'm honest about it instead of all the people who say, 'I don't care as long as the baby's healthy.' Bull. Men want boys and women want girls, and anyone who tells you otherwise is lying."

It was at this point that Bo threw Rufus into a cold shower and then shoved him into a car for the trip to Baton Rouge, where he met his newborn daughter and fell completely in love. "Sweet, sweet Charli," he cooed to the sleeping infant in his arms as tears coated his three-day stubble. "You are the love of my life. And I am gonna be a better man for you."

Rufus made good on his promise by joining a large group of Pelican's citizens at Ninette's Yes We PeliCAN! 10K Walk for the Cure. He even chose to be magnanimous about what part the Crozat Curse might have played in the dissolution of his relationship with Vanessa. But Ru didn't do a complete one-eighty. On his way to the restroom in Maggie's art studio, he spotted her caricature of Vanessa as a pregnant Valkyrie and gleefully used it as a substitute for toilet tissue.

The fundraiser was a huge success, and even more money was raised when Maggie auctioned off the diamond watch Quentin had told her she could keep. Artie and Cal, along with JJ of all people, chipped in for the winning bid. The watch would rotate between the three on a weekly basis. At the party after the event—because what event in Pelican didn't end with a party?—Maggie delighted her friends with the news that she'd received the Baylors' permission to let them adopt Brooke's and Jolie's offspring. Her one proviso was that Xander would still get to name the kitties and have first pick of a pet. Chret Bertrand then thrilled the crowd by announcing that he would match the money the Walk raised with a donation from his inheritance. "I'm still gonna keep on at the garage," he told the Crozats as his now-official girl-friend, Gaynell, stood beaming by his side. "But it's nice to have a little breathing room. And I'm gonna hire vets in the area to help me fix up the old Callette place. It'll be good for us. Like a kind of therapy. And my dad said he'd help. 'My dad.' Still feels weird to say that." A DNA test had proved Maggie's instinct correct. Fox was Chret's birth father, and the businessman was determined to form a bond with the son he never knew he had. To prove his commitment, he designated Chret as the beneficiary of Ginger's life insur-ance policy; an e-mail thread proved that he had doubled it not for nefarious reasons but because his financial advisor recommended doing so.

The party finally wound down. As the revelers headed to Junie's for an after party—because what party in Pelican didn't end with an after party?—Maggie watched them go from her perch on the veranda glider.

"Mind if I join you?"

Maggie looked up to see Bo, who was holding a paper bag. She moved over to make room for him. The two glided back and forth for a minute. "So . . ." he finally said. "I had a long talk with Whitney."

"I'm sorry. I never should have said anything. It was one of those stupid 'I may die so I'm going to open my big mouth' moments."

"No, I'm glad you did say something. She needs to deal with the reality of her life. I reminded her of all the reasons we got divorced in the first place and made it clear that romance was part of our past, not our future."

"I hope she's okay."

"She will be. She's flying out to Saudi Arabia to spend a couple of weeks with Zach. They need that. So I'll be a single dad for a while." Bo paused. "You didn't trust me, did you? You thought there was a chance I might be tempted to take up with Whitney again."

"What? No, I . . ." Maggie's protests sounded so hollow that she couldn't bear listening to herself. "Yes. Yes, I did. It's just that Whitney is so delicate and beautiful, and I'm . . . And then Johnny said . . ."

Maggie stopped herself. It seemed unfair to tattle on Johnny and drag him into her vortex of insecurity. But Bo's brown-black almond eyes narrowed. "What did Johnny say?"

"Nothing," Maggie responded meekly.

"Here's the deal with Johnny Tucker. He's a good cop and real entertaining, but he's the devil. Whit and I broke up for a couple of weeks during college, and he was on her in a white-hot minute. He can find a vulnerability and work his way into it. It's a great skill for interrogating suspects, but dangerous when it comes to women."

"Well, I'm nothing if not vulnerable," Maggie said. They rocked in the glider as Bo waited for her to continue. "I was devastated when my relationship in New York ended. Chris and I were together for six years. When I gave him some space to decide whether or not we should get married, and he used that time to hook up with someone else and marry *her*, it killed me." Maggie took a deep breath. "Wow, I thought time would make it easier to talk about this, but it still makes me feel sick inside. I thought I'd be planning my wedding, not living at home with my parents at thirty-two. I do love it here now, and I'm slowly finding my way, but . . . I have trouble trusting a relationship. I have trouble believing that anyone really wants me."

The only sound came from the glider creaking back and forth. Then Bo spoke. "I also told Whitney that I was in love with someone. Deeply in love. Someone who's smart and talented and generous and kind, and who always has paint stains somewhere on her, and usually smells a little bit like turpentine. She sometimes blurts things out without thinking, and I would not want to tick her off and get on the wrong side of her wit. But I know that she'd lie across train tracks for me and for Xander. She makes me feel safe and loved, and I would feel like my life truly had meaning if she could say the same of me one day."

Maggie gave up trying to control her tears as they streamed down her cheeks. "This may be the wrong time, but I've got something for you," Bo said.

He handed Maggie the paper bag. She reached in and pulled out a small, matte-glazed pottery vase. The background was of a blue-green shade that seemed nocturnal. A full moon peeked through the Spanish moss–laden branches of a repoussé oak tree. "Oh, Bo . . ."

"I talked to Lia about how I wanted to get you something personal and special, and then she told me about Newcomb Pottery. Look at the bottom."

Maggie turned the vase over. There it was—the mark of her great-aunt, Sylvie Doucet. "I'm trying to find the words that could tell you how much this means to me. But I don't think they exist."

Bo put his arms around her and kissed the crown of her head. A sudden rustling distracted both of them. They glanced toward Crozat's entryway and saw Xander standing in the doorway clutching a piece of paper, his face strained with anxiety. Maggie wiped her eyes with her hand. "Hey, buddy, no worries, these are tears of joy." Xander relaxed and wandered over to her. "What's that?" she asked, motioning to the piece of paper in his hand. He held it out, and she took it. "You named the kittens. That's great." Xander had spoken a few words since emerging from his selective mutism, but he had yet to form a full sentence. His psychologist recommended letting him proceed at his own pace but okayed the occasional gentle prompt. Maggie handed the piece of paper back to the boy. "Any chance you could read the names to us? There are only three."

Xander nodded solemnly. "Picasso," he read in his sweet voice.

Bo gave him a thumbs-up, and Maggie clapped. "I love it," she said. "I was afraid I was boring you when I threw in some art history with our lessons, but I guess not. What's the next one?"

Xander looked down at his list. "Skywalker."

"Wow, a completely different way to go," Maggie commented. "And also terrific. I can't wait to hear what you named the last kitten."

Xander started to speak, but stopped. He buried his face in his father's shoulder. Bo peeked at the list in Xander's hand, then blinked and cleared his throat. "You can do it," he whispered to his son.

Xander pulled himself away from Bo. Maggie gave the boy an encouraging smile. He handed her the list, and his small hand clutched hers. Xander looked her in the eye, maintaining contact for the first time since she had known him.

"I named the last kitten Maggie," he said.

Recipes

Turkey Dinner in a Braid

Ninette came up with a wonderful way to turn Thanks-giving leftovers into a delicious dish. She likes to serve this entrée with a simple side salad.

Ingredients

2 crescent roll packages (or use the new crescent
    roll dough packages instead)
2 cups turkey, chopped
1 cup chopped broccoli, peas, or string beans
1 cup diced potatoes (optional)
1 cup stuffing
2 tsp. gravy
½ cup cranberry sauce
½ cup mayonnaise
1 egg white, slightly beaten
2 tbsp. French-fried onions (the kind you
    use in a green bean casserole)

Instructions

Preheat the oven to 375 degrees.

Mix the turkey, gravy, mayonnaise, and cranberry sauce together in a medium bowl.

Line a large cookie sheet with parchment paper, leaving a few inches of space on each side.

Open and unroll the crescent roll doughs one at a time. Arrange the first horizontally across the width of the pan toward the top, then lay the second one below it, and seal them both together either with a rolling pin or clean fingers.

Cut the long sides of the dough into strips about 3" deep and 1½" wide. Important: you want to leave around 6" in the center for the filling, so adjust the strips accordingly.

Spoon the turkey mixture evenly over the middle section of dough. On top of the turkey, layer the stuffing, potatoes (if you choose to use them), and your green vegetable.

To braid the dough, lift the first two strips across from each other so that they meet in the center. Twist each strip once and then lay them both down on the filling. (You may have to pull or pinch the dough a bit to stretch it.) Continue to do this until you've twisted all the strips. Don't worry if it doesn't look perfect. Tuck the ends of the braid up to seal it on both ends. Brush the braid with the egg white, then sprinkle with the French-fried onions.

Bake 20–30 minutes, until a deep golden brown.

You can either serve it on the cookie tray or lift up both sides of the parchment paper to gently move the braid onto a serving dish.

Serves 8–10.

Bananas Foster Coffee Cake a la Ninette

Bananas Foster is an iconic New Orleans dessert created in 1951 by a chef at the legendary Brennan's Restaurant and named after a friend of restaurant owner Owen Brennan. The original dish is flambéed bananas served over vanilla ice cream. Many cooks have created unique recipes inspired by the original dessert, including Ninette.

Cake Ingredients

3 ripe bananas, sliced
6 tbsp. butter, divided (3 at a time)
2 oz. dark rum
1 oz. banana liqueur (note: if you don't have this, use 3 oz. rum)
2 large eggs, room temperature
1 tsp. vanilla extract
2 cups Bisquick baking mix

Streusel Ingredients

⅔ cup Bisquick baking mix

⅔ cup packed dark brown sugar

1 tsp. cinnamon

¼ tsp. salt

3 tbsp. cold butter or margarine

Cake Instructions

Preheat the oven to 350 degrees, with rack at center level of the oven.

In a large skillet, melt 3 tablespoons of the butter over medium-high heat. Add the dark brown sugar and stir to combine. Add the rum and cook for a couple of minutes, stirring often to blend the ingredients and keep them from crystallizing. Add the banana chunks and cook for 2–3 more minutes, gently stirring to coat the bananas with the thickening liquid. Scrape the caramelized banana mixture into a medium heatproof bowl. Use your spatula to break up the bananas into small pieces (but don't mash them into pulp). Stir in the remaining 3 tablespoons of butter until melted, then add the vanilla. Let the mixture cool down until moderately warm, then quickly whisk in the eggs.

Place the 2 cups of Bisquick in another medium-sized bowl. Add the wet ingredients to the Bisquick, then stir together.

Streusel Instructions
Combine the dry ingredients in a bowl, then cut in the butter. Use a pastry blender to combine ingredients until the streusel is crumbly.

To Put It All Together
Put half the cake batter in the cake pan. Top with half the streusel. Top that with the rest of the cake batter and then cover that with the rest of the streusel.

Bake for 35–45 minutes, until the center is firm.

Serves 6–8.

JJ's Jambalaya

Brown or red jambalaya? That's the eternal debate in Louisiana. Brown jambalaya is Cajun in origin while red jambalaya shows the Creole influence of New Orleans. JJ's Jambalaya is Cajun, of course!

Ingredients

2½ tbsp. vegetable oil
1 lb. boneless chicken thighs, in their juice
1 cup Andouille sausage, cut into bite-size pieces
6 oz. cup chopped heavy-cut bacon
2 cups finely chopped onions
1 cup finely chopped green bell pepper
    (generally 1 large pepper)
½ cup finely chopped celery
4 cups low-sodium chicken broth
1 tsp. ground thyme
¼ to ½ tsp. ground red pepper
1 tsp. smoked paprika

1 tsp. dried tarragon
¼ tsp. sea salt
⅛ to ¼ tsp. black pepper
2 cloves minced garlic
1 tsp. Tony Chachere's Creole seasoning—or
     any Cajun seasoning with salt
2 bay leaves
Dash Worcestershire Sauce
2 cups uncooked white rice
¼ cup finely chopped green onions
¼ cup finely chopped fresh parsley

Instructions

Season the chicken with the salt and pepper. Heat two table-spoons of the oil to medium-high in a large cast iron or Dutch oven pot. Sauté the chicken in the oil until it's thoroughly golden brown on each side (approximately four minutes per side). Turn off the flame, remove the chicken, and cut into bite-sized pieces.

Turn the flame back on to medium. Put the bacon in the pot (add a dash of vegetable oil if you feel it's needed) and cook the bacon until it curls. Add onions, bell pepper, celery, and garlic, then cook until the vegetables are softened, about five minutes. Stir to make sure everything cooks evenly.

Add sausage and chicken to the pot, then stir to combine with other ingredients. Then add the chicken stock, thyme, red pepper, tarragon, bay leaves, smoked paprika, Tony Chachere's seasoning (or your choice of Cajun seasoning), Worcestershire sauce, and rice. Stir to combine, then turn up the heat and bring to a boil, uncovered. Reduce heat to simmer, then cover the pot. Simmer for ten minutes, then uncover and fold the rice over once to make sure it's not sticking to the pot. Cover the pot and simmer for another ten minutes, or until the liquid is almost absorbed. Stir occasionally to prevent sticking, but not too much. You want to make sure the rice cooks through. Add a little more broth if you need to. (By the way, it's hard to avoid any sticking to the pot. It always happens to me.)

Stir in the parsley and green onions, then cook for another minute or two. Let sit for five minutes, then serve with French bread cut into slices. Have a bottle of hot sauce handy for any guest who prefers their jambalaya spicy.

Serves 6–8.

Or . . .

If you don't have the time to make jambalaya from scratch, do what I do. Make a packaged jambalaya and add your choice of ingredients. Trust me, it will be delicious!

World's Easiest Jambalaya

Ingredients
A box of jambalaya rice mix, like Zatarain's
   Jambalaya Rice, Original
2½ cups of water
A pound—or more—of whatever you want to
   throw in, like chicken, shrimp, or sausage

Instructions
Follow the instructions on the box to make the rice. Throw in
your meat. Stir it up. That's it!

Serves 6–8.

A Laginappe
about Body on
the Bayou

"Lagniappe" is a Louisiana term that means "a little something extra." For me, it's a way of sharing some personal
anecdotes about the wonderful region that inspired my
Cajun Country Mystery series.

The time I've spent in Acadiana has been filled with
unique experiences that cemented my affection for the
region. One occurred in the mid-1980s during a visit with
my friend Jan Gilbert, a noted New Orleans artist. We drove
up the east River Road to explore some plantations (one of
which was Ashland-Belle Helene, the inspiration for Crozat Plantation B and B). Worn out by the day's adventures,
we decided to take I-10, a much faster route, back to New
Orleans. But we got lost trying to find the interstate entrance

and wound up back where we started. We noticed an old gentleman walking along the side of the road and pulled over to ask for directions. He stared at us and then said in a thick Cajun accent, "I'm eighty years old, and I ain't never been more'n five miles up or down this road in my entire life."

I still marvel at a life so simple and circumscribed in this day and age. But when you live in such an interesting area, maybe five miles in either direction is all you ever need to go.

Naming characters in a book can be a challenge, but it's been fun for this series. Some names pay homage to an important person in my life. There is a real Gaynell Bourgeois, although her full name is Gaynell Bourgeois Moore; she's a very talented and dear friend. "Waguespack"—as in veterinarian Dr. Waguespack—is the maiden name of one of my closest friends from college. (I gave her first name, Charlotte, to Grand-mère.)

But one name was inspired by a legend I found fascinating.

On the outskirts of St. Martinville, Louisiana, there is an allée of trees known as Oak and Pine Alley. This once led to the grand plantation home of Charles Durand. Legend has it that when his daughters were to be married in a double ceremony, he promised them the most fantastical wedding Louisiana had ever seen. He imported a million spiders from China and gold and silver dust from California. On the eve of the wedding, the spiders were released to spin their webs between the oak and pine trees. In the morning of the wedding day—the actual date is murky—servants sprayed the webs with gold and silver dust, creating a canopy of intricate, glittering patterns and a spectacular exit for the newlyweds.

All that remains of Charles Durand's grandiose home is the alley of trees. A man motivated by a desire to one-up his neighbors, he was eventually ruined by the Civil War and his own hubris. The Durands in my series—arrogant Rufus and upstanding Bo—will meet a happier fate.

Acknowledgments

Thank you, Cameron and Kara Clanton, for sharing your wealth of automobile knowledge. And thanks to cousins Joan, Sandy, Paul, Sandra, Kevin, and Lucy for their support. A debt of gratitude is owed to those who helped me research the care and feeding of puppies and kittens: Holly and Donald P. Thompson, DVM; Polly Iyer and Daniel Iyer, DVM; Amy Shojai, CABC; and Sheila Boncham. As always, thanks to awesome agent Doug Grad and the fabulous team at Crooked Lane Books: Mathew Martz, Sarah Poppe, Heather Boak, Nike Power, and publicity phenoms Dana Kaye and Julia Borcherts. GoWrite gals Mindy Schneider, Kate Shein, Kathy McCullough, and Terri Wagener—bless your great notes. Same for you, fantastic Chicks on the Case Lisa Q. Mathews, Marla Cooper, and Kellye Garrett! And a shout-out to Margaret S. Hamilton for your invaluable thoughts. As always, thank you to my Louisiana crew, Kevin McCaffrey, Jan Gilbert, Laurie and Walter Becker, and Gaynell Bourgeois Moore, and my Texas buddies, Pam and John Shaffer (can't wait to go to the Barbecue Inn with you someday). Extra special love and thanks to Charlotte Waguespack Allen. Denise and Stacy Smithers, and Karen Fried, you are simply the best. Tom and Karen Moore, so lucky to have you in our lives. Kim Rose, your support is so appreciated, and Von Rae Wood, you are a forever friend—your optimism and enthusiasm always inspire me. A heartfelt thanks to Diane Vallere, Craig Faustus Buck, Jeri Westerson, Holly West, Stephen Buehler, Linda O. Johnston, Rochelle Staab, Nancy Cole Silverman, and all the members of SinCLA and SoCalMWA for welcoming me so warmly and sharing priceless information on the mystery world. More thanks to Catherine Respess and Red Mare Design for your website and design talent and creativity. Buckets of love to Mom, Tony, and David. And as always, infinity love to Jer and Eliza.

And finally, a big thank-you to my local Target stores. I do some of my best thinking aimlessly wandering those jam-packed aisles.